Praise for Catherine Bybee

Wife by Wednesday

"A fun and sizzling romance, great characters that trade verbal spars like fist punches, and the dream of your own royal wedding!"

—Sizzling Hot Book Reviews, 5 Stars

"A good holiday, fireside or bedtime story."

—Manic Reviews, 4 1/2 Stars

"A great story that I hope is the start of a new series."

—The Romance Studio, 4 1/2 Hearts

Married by Monday

"If I hadn't already added Ms. Catherine Bybee to my list of favorite authors, after reading this book I would have been compelled to. This is a book *nobody* should miss, because the magic it contains is awesome."

—Booked Up Reviews, 5 Stars

"Ms. Bybee writes authentic situations and expresses the good and the bad in such an equal way . . . Keep[s] the reader on the edge of her seat . . ."

—Reading Between the Wines, 5 Stars

"*Married by Monday* was a refreshing read and one I couldn't possibly put down . . ."

—. . . earts

Fiancé by Friday

"In this fantastic Weekday Brides installment, Bybee knows exactly how to keep readers happy . . . A thrilling pursuit and enough passion to stuff in your back pocket to last for the next few lifetimes, *Fiancé by Friday* is reminiscent of *The Bodyguard*, but way better because this story embraces unique personalities and they do not impede upon the plot. The hero and heroine come to life with each flip of the page and will linger long after readers cross the finish line."

—*RT Book Reviews*, 4 1/2 Stars, Top Pick, Hot

"A tale full of danger and sexual tension . . . the intriguing characters add emotional depth, ensuring readers will race to the perfectly fitting finish."

—*Publishers Weekly*

"Suspense, survival, and chemistry mix in this scintillating read."

—*Booklist*

"Hot romance, a mystery assassin, British royalty, and an alpha Marine . . . this story has it all!"

—Harlequin Junkie

Single by Saturday

"The fourth outing in the Weekday Brides series captures readers' hearts and keeps them glued to the pages until the fascinating finish . . . romance lovers will feel the sparks fly . . . almost instantaneously."

—*RT Book Reviews*, 4 1/2 Stars, Top Pick

"[A] wonderfully exciting plot, lots of desire, and some sassy attitude thrown in for good measure!"

—Harlequin Junkie

Taken by Tuesday

"[Bybee] knows exactly how to get bookworms sucked into the perfect storyline; then she casts her spell upon them so they don't escape until they reach the 'Holy Cow!' ending."

—*RT Book Reviews*, 4 1/2 Stars, Top Pick

Seduced by Sunday

"You simply can't miss [this novel]. It contains everything a romance reader loves—clever dialogue, three-dimensional characters, and just the right amount of steam to go with that heartwarming love story."

—Brenda Novak, *New York Times* bestselling author

"Bybee hits the mark . . . providing readers with a smart, sophisticated romance between a spirited heroine and a prim hero . . . Passionate and intelligent characters [are] at the heart of this entertaining read."

—*Publishers Weekly*

Treasured by Thursday

"The Weekday Brides never disappoint and this final installment is by far Bybee's best work to date."

—*RT Book Reviews*, 4 1/2 Stars, Top Pick

"An exquisitely written and complex story brimming with pride, passion, and pulse-pounding danger . . . Readers will gladly make time to savor this winning finale to a wonderful series."

—*Publishers Weekly*, Starred Review

"Bybee concludes her popular Weekday Brides series in a gratifying way with a passionate, troubled couple who may find a happy future if they can just survive and then learn to trust each other. A compelling and entertaining mix of sexy, complicated romance and menacing suspense."

—*Kirkus Reviews*

Not Quite Dating

"It's refreshing to read about a man who isn't afraid to fall in love . . . [Jack and Jessie] fit together as a couple and as a family."

—*RT Book Reviews*, 3 Stars, Hot

"*Not Quite Dating* offers a sweet and satisfying Cinderella fantasy that will keep you smiling long after you've finished reading . . ."

—Kathy Altman, *USA Today*, Happy Ever After

"The perfect rags to riches romance . . . The dialogue is inventive and witty, the characters are well drawn out. The storyline is superb and really shines . . . I highly recommend this stand out romance! Catherine Bybee is an automatic buy for me."

—Harlequin Junkie, 4 1/2 Hearts

Not Quite Enough

"Bybee's gift for creating unforgettable romances cannot be ignored. The third book in the Not Quite series will sweep readers away to a paradise, and they will be intrigued by the thrilling story that accompanies their literary vacation."

—*RT Book Reviews*, 4 1/2 Stars, Top Pick

Not Quite Forever

"Full of classic Bybee humor, steamy romance, and enough plot twists and turns to keep readers entertained all the way to the very last page."

—Tracy Brogan, bestselling author of the Bell Harbor series

"Magnetic . . . The love scenes are sizzling and the multi-dimensional characters make this a page-turner. Readers will look for earlier installments and eagerly anticipate new ones."

—*Publishers Weekly*

Doing *It* Over

Also by Catherine Bybee

Contemporary Romance

Weekday Brides Series

Wife by Wednesday
Married by Monday
Fiancé by Friday
Single by Saturday
Taken by Tuesday
Seduced by Sunday
Treasured by Thursday

Not Quite Series

Not Quite Dating
Not Quite Mine
Not Quite Enough
Not Quite Forever

Novellas

Soul Mate
Possessive

Paranormal Romance

MacCoinnich Time Travels

Binding Vows
Silent Vows
Redeeming Vows
Highland Shifter
Highland Protector

The Ritter Werewolves Series

Before the Moon Rises
Embracing the Wolf

Erotica

Kilt Worthy
Kilt-A-Licious

Doing *It* Over

A
Most Likely To
Novel

CATHERINE BYBEE

Text copyright © 2016 Catherine Bybee
All rights reserved.

Published by Montlake Romance, Seattle

www.apub.com

Amazon, the Amazon logo, and Montlake Romance are trademarks of Amazon.com, Inc., or its affiliates.

ISBN-13: 9781503950726
ISBN-10: 1503950727

33614059946540

Cover design by Shasti O-Leary Soudant

Printed in the United States of America

This one is for Kari
Because sometimes friends are the only family you need

Prelude

She'd earned the cap . . . and the gown, and there was no way Melanie was going to take them off until she fell into bed later that night. Tossing her cap in the air would have resulted in someone else grabbing it, so when Principal Mason of River Bend High had announced the graduating class, Melanie shot from her seat, waved a hand in the air, and screamed.

Hours later, Melanie hugged her yearbook to her chest and wiped the tears that threatened to take over what was supposed to be a night of celebration. She jogged from her car to Zoe's mom's double-wide. She pounded on the door before letting herself inside. As expected, Jo and Zoe already had the music pumped, the box of pizza opened between them.

"You started without me." She waved an accusing hand at her best friends.

Jo lifted a bottle of Jose Cuervo in the air. "Haven't even cracked the seal."

Melanie didn't want to know how JoAnne had managed a brand-new bottle of what they considered the *good stuff*. Then again, what self-respecting high school senior didn't have some connection somewhere to grab a bottle of booze?

Zoe still wore her gown, her cap sat beside the yearbook both she and Jo were studying. Jo had shucked her gown and tossed it by the front door . . . her cap was probably in the hands of an unknown senior . . . or worse, the custodian.

"Grab some glasses," Zoe said before Melanie made it into the room.

The three step detour had Melanie in Zoe's kitchen, the familiar space was marginally clean . . . the remainder of that morning's breakfast sat congealing on dirty dishes in the sink.

With two plastic cups and one made of glass, Melanie dropped on her knees before the coffee table and offered a pet to Gas Tank, Zoe's Pomeranian shih tzu mix. The mutt had repeatedly earned his name through the years.

"Did you see Mitchel Giesler after the ceremony?" Jo asked.

Melanie enjoyed the distraction gossip offered. "He was already shitfaced."

Zoe turned the page of her yearbook before taking a bite out of her pepperoni and cheese. "He's always shitfaced."

"So am I, but I knew better than to show up at graduation for everyone to see." Jo exaggerated, but both Zoe and Melanie knew better than to correct her.

"Not to mention your dad would have killed you."

Jo rolled her eyes as she reached for the bottle and twisted the cap as if proving a point.

Melanie sniffed the cup and looked around. "We're really going to drink this straight?"

Jo finished pouring Zoe's portion and set the bottle down. "Walking out of the house with lemons and salt would have been a dead giveaway."

"And walking out with the tequila wasn't?" Zoe asked.

"Whatever." Jo lifted her glass in the air. "To the end of high school. No more Mr. Edwards and his lisp."

"No more Mrs. Mothball and the smell of her musty closet that follows her everywhere," Zoe added.

"No more expectations of straight As to get into college." Melanie understood that expectation personally.

They shot back the liquid fire and set the glasses aside.

Jo refilled while Melanie grabbed a piece of pizza to calm the burn that was running down the back of her throat. She ate the pizza, not really tasting it.

Everything was about to change.

Everything.

All the planning and studying . . . her college dreams were about to come true.

Zoe and Jo were reading some of the other senior entries while Melanie's eyes swelled with tears.

The first sniffle had Jo glancing over. "God, don't start that."

"I can't help it," she uttered. "I'm going to miss you guys."

"It's college. You'll be back for holidays and summer . . . you'll probably see us more than your new friends."

Melanie's lips started to tremble.

She shook her head. "I-I won't."

Zoe and Jo both stared. "What do you mean?"

"My parents . . . they're moving. The house is going on the market next week."

The snarky smile on Jo's face fell.

Zoe wrapped the long length of her straight black hair behind her back. "Where are they going?"

That was the hardest part. "My mom said Connecticut . . . my dad said Texas."

"So which is it?" Jo asked.

There was no stopping the tears. "Both. They, uh . . ." She pulled the sleeve of her graduation gown over her eyes and sucked in a breath. "They told me they're both tired of fighting. That a divorce after I graduated from high school was for the best." Her older brother, Mark, was already out of college and living in Seattle, and she was the only thing keeping her unhappy parents together.

"Damn."

"That sucks, Mel."

"They've fought forever. I just thought that was marriage, ya know?"

Jo and Zoe exchanged glances. They both had single parents and didn't really know. Jo's mom had died young . . . car accident. And Zoe's dad was doing fifteen to life for armed robbery.

From the outside, the good people of River Bend thought everything was Norman Rockwell in the Bartlett family home. Like many kids, Melanie was encouraged to take all the college prep classes, take AP English, and join Associated Student Body. She'd been on the cheer squad in early high school but canned the chick club when she saw head cheerleader Margie Taylor kissing on Melanie's boyfriend. Melanie dumped them both and hooked stronger with her true friends.

"It was all for them," Melanie muttered.

Zoe moved from the couch to the floor and wrapped an arm around her.

The waterworks turned on high.

"College. They wanted me to get into a college far away so they could move on."

"California isn't that far," Jo reminded her.

"USC is a thousand miles from here, Jo. It takes two hours to drive to a flippin' airport from this town."

Zoe nudged her. "You got into USC. That's huge. Focus on that."

"And you won't have to choose which parent you're going to stay with," Jo added.

Melanie grabbed the bottle, added more to her cup. "Yeah. It's hot in Texas."

Jo lifted one side of her mouth in a half smile. "Connecticut sounds stuffy."

"It is." The liquor didn't burn as much this time. Her head started to swim, and the tears started to fade.

Jo twisted the yearbook around and flipped to a page they were already very familiar with.

A picture of the three of them, arms around each other: Jo attempting to act badass . . . Zoe wearing the wrong everything, but her head high anyway . . . and Melanie, blonde hair pulled back in a tight ponytail, her perfect teeth shining with a smile. To the side of the picture it said . . .

Melanie: Most likely to succeed.

Zoe: Most likely to never leave River Bend.

Jo: Most likely to end up in jail.

"Even these complete shitheads get where you're going with your life, Mel. You *are* the most likely to succeed."

Melanie shoved the book aside. "Lot they know. You won't end up in jail."

Yet as the words fell from her lips, Melanie knew it might happen. Jo had been trying most of her teenage life to buck her dad and just about everything he stood for. A small town sheriff's only daughter had two choices in life . . . rebel or conform.

Jo rebelled.

Looking around the paper-thin walls Zoe called home, Melanie reflected on her other BFF. She was wicked smart and had more going for her than she recognized, but Zoe probably wouldn't leave River Bend. Her part-time job at Sam's diner waiting tables and occasionally helping out in the kitchen helped her mom pay the bills . . . and then there was her boyfriend, Luke. They'd been tight forever, and chances were someone would forget the latex and a Junior Zoe or Junior Luke would have them married before they could legally drink with Jose and his friends.

"Yeah." Zoe pulled the bottle to her glass. "Jo won't end up in jail . . . and I wanna see the world. Can't do that staying in River Bend."

"Yeah!" The alcohol was already talking as they lifted their glasses in the air.

"We'll show this town." Jo drained her glass. "Let's make a promise . . . right here . . . right now."

Oh, the drama.

"What kind of promise?"

"Our ten year class reunion . . . we'll all come back to this one-shit town and show everyone how wrong they are about us."

Melanie started to smile. "Wait . . ."

"Not you, Mel-Bel . . . you're going to be fiiine. We just need our über-rich and famous . . . or successful whatever to stand beside us." Zoe was starting to slur her words.

Melanie still wasn't convinced she should drink to the toast.

"To showing your parents their timing sucked," Jo offered.

"I can drink to that."

They did.

Chapter One

Ten Years Later

Grants Pass killed her car. Melanie turned off the interstate and headed toward the coast, knowing the chances of passing other drivers once the sun set were nil. The noise from under the hood and the occasional coughing of exhaust that exploded from her tailpipe were evidence of her earlier conviction.

Grants Pass killed her car.

"C'mon, baby . . . only twenty-five more miles." She patted the dashboard and spoke in a soft voice to keep from waking Hope.

Melanie glanced at the backseat. Hope clutched her favorite stuffed animal, her legs curled under her and her head resting on a pillow. Her pouty pink lips slacked open and her eyes were closed.

The trip had started out as an adventure, but once they had been on the road for eight hours, Hope did what any seven-year-old would . . . she whined.

That was a day and a half ago. They stopped for meals and one night in a roadside motel.

The car sputtered, swinging Melanie's attention back to the road. Pine trees spiked toward the dusky sky, the clouds and smell in the air told her rain was close.

All she needed to do was coast into River Bend. She had enough money to stay at Miss Gina's Bed-and-Breakfast for a couple of nights. Hopefully Gina would offer an "old times' sake" discount in exchange for help in the kitchen . . . maybe the making of a few beds and she could stay a little longer.

All she had to do was limp her car into town and pray Miss Gina could take her in early. She wasn't expected for another week.

Melanie rounded the corner and immediately dodged a pothole that would have swallowed her front end had she not seen it. As she corrected the steering, a new sound rang from her already pissed off engine.

She held her breath and decided to ease up on the gas.

The noise stayed with her.

The next corner had the occasional "check engine" light turning a steady red. Melanie tapped her dashboard, hoping it was wrong.

Twenty more miles. Twenty more miles.

Hope's sleepy voice pulled Melanie from her silent chant. "Mommy?"

"Hey, sweetie."

"Are we there yet?"

"Almost." She offered a weak smile over her shoulder.

"When did it get dark?"

Good question . . . *When I wasn't looking.* "Not long ago."

"I'm hungry."

"I know . . . we're almost there."

Her piece of crap car sputtered and slowed. "No, no, no."

"Is the car sick again?"

"No . . . yes . . . just a little longer." Worry etched up her spine as rain started to fall.

She reached for her cell phone and cussed under her breath. *No Service.*

Of course not. Why would River Bend bother with updated cell towers when two-way radios worked just fine?

"Hope, honey, I want you to look at Mommy's phone and tell me if we get service."

Hope reached for the phone and placed it in her lap.

Less than a mile later, Hope said, "One bar . . . wait . . . no, it's gone."

A second light on her dash sprang to life. This one flashed, as if calling Melanie an idiot for continuing to drive. "I have no choice," she said as she hit the dash again.

Seemed the car took offense and coughed one last time before the engine gave up altogether.

"No. C'mon . . . no!"

"That's not good," Hope said.

"Not good at all." Melanie managed to pull off the road by a good two feet. She shoved the car in neutral and attempted to start her again.

Click.

Click.

She rested her head on the steering wheel and closed her eyes. Eighteen more miles. That's all she'd needed. The desire to roll into a ball and block out her situation nearly took over her good sense.

"It's okay, Mommy. We can walk."

Melanie released a frustrated laugh. "No, hon . . . it's too dark." *And too far.*

Hope undid her seat belt and handed her the cell phone. "You can call someone."

She attempted a smile and glanced at the phone.

No Service.

She waved it in the air.

Nothing.

She shoved the door open and stood alongside the dark road waving her phone in the air. The ambient light lit her face, but still, the words *No Service* mocked her.

Melanie reached into the car and popped the trunk.

As the rain settled in, she pulled a sweatshirt from her suitcase and another from Hope's bright purple bag.

After turning on her flashers and popping the hood as a sign to anyone who might drive by that they could use help, Melanie climbed into the backseat with her daughter.

She shook her rain-soaked hair and pulled Hope's sweatshirt over her head. "It's going to get a little cold."

"We can run the heater."

"It only works when the engine runs, sweetie."

"Oh."

Melanie found the remainder of their road trip food and offered the last of the cheesy crackers and gummy bears to her daughter. Someone would come along, she told herself.

She dialed 911 and pressed Send on the off chance the *No Service* notice was as out of order as her car.

It rang once, and then went dead . . . Melanie tried a few more times before giving up.

"Do you know where we are?" Hope asked with a mouth full of crackers.

"River Bend is only a few miles away."

Hope wiped the sleeve of her shirt against the condensation on the window and peered out. "There's a lot of trees."

Melanie found herself smiling. "Yeah. I missed them."

"Our trees are smaller."

"When I was about your age, I used to climb some of these trees."

Hope's blue eyes grew wide. "You climbed a tree?"

"Took a week to get the sap off my hands."

"I wanna climb a tree."

"My friend Zoe had the best climbing tree in the field by her house."

"You think it's still there?"

"Not a lot changes in a small town. My guess is, it's still there and waiting for another little girl to climb it."

The pounding of the rain on the hood of the car intensified. Both of them looked up and Hope started to squirm.

Oh, no.

"Mommy?"

Melanie closed her eyes . . .

"I need to go to the bathroom."

As if on cue, the sky flashed and thunder shook the car.

Melanie waited until Hope was squirming around the backseat before she shoved the both of them into their jackets and flung open the back door away from the road. Not that it mattered, no one had passed in the forty minutes they'd been sitting there.

One foot outside the car and Melanie was up to her ankles in wet muck. A marsh more than a puddle sat right outside the door.

She reached for her daughter and did her best to lift her away from the majority of the gunk. "We don't want to leave the car, Hope. You're going to have to pee here."

Hope squished her nose and looked as if she was about to object.

The rain that was coming down in steady sheets picked up speed and Hope reached for her jeans.

Melanie held Hope's arm to keep her from falling and waited. A blast of cold air had her teeth chattering.

She was about to encourage Hope to hurry when she stood upright and pulled up her pants. Rather than walking through the mud a second time, Melanie directed her daughter around the back of the car and helped her into the backseat.

Instead of popping in beside her, Melanie moved to the driver's seat and opened the trunk. They'd both have to change into dry clothes or spend their first week in River Bend sick with the flu.

"Damn rain," she said once Hope was out of earshot.

She tossed Hope's smaller case into the front seat and went back for the second when light flittered across the trees above her car. For a brief second she thought it was lightning, then the sound of an engine met with the lights.

Melanie dropped her suitcase beside her when a twin cab, long bed truck took the corner a little fast.

She shielded her eyes from the light with one hand and waved with the other. "Please stop," she whispered to herself. *And don't be an ax murderer.*

Her heart kicked hard when the truck splashed up a puddle in the middle of the street, spraying her already soaked frame to the bone. Just when she was sure the driver of the truck was going to pass her by, she heard a screech of brakes, and the red taillights filled the dark night.

"Thank God."

The words no sooner left her lips than the truck gunned in reverse and did a thorough job of ensuring not one inch of her was dry.

The tall frame of a man stepped out and peered at her from over the bed of the truck.

"I-I think you missed a spot," Melanie chattered.

"What the hell are you doing standing on the side of the road in the rain?" The stranger was actually yelling at her.

She couldn't see his features under the hood of his coat . . . she glimpsed a bit of facial hair from the light inside the cab, but she couldn't tell if it was *I'm a mountain man hermit who chops up body parts of stranded women and children* hair or a fashion statement.

"I'm enjoying a walk," she yelled back.

"What?"

Melanie shook her head. "My car broke down."

Just then, Hope opened the back door.

"Mommy?"

"Get back in the car, Hope."

"Do we have a ride to town?"

Melanie shot a look at the stranger. "Get back in the car."

"But . . ."

"Hope!" She used her Mom voice and her daughter closed the back door.

She thought she saw the flash of the stranger's teeth. The dark hid his eyes and didn't give her any hint about their safety with the man.

"Listen, lady . . . I can give you and your daughter a ride into town. It's not very far."

Melanie wrapped her arms around herself and attempted to hold in a full body shiver. "Uhm . . . yeah . . . but you could be a parolee from Sing Sing."

The man laughed. "A parolee wouldn't have stopped."

Maybe.

"I-I'd feel better if you'd send a tow truck after me once you got into town."

"You want me to leave you out here?"

She shivered again. "A tow truck is closer than Sing Sing. I'd appreciate the call," she told him.

The man shifted his head toward the road, then back to her and her broken-down car. "Suit yourself." With that, he jumped back into the cab of his truck and started to drive away.

He got as far as a few yards before pulling off to the side of the road and turning on his hazard lights.

She wasn't sure what the man was up to, but she didn't see the point of standing in the rain any longer to figure him out.

With her suitcase back in the trunk, she crawled in beside her daughter and closed the wind outside. Reaching over Hope, she locked the door and swiped her wet hand across the window to keep watch on the truck . . . or more importantly, the stranger inside.

"Is he calling for help?" Hope asked.

"I think so."

Melanie kept one eye out the window and fished a dry sweatshirt and leggings from her daughter's clothes. One layer at a time, she managed to help her little girl into dryer clothing, shivering the whole time.

She was tossing wet clothing onto the floor of the front seat when a fist knocked on her window.

Melanie jumped.

Outside, there wasn't any evidence of another car . . . a tow truck . . . anything. Only the tall frame of the stranger. Since she couldn't roll the window down to talk to him, she debated what to do.

"Aren't you going to open the door?" Hope asked.

"I, uhm . . ."

He knocked again.

She jumped . . . again.

The sound of the rain on the car made yelling through the steel impossible.

Melanie opened the door but kept both hands on the door handle, ready to slam it closed.

When he didn't attempt to open it farther, she relaxed slightly.

"The tow truck is an hour away. You sure you don't want a ride?"

The man was still a shadow, though his voice was somewhat soft.

"An hour," Hope whined beside her.

"Hush."

"I'm not going to hurt ya, lady. I swear." He lifted his hands in the air.

"I bet Jack the Ripper said the same thing."

The man scratched his head.

"You can move along. We'll be fine."

The man grumbled, turned on his heel, and marched back to his truck.

Melanie closed the door, locked it again, a wiped the windows to keep an eye on the stranger.

"He seemed nice," Hope added her opinion.

"He might be, but I'm not taking any chances." She noticed exhaust come from the tailpipe of the truck but it made no move to drive away. "Let this be a lesson for you, young lady. Don't get in a car with a stranger."

"Won't the guy in the tow truck be a stranger?" Hope asked.

"Well, yeah . . . but that's different."

"How?"

It was time for Melanie to scratch her head. "It just is."

"That's a Mom answer."

Melanie rolled her eyes at her wise daughter. "Tow truck drivers are there to help you when your car breaks down. They are doing their job."

"Like a policeman or a fireman?"

"Yeah."

"They aren't the only people that want to help strangers."

"I know, honey. Maybe that man just wants to help, but I don't know him." *Trust is earned, not given freely. Even when it's earned, it's sometimes blown to tiny bits.*

Five minutes ticked by in silence when Hope ran out of questions about strangers and matters of trusting them.

The stranger turned off his engine and sat in his cab.

Melanie watched his shadow like a hawk.

Less than twenty minutes later, the road flashed with red and blue lights as a sheriff's squad car pulled around the corner and tucked in behind Melanie's hunk of junk. "Stay here," she said for the second time that night.

The rain had let up to a steady fall instead of sheets, not that her body felt the difference.

The officer pushed out of the car, placing a plastic-covered hat on their head.

"Looks like you're having some trouble." Melanie heard the voice of a woman and felt her shoulders slump in relief.

"Stupid car." Melanie kicked the tire as she walked by.

The officer shone her light on the car, then up into Melanie's face. "Mel?"

Melanie sucked in a breath. "JoAnne?"

Jo shoved the light in her own face, giving Melanie the best relief of the night. "Oh, my God. I knew you were the sheriff, but . . . wow! Just look at you!"

Her gun toting, flashlight shining BFF squealed like any friend should, and moved in for a hug.

"Looks like you have it from here, Sheriff," the voice of the stranger sounded in the drizzling rain.

"Melanie's an old friend. Thanks for the call, Wyatt."

So his name is Wyatt.

"Might wanna teach your friend that not everyone wants to cut her up."

"I'll do that," Jo yelled as Wyatt slid back into his truck and left.

"What's he all about?" Melanie found herself asking.

Before Jo could answer, Hope was ducking her head out of the backseat again. "Can I come out now?"

Melanie waved her daughter from the car and she came running.

Chapter Two

Jo insisted Melanie and Hope stay with her until morning. It wasn't hard saying yes when Hope all but begged for a hot meal and a warm house.

With Jo back at work, Melanie settled into Jo's childhood home. The bungalow's footprint was the same, but the furniture had changed and the walls were free of floral patterned paper.

Once Hope was tucked into the guest room, fed, showered, and exhausted, Melanie pulled the cork on a bottle of wine and lit a fire.

The house felt smaller than she remembered . . . quiet. She'd never spent any time in the Ward home without her friend. She found herself looking around, waiting for Sheriff Ward to walk in the door and read her the riot act for drinking. Didn't matter that she was twenty-eight now, well past the legal age to drink . . . your parents, or even your friend's parents who knew you before you could wear a bra, intimidated you into believing you were still ten.

Melanie wiggled sock-covered toes and let the flames warm the last part of her that still felt chilled.

She couldn't remember the last time she sat in front of a fireplace. Probably right after Hope was born when her mother sent her tickets to fly to the East Coast to visit. What a mess that was. Whatever maternal instinct her mother had when she was growing up had disappeared the day her divorce was final. The free trip to Connecticut was to ease her mother's guilty conscience. Melanie went to try and give Hope a grandmother.

By the time she boarded the plane back to California all hopes of a normal grandparent for her daughter had vanished.

Felicia Bartlett sent her a hundred bucks and a generic birthday card every year . . . sent another check for Christmas. If Melanie could afford to deny the money, she would. But pride didn't put food on the table. If it were just her, she'd probably send it back. Instead, she put every dollar in a savings account for Hope. It wouldn't add up to much, but maybe by the time her daughter was driving, she could afford a running car for her.

She didn't even want to think about college.

The jiggling of the lock in the door told her Jo was home.

Melanie lifted both hands in the air, one held her wineglass. "I didn't do it," she said as Jo closed the door behind her.

Jo offered a laugh as she pulled her overcoat from her shoulders. "The guilty always say that."

As Jo removed what looked to be a twenty-pound belt from her waist and draped it on a side table, she slowly started to look more like Melanie's old screw-the-establishment friend and less like a cop.

"Thanks for letting us stay here. Hope was exhausted."

"You looked like something the cat drug home yourself."

Melanie pulled herself off the couch and grabbed a glass from the kitchen. She splashed some of the wine for her friend. "I've had better days."

"I'm glad you're here. It's been way too long."

Melanie sat back down, tucked her feet under her. "I know . . . I'm sorry."

"What are you sorry about?"

"I didn't even come back for your dad's funeral." Her eyes traveled to the mantel above the fireplace. There, in a triangle frame, was what had to be the flag that had draped over Sheriff Ward's casket.

Jo fell into a chair across from her.

"I didn't come when Hope was born. We're even. Besides . . . funerals suck, and screaming women in labor aren't pleasant either."

They both laughed at that.

"She's beautiful. Looks a lot like you did when we were kids."

"She's amazing . . . smart, so damn smart."

"Just like her mom."

Even after seven years with the title, it was hard to hear.

"Her mom wasn't smart enough. Didn't even graduate from college."

Jo waved her glass toward her. "Not your fault. You didn't flunk out."

No, she hadn't flunked. She'd made the grade, but once her parents separated and sold the house . . . they decided they couldn't afford the fancy school. Her parents made too much money for financial aid, but not enough to pay the entire bill. When Melanie realized how quickly she was going into debt with student loans, and no clear path on what she wanted to do with her life, she'd dropped out. Torn apart from her family, her friends, Melanie turned to a guy. Her train to the future derailed and the piece left over was asleep upstairs.

"Life isn't like any of us thought it would be," Jo said. "Does that prick ex-husband of yours help at all?"

"Nathan?"

Jo looked over her glass. "Do you have more than one ex-husband?"

It was time to come clean. "No . . . I—" She drew in a deep breath. "I don't even have one of them."

"One of what?"

"Ex-husband. I never married Nathan."

Jo lowered her glass to her lap slowly. "But you said—"

"I know what I told you . . . what I told everyone. I was embarrassed, scared. I knew the minute I told Nathan about Hope that he wasn't going to stick. He said we should get married. I told him I'd think about it. Within a month he was telling everyone I was his wife."

"So there was no justice of the peace?"

Melanie took a big drink of her wine. "Nope. If we could make it through Hope's delivery . . . the first year . . ."

Jo's eyes never left hers. "I thought you'd fallen for Mr. Right."

"I was so messed up after USC. I found a weekend job waiting tables until I could serve alcohol, then I switched to the bar circuit. Serving drinks and getting my ass pinched was a nightly affair. I spent the weekdays trying an online community college. It didn't take long for Nathan to convince me to work two jobs so he could concentrate on school. Then he was going to work so I could go back . . ." She lost her voice. For a brief amount of time, she'd thought it could work.

"I remember you telling me you were going to hold off for him. Pissed me off. I thought you were stronger than that."

Melanie scoffed. "You leave high school believing you can conquer the world. Then she kicks your ass."

Jo lifted her glass. "I can drink to that."

They sat watching the flames lick the log in the fireplace.

"So Nathan doesn't help you at all?"

"Once he realized raising a baby meant one of us had to be home at all times . . . that I couldn't work to support his school, and he couldn't party when I worked, he stopped playing house. He left the apartment, moved in with a friend. He gave me cash once in a while for the first year . . . then one day he came over and started an argument . . . said he always doubted if Hope was even his."

"Bastard."

"Yeah . . . then he left." Melanie shook the memories away and refilled her glass. The wine was already swimming in her head. She didn't often drink since there was no one else to take up for Hope if something happened. Having Jo there gave her some peace to relax.

"I'm really sorry, Mel."

She shrugged. "I am, too. Not about Hope. I mean sure, at first, the enormity of becoming a parent before I got my shit together scared me to death. It's been hard, but I wouldn't trade her for anything."

"You always hear parents say that."

"You'll see when you have a kid, Jo. It changes you."

Jo finished her wine and set the glass to the side. "I have enough responsibility. Last thing I need is a kid."

"That's what I said."

"How are things now? From the looks of the suitcases you and Hope brought, your stay here is going to be longer than a week."

The wine was making her weepy. "I don't know what the hell I'm going to do. The cost of living in California is stupid, even in nowhere Bakersfield. The school Hope was in was crap . . . the neighborhood would keep *you* busy until you're eighty."

"What about your job?"

"Phew . . . my job? I'm tired of my ass getting pinched."

Jo moved from her chair and sat next to Melanie with an arm around her shoulders. "Sounds like you need a fresh start."

Melanie wiped a fallen tear. "I do. I don't know if it's here, but I knew it wasn't there."

"You can stay with me. I have plenty of room."

Melanie shook her head. "I can't do that, Jo."

"Yes you can."

"It would be too easy. Like bumming off your parents. If my fresh start is back here in River Bend, then it has to be on my own two feet . . . not yours."

Jo frowned, then sighed. "I get it. The offer is always open."

Melanie moved in for a hug.

They both stretched out with the empty bottle of wine between them.

Through the quiet, Jo muttered, "I don't remember the last time someone pinched my ass."

~

Hope bounced on Melanie's bed at the butt crack of dawn. "You're wasting our vacation sleeping, Mommy."

"I'm up. I'm up." She ran a hand over the sand in her eyes and attempted to shake sleep away. Hope was already across the room and pulling the drapes open.

"Oh, Lord." One too many glasses of wine. *I'm such a lightweight.*

"It's not raining," Hope announced.

And the sun was burning her eyes like a vampire's. Shoving the blankets to the side, she padded across the room and slipped into a bathrobe.

"C'mon, sweetie, let's find you some cereal and a TV." To quiet and entertain her while Melanie sought out a shower.

The smell of fresh coffee warmed her senses before she reached the bottom floor.

Jo had made a pot and left a note.

> *Make yourself at home. I'm at the station . . . you and*
> *Hope should stop by. Your car is at Miller's . . . yes it is*
> *still Miller's and in the same place. Feel free to use my car.*
> *I have the black-and-white. I'm really glad you're here.*
> *Jo*

Melanie played with the keys as she read the note. "I'm glad I'm here, too."

After finding a cartoon channel and setting Hope up with breakfast, Melanie worked her way to the bathroom.

An hour later Melanie had Hope by the hand and the two of them were walking through town. JoAnne's car was still safely tucked in her garage. After hours of driving the past few days, it felt good to take the slow route. As they walked through town, memories did a fine job of making her smile. The wooden white gazebo sat in the center of a small, grassy park in the center of town. The memory of her and Mark playing tag as children had her hearing his laugh. She could almost smell the hot popcorn that accompanied every holiday spent outside in that very spot. Melanie pointed at storefronts, told Hope what had occupied each space when she was a kid. Most of them were the same. Fresh coats of paint, a new facing on the building, but everything felt familiar.

They rounded on Second Street down to Miller's Auto Repair. The tow truck occupied one parking space, an old Ford pickup sat beside it. Inside one of the two stalls in the garage was her car. The hood was open, a light hung from inside where the mechanic must have left it. Inside the garage, loud heavy metal music blared.

When Melanie didn't see anyone, she attempted to call over the music. "Hello?"

Silence . . . well, from a person who wasn't on a radio in any event.

Melanie stepped deeper into the shop. "Hello?"

"Hold up." She heard the voice of a man.

She stopped in front of the open hood of her car. Whoever had been looking at it had taken off bits and set them to the side. Computer code would be just as foreign as the underside of a car. She didn't know her way around an engine and wasn't going to pretend to now.

The volume of the music diminished and someone called, "Hey there."

Melanie turned to a familiar face. "Hello, Mr. Miller."

Mr. Miller had owned the shop for as long as Melanie could remember. He worked on everyone's car in town at some point. At six two or better, with a good extra forty pounds on him, Mr. Miller had always appeared intimidating. Until he smiled like he was now. Then he was a big teddy bear. "Melanie Bartlett? Richard's girl."

"That's right, Mr. Miller."

"Well I'll be. You are all grown up." He pulled a shop towel from the side of her car and wiped his hands. Not that the stains would disappear after five years of hard scrubbing.

"Ten years has a way of doing that," she said with a grin.

"And who is this?" He smiled at Hope.

Hope held her hand tight.

"This is my daughter, Hope. Say hello, honey."

"Hello, Mr. Miller."

"So polite, too." He winked and Hope attempted to wink back.

"How is Mrs. Miller?"

"Fine, just fine. I'm sure she'd love to see you. You'll have to drop by the house and bring this cutie with you."

It was hard not to smile. Mrs. Miller loved to bake, hence Mr. Miller's slightly large girth. Dropping by was a favorite pastime when she was a kid and always resulted in a take-home package of something sweet.

"We'll do that."

Mr. Miller rounded in front of the car. "This yours?"

"Sorry to say."

He made a few tsk-tsk sounds and his smile started to fade.

"That bad?"

"It's not good. Luke is digging deeper to make sure, but . . ."

She had to wade through the bad news before the name Mr. Miller had used sank in. "Luke is still here?"

"Of course."

Despite her dead car, she smiled again. She couldn't wait to catch up with her old friend.

Mr. Miller started talking about oil levels and starters . . . something about a block. Everything he said was all over her head.

The sound of a motorcycle drew their attention to the front of the garage.

Luke still wore black and leather . . . his frame had filled out in ten years, but he still had that swagger that drove Zoe crazy in high school. Melanie always thought the two of them would ride off into the sunset on his bike.

Life happens, and that wasn't their path.

"Mel?"

She dropped her daughter's hand and accepted his hug. "Luke!"

He picked her up and swung her around. "Jesus, look at you."

She knew she didn't look bad. Ten years had filled her curves out as well. Staying in shape was easy when your car broke down all the time and walking was a better option than taking the city bus.

She punched his arm when he set her back down. "Look at me? Look at you. There should be a law for looking better than you did in high school."

Luke winked, just like his dad, and swung an arm over her shoulders. "Good to see you, too." His eyes traveled to Hope. "This must be your girl."

After introductions and another attempt at winking out of Hope, they started back into the garage. "Jo dropped in earlier, said this was your car. I took the liberty of taking it apart."

If there was one person she could trust under the hood more than Mr. Miller, it was Mr. Miller's son.

"Your dad says it's bad."

"Our car died," Hope said from the side.

"It sure did," Luke agreed.

"What are we going to drive if our car is dead, Mommy?"

Melanie glanced at Hope. "I'm sure Luke and Mr. Miller can fix it."

Only one look at Luke and that assurance blew away. "Or not."

Hope drew her brows together with worry. "But we need a car."

"It will be okay, baby."

"Hey, Hope?" Mr. Miller distracted her. "Do you know what the best part about having a broken car is?"

She shook her head.

"Auto shops always have fresh donuts. Do you like donuts?"

She bobbed her head and took his hand, before Mr. Miller led her down the hall and into the office.

"Is it that bad?" Melanie asked once Hope was gone.

"Nothing that a little C-4 and the back of Grayson's farm won't take care of."

"C'mon . . ."

"How long was the oil light on, Mel?" Luke ran a hand over his slightly long hair and stared at her.

"It's always on. I topped off the oil in Redding."

"Topping off means some of it ran out . . . did it take the entire quart?"

"Yeah."

"Did the oil light go off?"

"No. It went on in Modesto, flickered on more than off ever since."

Luke rolled his eyes. "You can't ignore the oil light, Mel."

"I didn't ignore it. I gave it oil."

Luke stepped over to a workstation and waved a part in front of her. "Your oil pan had a hole in it. The slow leak gave you a nice trail to follow back to Bakersfield. Do you know what happens when your engine doesn't get oil?"

"It's like gas, right? The car stops running . . . but you put oil in and it's all good."

Luke squeezed his eyes shut and shook his head. "Oh, Mel."

"I'm not right?"

"Nowhere close. A car without oil can only run dry for so long, then after miles of sputtering and bitching at you, she flips you the bird and cracks. You cracked the block, Mel."

"That's bad?" She really didn't know.

Luke lifted one brow in the air. "Do you have any idea how bad I want to tell a blonde joke right now?"

"How do you fix a cracked block?"

"You don't," Luke told her. "You put in a whole new engine. With the condition of this car, our advice is to cut your losses and start over."

"I can't afford a new car, Luke."

He sighed. "That's what I thought."

"How much does a new engine cost?"

"These foreign cars usually run a good twenty-five hundred just for the engine."

Melanie felt her eyes widen. "Dollars? Twenty-five hundred *dollars*?"

"See why I think you should find another used car?"

If she had twenty-five hundred bucks, she probably would. At least her decision was an easy one. She couldn't afford the repair, so C-4 in a back field it was.

She reached into her purse and removed her wallet.

"What are you doing?" Luke asked.

"Paying for the tow and what you've done."

Luke waved her off. "Your money isn't any good here, Mel."

"I can afford to pay for your time."

"My time is cheap. Buy me a beer at R&B's."

She knew she wasn't going to win, so she returned her wallet. "You're on."

Chapter Three

It was well past noon when Melanie pulled Jo's Jeep into the driveway of Miss Gina's Bed-and-Breakfast. Like everything else in town, the footprint was the same. The shrubs had grown, a new tree planted here, a new rosebush there . . . the place could use a coat of paint and the gravel on the driveway was in need of a dusting of whatever it was they used to maintain it.

As Hope and Melanie walked up the stairs, she realized the place needed a bit more than paint. It wasn't run down . . . not like the motels in Bakersfield, but it wasn't exactly what Melanie remembered.

The bell on the door rang as she and Hope stepped inside. Like most B and Bs, the old Victorian was made up of small rooms, each of which served a purpose when the house was built at the turn of the twentieth century. To be fair, they served a purpose now . . . only one was a large dining area where a parlor once stood.

When she was a kid, Zoe would sometimes pick up a few hours

of work with Miss Gina. Mainly in the kitchen on busy holidays and summer weekends. Jo would complain as she raked leaves in the fall, and Melanie would answer phones and occasionally make a bed or clean a floor. The three of them had enjoyed hanging with Miss Gina and her colorful mouth. The lady never treated any of them like they were kids. She treated them as equals. In a small town, that went a long way.

Before Melanie moved past the threshold, she knelt down to her daughter. "I've known Miss Gina for a very long time. She's harmless, even though she uses bad words sometimes. Be polite."

"Sometimes you use bad words."

"Not like Miss Gina," Melanie all but mumbled.

Hope sent her a look she'd seen in her own face more times than she'd care to admit. Disbelief manifested in a high brow and a cock of the head. Melanie would laugh if Hope's subtle attitude wasn't spot-on.

"C'mon." She dragged her daughter toward the abandoned registration desk. "Miss Gina?" she called.

Silence.

Thud!

Melanie shrugged at her daughter and peered at the ceiling. "Miss Gina?" she called toward the stairs.

A larger thud and a distinctive crash had the two of them running.

They made it halfway up before Melanie heard the smoky voice of Miss Gina. "Son of a bitch!"

Before Melanie made it into one of the guest bathrooms, water sprayed toward the door, a puddle pooled at Miss Gina's feet.

She held a broken pipe with both hands, unsuccessfully attempting to hold the water in. "Towel," she yelled the second Melanie ducked her head into the room.

She grabbed one from the far rack and handed it over.

As Miss Gina scrambled to keep the spray from removing the wallpaper, Melanie dropped to her knees to find the shutoff valve for the vintage Elizabethan toilet.

"It's at the top." Miss Gina pointed with her chin.

Melanie switched direction, climbed on the commode, and found the crank.

By the time the water stopped trickling, Miss Gina dripped like a leaky faucet, Melanie felt as if she'd had a second shower for the day, and Hope stood in the doorway with wide eyes.

"Are the extra towels still in the hall closet?" Melanie asked.

"Damn pipe . . . I just knew this was going to happen."

"Miss Gina, the floor? We gotta get this up or your reception area is going to need a new plaster job."

Miss Gina was a tiny woman who smoked more than she ate, laughed often, and cussed like a sinner on Saturday.

"Yeah, yeah . . . hall closet."

Depleted from the mess, Miss Gina slumped against the vintage tub while Melanie hustled from the room. She piled towels in Hope's arms and filled her own.

Hope mimicked her to help mop up the mess.

On all fours, Melanie sloshed up one puddle before tossing the soaked towel into the tub.

Hope handed her towels as if she were the towel girl at the spa.

"This is awful," Miss Gina started. "I finally have a fully booked week and now this."

"I'm sure you can get someone out here to fix it."

For the first time since Melanie walked into the fray, Miss Gina looked her in the eye.

With a pause and a cock of her head, she wiggled a finger in the air. "Melanie Bartlett? Is that you?"

Melanie paused in her effort to clean the floor and smiled. "Hi, Miss Gina."

Miss Gina jumped from the edge of the tub and threw her tiny arms around Melanie's shoulders. "Oh, little girl . . . look at you." She backed away and held her face. "You look tired."

Melanie felt a laugh deep in her stomach. Leave it to Miss Gina to point out the obvious.

"Mommy's always tired," Hope said.

Miss Gina took in Hope with narrow eyes. "My Lord, she looks just like you did at her age. How old are you, doll?"

"Seven."

Melanie held out her hand for another dry towel and Hope delivered it without taking her eyes from Miss Gina.

"I'm going to be eight at the end of summer."

"Oh, don't rush aging, little girl. It happens without your encouragement."

Hope simply stared in bewilderment.

Melanie sat back on her heels once the majority of the water was off the floor. "I think the lobby is safe now."

Miss Gina blew out a breath. "Yeah, but now I'm down one room."

"It's only one bathroom."

"People don't want to share bathrooms in a B and B."

Melanie sucked in her bottom lip. "True." She took another look around the familiar space. The wallpaper had changed from a floral print to one with muted stripes, but the art still held the flower motif she remembered. "How about offering it at half price?"

"I don't know if that will work. Probably have to cut that down more. Besides, that would mean sharing my bathroom until I could get this one fixed."

Looked like Miss Gina's bad plumbing was Melanie's good fortune. "We'll take it."

"Oh, no, no, no." Miss Gina stood and wiped her hands on her shirt as she walked out of the room. "I can't give an old friend castoffs. That wouldn't be right."

Melanie scrambled in front of her. "Really. We don't mind. I was actually hoping Hope and I could stay in town longer than just the class reunion weekend. I can't afford a full price room for that many days."

"I couldn't charge the person in this room. I'll have plumbers coming and going. It's too much to ask of you." Miss Gina attempted to move around her, and Melanie planted her feet in the doorway.

"I don't mind. Really. You'd be doing me a favor charging half."

Hope pulled on Miss Gina's skirt. "Mommy's car broke."

"It did?"

"Ah-huh."

"You don't have a car?"

"I'm using Jo's until I figure out what to do with mine."

"Can you believe our Jo is the town sheriff? I still pinch myself when I see her all geared up and wearing a gun."

"Everything changes," Melanie said with a glance at her daughter. "I'll take the room, Miss Gina. I could use the extra time in town."

Miss Gina glanced at Hope and back. "Fine . . . fine . . . but I'm not charging you for a crappy room. You can lend me a hand around here like the old days."

"Oh, I can't—"

Miss Gina stopped her with a hand in the air. "Not another word. It's this room for free, or another one full price."

Melanie bit her lip. "I'll take it."

Miss Gina's grin gave Melanie pause. "Perfect. Hope, grab some of those wet towels. Let me show you where the washer and dryer are." Miss Gina snapped her fingers with a wave of her hand.

Hope didn't hesitate.

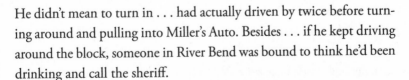

He didn't mean to turn in . . . had actually driven by twice before turning around and pulling into Miller's Auto. Besides . . . if he kept driving around the block, someone in River Bend was bound to think he'd been drinking and call the sheriff.

Not that Jo would do anything but laugh.

The crappy car he'd seen on the side of the road the night before was shoved outside of the garage doors and being lifted on the back of Miller's tow truck.

Wyatt stepped out of his truck, shut the door without even taking the keys with him. River Bend was this side of Mayberry in terms of crime. The chances of someone jumping in his truck and taking off were nil.

"Luke?"

Luke was currently positioned between the undercarriage of the wreck and the chains of his tow truck.

Wyatt placed a hand to the side of the car and ducked.

Luke noticed him and tossed the hook his way. "Hey, Wyatt. Hook that up, will ya?"

He clasped the chain, made sure it held, and backed away from the car.

Luke wiped his hands on his faded jeans before grasping the automated controls of the tow to lift the car off the ground. "Thanks."

"No problem."

While the belts and hydraulics kicked in, Luke asked, "What brings you by?"

"Saw this car on the road last night . . . just wondering how it all turned out."

"Mel is an idiot," Luke said with a laugh. "Leave it to a woman to run a car without oil."

The familiarity of Luke's words about the owner gave him pause. "Mel?"

"From Modesto to River Bend with an oil light blinking at her . . . who does that?" The hydraulics lifted the car as far as it would go before Luke tossed the controls on the bed of the lift. He fiddled with a few more chains while he worked.

"Is that a rhetorical question?" Wyatt asked.

Luke offered a grin. "Women!"

Wyatt had to agree. A man wouldn't let the oil run dry. Not a self-respecting man who did more than shove a key in the ignition and fill a gas tank. Thankfully, small towns weren't filled with lawyers, doctors, and white-collar workers who fell into that category.

Women, on the other hand, didn't have to hold six-figure careers to be deemed clueless when it came to cars.

"Can it be fixed?" Wyatt wasn't completely sure why he asked.

"Cracked block."

He blew out a long breath. A long look at the late model sedan had him shaking his head. "More trouble than it's worth."

"Yeah." Luke shook his head. "Hated breaking that news to an old friend." He shrugged and leaned an arm over the car. "It's not a complete loss. She'll make a great target out back of Grayson's farm."

Wyatt huffed. The image of a drowned shadow of a woman with wide eyes and fear swam into his head. She'd accused him of being an escapee from Sing Sing . . . Jack the Ripper, even. She had the right lines, but not an ounce of trust in a stranger. To hear she was an old friend of Luke's made Wyatt wonder. "I'm sure your friend enjoyed the thought of her car being used as target practice."

"She's smarter than her cracked block implies." Luke nodded toward Wyatt's truck. "Where you headed today?"

"Miss Gina's. I've been telling her for two years her roof needed to be replaced. Buckets in her attic after last night's storm proved me right."

Luke rolled his eyes. "That woman is still living in the sixties. Let me know when you find her pot plants."

Wyatt had his head in the same place.

Miss Gina had a way of waving away problems as if she were high on something most times.

"I'll do that."

Wyatt pushed Mel and her cracked block from his head as he turned his truck back onto the main road through town.

Every year the annual high school reunion brought in new faces and the occasional casual hookup. Small towns had a way of limiting a single man's sex life. Yeah, he could drive up the coast, or worse, up the five and hit Eugene in a little over an hour, but those encounters didn't repeat.

When he'd first moved to River Bend the last thing on his mind was women or what he might be missing from a big city. He'd grown up just outside of San Francisco and had his share of traffic, crime, and noise to last a lifetime. The best memories of his life were those from when he was young and his parents had taken him and his little sister on camping trips to Sequoia or the Redwood National Park. The quiet and calm grounded him and reminded him of happy times. He vowed that as soon as he acquired a trade that would set him up with a nice, comfortable living in a small town outside of the state of California, he'd find one and move. A simple place that didn't require him to drive through a desert to reach an airport.

That was five years ago.

A general contractor license was complete overkill for a small town where no one cared if you were licensed and bonded so long as you showed up when you said you were going to . . . and did the job as promised.

The nuance of small town living became obvious the first time he'd done a simple plumbing job for a widow who lived just outside of River Bend. Mrs. Kate offered a pot roast and an apple pie as payment.

He'd really thought that only happened in movies and novels.

Apparently not.

Having a deep respect for an older woman, especially a widow in her late seventies, Wyatt enjoyed the pot roast, ate the pie, and took the rest home that night at Mrs. Kate's insistence. To this day, he made a point of stopping by Mrs. Kate's on the first Sunday of every month with a toolbox and an empty stomach.

Unlike Mrs. Kate . . . Miss Gina offered horizontal naked favors as payment. With one look of *hell no*, Miss Gina offered a wink and cut a check. The woman still flirted like she was thirty and he was a teenager, but she never took it any further.

Thank God!

Mrs. Kate and Miss Gina were worlds apart and yet only a few miles away from each other. Wyatt appreciated both of them.

Wyatt turned down Miss Horizontal Naked Pot Lady's B and B drive and dodged a pothole before the pavement turned into ground-up asphalt that resembled a driveway.

He recognized Jo's Jeep and Miss Gina's VW van in a vintage teal and white paint with a tuck and roll interior that looked like it just came off the showroom floor. Miss Gina loved her throwback from the sixties vehicle more than anything . . . and even after a storm the van appeared as if Miss Gina had been out polishing the thing the moment the precipitation dried up.

Wyatt didn't bother walking into the inn. He stepped around the west side of the old Victorian and dragged his largest extension ladder with him. He knew months ago exactly where the roof was going to fail, but Miss Gina didn't want to fix it until after the cosmos told her it was time.

The previous night's storm was Miss Gina's sparkling sign.

With a tool belt secured around his hips, he climbed up onto the roof of the three-story house and pulled himself higher on the brittle composition shingles.

The recent warm summers and lack of maintenance had blown free a good five-foot section the night before. This close to the coast, the weather did a number on every house. Miss Gina's stood taller than most, had a decent ocean view from the widow's walk on a clear day, and therefore took the brunt of every storm nature delivered.

Wyatt balanced on one knee while he wrote down the dimensions of the minimum of work that needed to take place to keep Miss Gina's guests dry. He was extending his tape measure for the fourth time since climbing on the steep roof when he heard a noise behind him.

He twisted, caught himself as he slid half a foot.

"Wow . . . this is awesome."

A little girl . . . seven, maybe ten, he couldn't tell . . . had climbed up his ladder and was perched way too close to the edge of the brittle roof.

"Jesus!" He wasn't sure where the kid had come from, but given how she was flipping around on the steep grade, she had no idea of the drop below.

"Climbing a tree must be like this," he heard her say.

Wyatt felt his nose flare, took a deep breath. "Hey," he said in a voice five times calmer than he felt.

"This is better than climbing a tree, isn't it?" the kid asked as if they were in the middle of a conversation.

He wanted to counter her . . . say that if she were in a tree and fell the branches would break her fall, possibly end with a broken leg, not a broken neck.

To his dismay, the kid started to climb higher. "Can you see the ocean?" she asked as if they were sightseeing.

"Hold on!" This time Wyatt used a stronger voice.

The kid hesitated and slid a few inches.

Wyatt's breath caught before the girl stopped herself and continued to climb. "Miss Gina said there was a leak . . . are you fixing the leak?"

"Yeah . . . you, you shouldn't be up here."

The tiny girl kept climbing and Wyatt felt his limbs crawling closer to the kid.

If he had a crew on this roof, he'd have to have scaffolding, rails to ensure the safety of his men. He didn't hold any concessions for himself . . . but a little girl without any idea of the danger of dangling off the side of a roof was a complete risk.

"Stop!" He found himself almost yelling when the kid moved closer to the failing shingles.

Her big blue eyes grew wide, her feet stopped moving.

"It's not safe up here for little girls."

Her brows drew together and Wyatt knew he'd said the wrong thing.

"Girls are just as strong as boys. More so." She started to climb again. Determined.

Suddenly the world moved in slow motion. He saw her hand grip an unstable shingle, her feet lose balance . . . and a shriek sounded from below, drawing the child's attention away from holding on.

With one hand dragging behind him, he let his boots lose their grip and took out a good twenty feet of Miss Gina's roof before grasping hold of the kid's hand and stopping the both of them on the gutter of the inn before they could take a two-for-one special ride to the nearest emergency room.

"Hope!"

"I got her." Wyatt wrapped an arm around the kid and didn't take another breath until he knew neither one of them was going over the edge.

Good God.

The little girl grabbed his chest with tiny nails and all but crawled up his neck.

"Hope?" A woman's frantic cry had Wyatt opening his eyes.

Three stories down stood a blonde woman who had to be Hope's mother. Before Wyatt could encourage Hope's vise grip to leave some circulation in his neck, Miss Gina was beside the blonde.

"What the hell is going on?"

The blonde pointed up.

With her long skirts flowing behind her, Miss Gina tried to hold her hair back as the wind pushed against it.

"Hope, what are you doing up there?" Miss Gina asked.

"Climbing a tree," Wyatt heard her say.

"This isn't a tree, sweetheart," he told her.

Hope had figured that out and all the bravado that had passed her lips a few minutes before was gone now. She glanced to the ground and quickly buried her head into Wyatt's chest.

"Don't let her go!" the voice of Mom called.

"You're not going to let me go, are you?" Hope asked in a small voice.

Where had the strong, tiny girl who was there a few minutes ago gone? She'd been brave, managed quite the climb before a slip.

"No," he told her. "We're going to climb down together."

She held on fast.

Wyatt had to anchor his feet tighter to keep from sliding.

He inched closer to the ladder, Hope nothing but a barnacle on the hull of his frame.

"Sweetie," he said once they reached the ladder. "I need you to let go."

She held tighter.

"Hey," he said in a voice only she could hear. "You climbed up here. Let go and just sit while I step on the ladder and help you down."

Those doe eyes blinked a few times before her grip loosened.

He started to let her go and she clasped on.

Distract . . . get her to stop looking down.

"How old are you?" he asked.

"Se-seven," she stuttered.

"Really? I thought you were at least a teenager, climbing up here like you did." Her grip let loose again.

Wyatt kept one hand on her as he positioned himself on the ladder.

"I'm just seven," Hope said in a much calmer voice. "Gonna be eight in August."

Once his feet were secure on the second step down the ladder, he waved Hope over.

She scrambled like she had earlier.

No fear.

"August is a good month for a birthday."

Hope nodded as she turned her back to him and started a slow descent.

"My friend Lorna's birthday is two days before Christmas. That just sucks."

The second story passed them as they talked their way down.

"Christmas birthdays always suck."

"Yeah."

"Birthday gifts get lost in Christmas wrapping."

"Yeah."

Wyatt felt the ground beneath his feet before he lifted Hope from the last few steps. He hadn't let go when Blondie clasped the kid to her chest like a life raft in a turbulent sea.

"Don't ever do that again," she scolded without an ounce of anger.

"She's fine, Melanie. You've climbed trees higher than my roof," Miss Gina said.

Wyatt took a step back.

So this was Mel . . . Melanie . . . friend of the town sheriff . . . old friend of Luke . . . owner of a car destined for destruction in the back of Grayson's farm.

The woman who kept him locked in a cold truck half the night.

Her amber eyes found his over the head of her daughter and held.

Chapter Four

She wanted to kill her, hold her . . . strangle her . . . scold her . . . love her to death.

Good night, parenting was a bipolar disorder.

Melanie knelt down to her daughter's level and clasped her face between her palms. "Don't *ever* do that again. You hear me?"

"But—"

"No buts, Hope! What you did was dangerous and you could have gotten really hurt."

"But—"

Melanie let her hands slip to her daughter's shoulders and tighten. "Never again!" she yelled.

Hope's big eyes started to moisten and her bottom lip started to tremble. Melanie wanted to comfort her but didn't want her point to be lost.

"Hey, Hope." Miss Gina placed a hand over Melanie's. "Why don't we go inside and make some lemonade?"

Hope nodded and took Miss Gina's hand.

Melanie watched her daughter walk out of sight before the adrenaline of the moment dumped into her system all at once. Her head grew dizzy and her eyes misted over. Before she could fall, she went ahead and let her knees bend until she felt the damp soil under her butt.

"You okay?"

Melanie squinted up at the stranger who'd kept her daughter from what would have been a very painful fall and sighed. "I'm going to be gray before I'm thirty," she said.

He ran a hand through his brown hair before releasing the tool belt from his waist and dropping it to the ground. He pushed up a spot of grass beside her and rested his forearms on his knees. "You have had a rough couple of days," he told her.

"Boy have I ever." It took Melanie a full thirty seconds to register his words. "Wait . . . how would you know about my week?"

The stranger smiled, flashing dimples, and reached out his hand to shake hers. "Name's Jack . . . Jack the Ripper. I'm on a work release program out of Sing Sing. Save little girls to keep my parole officer happy."

She placed a limp hand in his and peered close. It was the stranger from the night before, minus the rain-soaked coat and pissy attitude. "Oh, God. I'm sorry . . . I mean . . ."

Melanie clasped his hand tighter and felt a laugh deep in her belly. It didn't take long for that adrenaline to release in laughter. "I'm sorry I kept you out in the rain. Thank you for all your help last night."

"I couldn't exactly leave you there."

"Lots of people would."

He had the kindest chocolate brown eyes. His hair was long on top, a surfer style Melanie saw a lot in California. He had a decent tan, considering he lived in Oregon, and he was thicker than a pencil pushing desk jockey.

Fit, definitely fit.

A byproduct of his job, she guessed.

Wyatt lifted her hand, which still held his. "Can I have this back?"

She released it as if he stung. "Sorry."

"S'okay. You've had a hard couple of days," he said again. "The name's Wyatt, by the way."

"Right. Jo said that last night."

He rested his elbows on his knees but kept his eyes on her. "And you're Melanie."

"How do you know?"

"I saw your car at Luke's shop. He told me you were old high school friends. I assume you're here for the reunion."

Melanie glanced up at the Victorian. "Yeah. I can't believe it's been ten years. I promised my girls I'd be here."

"You have more than one daughter?"

She shook her head. "No, no . . . Hope is my only child. I mean Jo and Zoe. We were like sisters growing up. Couldn't let them down."

"Even if it killed your car."

"Even if it killed my car," she said matter-of-factly.

They both stared at the roof of the inn before the silence between them took weight.

Melanie felt Wyatt's eyes before she confirmed with a twist of her head he was staring at her.

Something she hadn't felt in forever stirred deep inside her. She couldn't tell if he was flirting with only a look, or if the dimple that deepened on the right side of his cheek was something he always wore. He was younger than her, if she wasn't completely off her game . . . and she had a kid.

Flirting wasn't something a man who looked like him did with a woman like her.

So when his eyes flitted to her lips, and then popped back to meet her gaze, Melanie attempted to push to her feet. Her hands slid in the mud before she caught herself and stood.

"I should make sure Miss Gina isn't spiking the lemonade."

Wyatt laughed as he stood beside her. "The special batch is always in the red pitcher."

A teenage memory of that red pitcher made Melanie smile.

"Well." She extended a slightly dirty hand to him again, felt a buzz of current when he took it. "Thanks for not letting Hope plunge to an early death."

His hand was warm . . . comforting.

"My parole officer would have sent me back if I had." He winked.

Melanie released his hand and bit her lip as she smiled. Maybe she had a little flirt in her after all. "I'll be sure and tell him you were our hero."

Wyatt reached for his tool belt and fastened it around his slim hips.

He caught her watching his slightly damp ass as he turned to look behind him before climbing up the ladder.

"Going . . ." She stumbled on her own feet as she scrambled away. "Check on Hope."

Wyatt the Ripper . . . from Sing Sing . . . laughed as she disappeared inside.

~

The lemonade was from a powder and not nature's fruit.

With vodka . . . it was perfect.

Jo turned up after her shift and poured from Miss Gina's giant red pitcher while the three of them kicked back in conversation. The inn was quiet. Hope was asleep, sent to bed early for creating several wrinkles in her mother's face.

Melanie smothered Hope with a hug before making her go to bed early. The thought of her daughter hanging on the edge of the three-story Victorian would live with her forever.

"I wanted to kill her."

"You haven't stopped holding her since she climbed off that ladder." Miss Gina released a long stream of smoke from her lungs as she spoke.

They sat on the back porch, the twilight and several strings of white Christmas lights running across the length of the wraparound porch offering enough light to drink and chat by.

"Doesn't mean I didn't want to strangle her." Melanie sipped her drink, laid her head back against the wicker chair, and closed her eyes. "I will never have sex without a condom again," she declared.

Jo started to laugh. "I think I need to quote that."

Melanie pointed her glass in Jo's direction without opening her eyes. "You do that! I'm done. One kid is more than enough for me."

"I can beat that," Miss Gina said.

"That's a shame," Jo told their host. "You would have been the best mom ever. You never get mad . . . take everything in stride . . . why do you think we hung out here all the time?"

Melanie lifted an eyebrow and saw Miss Gina lift her glass. "Might have something to do with the giant red pitcher in my fridge."

"It was more than that. We could be ourselves here."

Miss Gina waved her cigarette in Melanie's direction. "You remember that for your own daughter."

That was different . . . wasn't it? "I need to keep her safe."

"Safe, not smother her."

"The world is different than when we grew up."

Miss Gina shook her head. "Not in River Bend. We don't change here. Other than a few businesses that have gone under, and the occasional bust Sheriff Nosy gets herself into, this town doesn't change."

Jo didn't bat an eye at Miss Gina's dig.

"Bakersfield was crime central. I couldn't let Hope walk to school alone." *So different from our childhood.*

"Why are you there?" Miss Gina asked.

"It's where I ended up."

"*Ended up* is such a cop-out," Miss Gina chided. "You're an adult. Take charge, girl. How can you be a role model to that little girl if you're the mom who *ended up* somewhere?"

The direct, cut-the-bullshit trait Melanie loved most about Miss Gina did a fair job of raising the hair on the nape of her neck. Even though she knew the woman was right.

"It wasn't my plan—"

"Change the freakin' plan."

Jo sat silent until then. "She has a point."

"I'm here, aren't I?"

"For a high school reunion," Miss Gina reminded her.

"I might stay." The emerging stars above started to pull down as two of the most influential people in her life stared in judgment.

"*Might* means shit in my book," Miss Gina said.

"I don't have a job here."

"So get one." Miss Gina wasn't letting go.

"Fine!" Melanie sat high in her chair, the hair on her neck now a hard stone ready to ward off any impending doom. "I need a job, Miss Gina. Is the inn hiring?"

A soft lift to Miss Gina's left eyebrow and a twinkle in her eye told Melanie she'd been outsmarted by the older woman. "I could use some help. Not getting any younger."

"Good! This place could use some help."

"It could."

"Good!" Melanie wasn't sure why she was upset. She'd managed a job while sitting on the back porch drinking spiked lemonade.

"Good!" Miss Gina finished her glass and poured another.

Jo lifted her glass. "Well, that was entertaining."

~

"I'm a chef," Zoe all but yelled at the TSA agent. "My knives are an extension of my hands." She'd ship her pots and pans if they weren't so bulky.

The man judging the contents of her checked bag looked as if he lived on McDonald's and Budweiser—which she could relate to and appreciate—but he had no idea what her set of knives meant to her.

She'd learned, years before, to simply identify herself, the contents of her bag, and her reason for shipping her personal arsenal with every business or extended trip she took. A return to River Bend for a week away from her personal life she considered an extended trip. There was no way she wouldn't find herself in someone's kitchen cooking something while visiting . . . hence, the knives.

"What show did you say you were on?" The secondary TSA agent who'd been called over had his balding head bent over his phone.

"*Warring Chefs*, season one." She didn't bother telling the man about the dozen-plus other shows she'd been featured on since. *Warring Chefs* had made her . . . if Google was going to pick up any hits with her name, it was that.

The confusion on the agent's face lifted and his eyes narrowed.

"You came in second," he said, his voice flat.

Right! Thanks for the reminder.

"Can I get on the plane now?"

The second TSA agent waved at his colleague and her luggage was shoved back in her bag before being zipped up and moved onto the conveyer belt behind the counter.

Dallas to Eugene wasn't a long flight, and thankfully she'd managed enough frequent flyer miles to sit in the first-class cabin. The fact that she was returning to her ten-year class reunion with a suitcase full of knives that had set her back well over a thousand dollars, and wearing a dress that cost over three hundred bucks, and heels that cost half that, wasn't an accident.

She hadn't been back to River Bend in seven years. Sheriff Ward's funeral.

What a crappy week that had been.

A town in mourning, one of her best friends taking a swan dive off the deep end.

And Luke.

The real reason she never returned to her hometown. She kept hoping she'd hear about him hooking up with some lucky woman and making her a mama.

Maybe she'd learn of a Mrs. Luke on this trip.

Maybe Jo was avoiding the Luke conversation on their occasional phone calls in an effort to save Zoe's feelings.

She wove through security, taking the fast-track service that came with a first-class ticket, and made her way to the terminal for her departing flight.

Airports had become her second home. Between guest spots on Chef Monroe's weekly show, talk shows, and special events where she would slave away for hours or days on end for a charity event in a foreign country, Zoe was a seasoned traveler.

Her frequent flyer miles almost always upgraded her ticket, and when they didn't, she would spring for first class if the flight was longer than a couple of hours. No one wanted to resemble a sardine after traveling if they could avoid it.

Zoe could afford to avoid it.

She stepped into her designated window seat, tucked her purse in the space provided in front of her, and slid the lap belt over her hips.

The flight attendant handed her a glass of wine before the coach passengers boarded. For the longest time, Zoe thought she'd have a silent trip home, until halfway through the coach seating a middle-aged man sat beside her. He offered a quick hello and attempted to tuck his carry-on in the overhead compartment.

He sat with a little flourish. "I hate Dallas traffic."

"Could be worse," she told him as she glanced out her window at the baggage handlers loading the plane.

The man wore cotton pants and a T-shirt with a parka. He looked nothing like those in Dallas. "Compared to New York and LA . . . yeah, could be worse. But not much."

"I take it you don't live here."

"Couldn't pay me to," he told her. "Live just north of Eugene. Ten acres of silent, wooded bliss."

Dallas wasn't Eugene—that was certain. But both cities had their share of traffic and issues. In terms of her line of work, Dallas offered more.

Even if the heat of the summers was starting to wear on her.

Even if she was itching to find another green pasture to explore.

Even if the moist, cool weather of the Oregon coast sounded ideal after years of avoiding it.

Even if . . .

It wasn't long before the captain asked that everyone fasten up, prepare to depart Dallas, and for Zoe to lose feeling in her toes from holding her breath.

She didn't mind flying . . . it was the destination.

Her Dallas hating, Eugene loving seatmate offered a look of sympathy . . . or maybe he was worried she'd puke on him. "You okay?"

"I'm . . . it's been a long time since I went home."

He wiggled eyebrows as the engines on the plane started to speed up. "Family drama?"

He had no idea. Her mother and siblings had actually been supportive over the years. Outside of her youngest brother, who was doing his level best to join her father in prison, everyone else stayed on the sidelines of her life and didn't ask for much.

She'd flown the lot of them out to visit her two years ago. It was then she realized that a two-bedroom apartment wasn't nearly enough space to entertain a family. How on earth had she grown up in a home, a double-wide, with only one bathroom and two bedrooms?

She'd stayed away from home . . . spent her time at Miss Gina's . . . Luke's house . . . even Jo's when her dad was working. There was the occasional sleepover at Mel's, but as much as her BFF lived with the appearance of money, the place wasn't inviting in the least. Seemed the only one surprised by the Bartlett divorce was the lone daughter.

Zoe couldn't wait to see Mel.

She knew from the few e-mails and even fewer phone calls that Mel was struggling.

In ten years Zoe saw Mel only once, shortly after Hope was born. One look at that arrangement and Zoe knew the relationship between her and Baby Daddy wouldn't last. As much as Zoe wanted to perform a solo intervention, Mel wasn't going to listen. And how could she? She was a new mom . . . jobless . . . listening to a jerk. The news of her divorce made Zoe happy, even if it was completely non–politically correct to feel so.

Somewhere over Colorado, her seatmate gave up on small talk, ate the first-class lunch, and plugged into the online movie selections.

Zoe watched the Rockies from twenty-five thousand feet and found her smile.

The *most likely to* never leave River Bend was returning home for her ten-year class reunion in a first-class seat from a city much bigger, a place more full of opportunity than the town she'd left. Much as she hated herself for it, she looked forward to rubbing a few noses in her success.

Those she cared about, the ones who actually kept her away . . . she didn't want to rub in anything.

Some people she would like to avoid.

Avoid the pain of seeing them . . . seeing his eyes . . . feeling the disappointment all over again.

Chapter Five

The noise in R&B's was greater than most nights. The influx of graduates from ten years past filled all the stools at the bar . . . making Josie
run like a wild woman with trays of drinks without a passing smile to
the regulars.

Not that it mattered, Wyatt and Luke sat at one of the high-top
tables in the thick of the crowd. Josie kept the longneck beers coming,
didn't even ask if they needed another round as she handed them off
while she passed by.

"This is crazy." Wyatt looked around the standing room only space.

"Happens every year." Luke tipped his bottle back and kept glancing at the door.

"You recognize most of these people?" Wyatt asked.

"Some."

"Friends . . . enemies?"

"Not a lot of enemies. Can't say they were all friends." Luke focused his attention back on Wyatt. "The problem and curse of a small town is everyone knows everyone. There isn't one secret that everyone doesn't know, and they never let them die. Especially ten years later."

"Doesn't seem like anything dies in this town."

Luke shrugged. "The good stuff doesn't. What else would the bridge club at Miss Gina's gossip about if it did?"

"Miss Gina doesn't play bridge."

Luke laughed. "That's what she calls it."

"Drunk night where most of her *club* uses her rooms to sleep off her special lemonade."

"Love her lemonade. Sucker punched me a few times when I was a kid. The only one who seemed immune to it was—"

"Me!"

Wyatt glanced up and noticed the town sheriff nudging Luke's hand away from his beer before she took a swig.

"Hey!" Luke swiped the beer back with a wink.

It wasn't often that Wyatt saw the sheriff at R&B's. Unless it was in uniform breaking up a fight or helping Josie and her staff *encourage* a patron to take an offered ride home.

Tonight JoAnne Ward wore tight blue jeans, a cotton shirt that sat snug enough that the world knew she was a woman but wasn't advertising it. Her hair was down, but most importantly, uncovered by that hat she always wore while on duty.

"Hi, Wyatt," she said with a smile.

"Sheriff."

"It's Jo tonight."

She leaned in and said something in Luke's ear before Luke's eyes traveled toward the door and the expression on his face froze.

Wyatt followed his gaze to find Melanie at the end of it. Her honey blonde hair was down in a clean sheet to her shoulders. At her side was an opposite bookend. Tall, sleek with dark hair and an air of confidence in the way she held her shoulders back. "Who's that?" he found himself asking.

"Zoe." The soft answer was hard to hear coming from Luke.

Melanie and Zoe stopped by a group closer to the door.

From across the room Melanie attempted to look above the heads while nodding to whatever the group surrounding her was talking about. Her gaze found his and she tilted her head.

Jo signaled the women over.

"You gonna be okay?" she asked Luke.

Wyatt returned his attention to Jo and found Luke studying his beer. "Long time ago, Jo. Old news."

Before Wyatt could question what the two of them were talking about, Melanie and Zoe stepped up to their table.

Both Luke and Wyatt slipped out of their bar stools.

"I can't believe Jeff lost his hair already. He's only twenty-eight."

"It was gone at twenty-four," Luke told Melanie.

"Bad genes," Jo said.

Wyatt returned Melanie's smile. "I didn't know you were going to be here," she said.

"It's this or senior bingo night."

There was a moment of pause before Wyatt noticed the locked expressions on Luke and Zoe's faces. Hard, controlled, and full of emotion all at the same time.

"Hi, Luke." Zoe had a smooth texture in her voice that softened the hard line of Luke's jaw.

"You, ah . . . you look amazing."

"And you still have your hair."

Luke laughed. "Good genes."

Zoe opened her hands and Luke engulfed her in a hug. Even from the side, it looked like neither of them knew how to act.

Luke offered her his chair while Wyatt pushed his toward Jo and Melanie. "I'll see if I can find another one."

Wyatt turned over a stool for Jo and joined the conversation.

"We haven't met." Zoe reached across the table. "I'm Zoe."

"Sorry." Jo took over. "Zoe Brown, Wyatt Gibson. Wyatt moved here about what . . . six years ago?"

"Five."

Josie stopped at their table, swept an empty bottle away. "What can I get . . ." Josie stopped talking and squealed. "Mel? Zoe?"

The high-pitched girl noises had Wyatt and Luke pulling back. "Women!" Luke said.

Even Jo rolled her eyes.

"Good God, Zoe? I hardly recognized you. Hollywood must be agreeing with you."

"Dallas, actually."

Wyatt leaned over to Luke. "Hollywood?"

"She was on one of those chef reality shows years ago," Luke whispered.

"Oh."

Josie turned her attention to Melanie. "You haven't changed one bit. What are you doing these days?"

Melanie blinked a few times. "Been busy."

"I heard you were married to some lawyer or something."

"Uhm . . ."

Jo wiggled into the conversation. "Mel has an adorable little girl. Looks just like her."

Josie kept smiling. "Did your husband come with you?"

Zoe crowded in front of Melanie. "She dumped him years ago."

Josie seemed lost. "I guess that's a good thing then."

"How about some drinks?" Wyatt asked when silence filled the table.

"I'll have another one of these," Luke said, waving his beer in the air. "Zoe? Rum and Coke?"

"Perfect," Zoe said.

"What about you, Mel?"

"I'm driving everyone home. I'll have a Sprite."

Jo and Wyatt ordered two more longnecks before Josie sauntered off.

Melanie held her head in both hands. "That's going to get old fast."

"Let it roll, Mel."

Melanie shook her head, Zoe patted her on the back, and Jo kept talking. "None of these people have lived the perfect life."

Wyatt felt like a third wheel. "What needs to roll?"

Luke opened his mouth to talk, and Melanie cut him off. "I was supposed to be the one who left here and came back rich and powerful."

Wyatt met Melanie's eyes and saw the raw disappointment in them. This meant something to her . . . this censure from her peers of the past.

"The problem with class reunions is everyone judges the others on wealth and the size of their waists. Personal happiness and health never seem to be a part of the measurement. Are you happy, Melanie?" Jo asked.

Melanie glanced at Wyatt, the smile on her lips finally met her eyes, and his stomach twisted. "I'm working on it."

Wyatt saluted her with his beer before taking a swig.

Bed-and-breakfasts didn't often have a rush . . . but Miss Gina's was the exception on the Wednesday before the high school reunion. It helped that the closest motel was a good ten miles outside of town, and a handful of RV parks rounded out the accommodations for visitors.

Melanie forced herself to smile in the face of her high school nemesis. "Hello, Margie."

"My goodness, just look at you." Margie Taylor stood beside her fiancé, her arm looped through his as if she were the prize. "You haven't changed a bit."

Melanie found her eyes traveling to Margie's excessive cleavage. Cleavage that certainly hadn't been there in high school. Cleavage Mel was used to seeing in the big cities of Southern California, but saline cleavage that didn't exist in River Bend.

"We've all changed." Melanie attempted to smile and look beyond the boobs. She suddenly felt like a member of the opposite sex. Who knew boobs had such radar.

"Jonathan, Melanie and I were on the cheer squad together." Margie draped an arm over her fiancé's shoulder, pressing her massive rack into his arm.

Jonathan had to be a good ten years older than Margie, the suit he wore wasn't terribly expensive from what Mel could tell, but it wasn't ill-fitting either. He was reasonably attractive with a strong jaw and completely disinterested eyes.

"I quit cheer my sophomore year," Melanie reminded her.

Margie waved her hand in the air. "Splitting hairs, Melanie. Once on the squad, forever on the squad."

That wasn't how she remembered it. Instead of offering an argument, Melanie pulled out the key for Margie and Jonathan's room and set it on the registration counter. "Miss Gina has you down as staying through Sunday."

"It's so nice of you to help Miss Gina out. Poor woman isn't getting any younger."

Don't let her hear you saying that sat unsaid on Melanie's lips. Let Miss Gina overhear Margie and see how fast it would take for Margie and her suit-wearing fiancé to find themselves at the RV park inside their car.

"Do the rooms have Internet access?" Jonathan finally spoke.

"The house has Wi-Fi access throughout," Melanie told him.

"Is there a code?"

Melanie forced herself not to laugh. "No one is concerned with stealing Miss Gina's Internet service."

"I told you it was a small town, darling," Margie said.

Jonathan let his eyes wander the foyer without an ounce of amusement.

"It's only a few days."

Melanie clicked a few keys on Miss Gina's computer and removed a receipt for Margie and her reluctant fiancé's room.

"Breakfast is from seven to nine thirty. There are refreshments in the sitting room throughout the day, and a wine and cheese reception between five and six thirty on Friday and Saturday."

Margie offered a plastic smile to match her plastic breasts. "That's lovely . . . isn't that lovely, Jonathan?"

Jonathan didn't comment as he grumbled and let Margie pull him away.

"The garden view room is on the second story, first door on the left."

Jonathan said something about a lack of a bellhop, and Margie tugged on his arm.

"Thank you for waiting." Melanie addressed the young family standing in the space Margie and her squeeze had just vacated. A boy, not more than six, attempted to climb up onto the counter.

"Is it our turn?"

"Samuel . . . get down." The young mother removed her son from Miss Gina's desk with an arm around his waist. "Sorry."

"It's okay . . . been there."

"He's been in the car for hours." The man Melanie assumed was Dad removed a wallet from his back pocket as he spoke.

"My daughter's the same way after a long car ride." Melanie took his credit card and checked his name. "Wait." She snapped her eyes back to the man. "Mitchel Giesler? Holy cow . . ." The man was no longer the boy. He had an extra thirty pounds and a beard.

"Melanie Bartlett," she said, pointing at herself.

"Oh, hey . . . how are you?"

"Good. Not bad." She looked down at the boy again. "Is this your son?"

"Yeah, and my wife, Letty."

Melanie glanced between the three of them. "Wow, how much we've all changed. Last time I saw you was at graduation . . . you were really . . . celebrating."

"Yes," he said with a knowing smile. "I certainly was."

Samuel was pulling out of his mother's arms with enough energy to power the house.

"Settle down."

"I wanna go outside," the child whined.

Melanie glanced at her old classmate and lifted her voice to the back of the house. "Hope, honey?"

"Yeah?" her daughter answered.

"C'mere, sweetie."

Hope ran from where she was perched in Miss Gina's kitchen. Her hair in a ponytail, the smile she'd worn since they'd arrived in River Bend painted on her lips.

She moved alongside Melanie's leg and glanced at the guests.

"Hope, this is Samuel."

Her daughter gave a little wave and Samuel smiled.

"Why don't you take Samuel out back and show him Miss Gina's garden."

Samuel wrinkled his nose. "Flowers? Yuck."

Hope shook her head. "No, silly . . . dirt and worms."

Samuel's eyes grew wide.

"If it's okay with you?" Melanie glanced at Mitchel.

Mitchel placed a hand on Samuel's back and shoved. "Go, buddy."

That was all the encouragement the kids needed before they were running out the back door. The sound of the screen slamming had both parents releasing long-suffering breaths.

"Kids and cars don't mix. Now, where were we?"

Chapter Six

The guests were checked in, the rooms were all clean, and Melanie sat on the back porch watching Hope and Samuel do their best to ruin their clothes with dirt.

"There you are," Zoe's voice rang from inside the inn. She pushed through the back door and let it slap shut.

Melanie swatted her palm against the double swing she was perched on in invitation. "I thought you were going to spend the day with your mom and sister."

"I did, too, but she didn't bother asking for time off work while I'm here and Zanya's pregnancy is kicking her butt. Guess I'll just squeeze in a few hours when I can." Zoe stretched her long legs out and dropped her purse on the deck. The long expanse of the lawn held a large maple tree with a lone wooden swing. The forest bordered the grass without a single fence blocking the view. A pathetic attempt at a vegetable garden sported mostly weeds and a pile of dirt. The beginnings of a tomato plant, one probably volunteering its efforts from the previous year, sprang from the earth. The only thing that had changed from her childhood was the size of the tree. "It's so quiet here. Was it always this quiet?"

"We were too busy yakking to notice. But yeah, I think it was. It's not quiet in Bakersfield."

"Not in Dallas either."

The two of them watched the kids playing for a few minutes. "She's just like you."

"I don't know about that. I didn't play in the dirt a lot."

"You grew out of it," Zoe corrected. "Decided cheer squad and lip gloss were better pastimes."

Melanie closed her eyes and shook her head. "Don't remind me. Guess who is staying here this weekend?"

Zoe glanced to the clouds as if they held the answer. "Enlighten me."

"Margie Taylor."

"No!"

"Yes . . . with a stuffy fiancé perfectly suited for her."

Zoe gave the swing a little push. "I thought her parents were still in town."

"They are. I'm not sure why the two of them are staying here."

"More money for Miss Gina." Zoe made a show of looking behind her shoulder. "Where is she, anyway? I did not see her van when I pulled in."

"She said she had an appointment in Eugene. I told her I'd keep everything running. I'll do anything to avoid reunion setup. My guess is I'll get a chance to do all of that next year if I'm still in River Bend."

"You're really going to stay?" Zoe asked.

Melanie shrugged. "There's nothing for me back in California. Hope deserves a little more of this. Open, safe space to run and play. People she can trust close by. Rain. I don't think Miss Gina needs a full-time employee since this place only fills up a few times a year, but maybe this summer will help me figure out a few things."

The grandfather clock inside the house chimed twice. She unfolded from the swing. "Hope?"

Her daughter glanced up, her face was smudged with dirt. "Yeah?"

"I'll be in the kitchen. Don't wander off."

"'Kay!"

"Mel in the kitchen?" Zoe asked while they walked inside.

"Afternoon cookies," she reminded her friend. "Miss Gina's schedule hasn't changed."

"But you don't cook."

"I manage." Kids had a way of making cooks out of their parents. Even if that cooking was often out of a box with *just add water* instructions.

The retrofitted kitchen was home to modern conveniences Miss Gina added when she turned the old Victorian into a B and B. The restaurant grade stainless steel refrigerator and range stood in contrast to the white cabinets and poured concrete countertops.

"Is it wrong that walking into this kitchen feels more like home than my mom's?" Zoe asked.

Melanie removed two baking pans from a lower cabinet and set them on the counter. "Food at your mom's was pizza or whatever she brought home from the diner. Miss Gina always had raw ingredients that had your hands flying to grab them."

Zoe opened the refrigerator and giggled. She reached for the red lemonade pitcher and set it aside. "God bless Miss Gina."

Melanie handed her friend a glass and moved around to dig inside the fridge herself. "It's like coming home, isn't it?"

"Sure is." Zoe topped her glass off, sat, and took a drink. "So good."

"It still bites you," Melanie warned.

The premade cookie dough came in a tub. According to Miss Gina, she bought the stuff off the school fundraiser and stocked herself up twice a year.

Melanie set the tub on the counter and turned to the sink to wash her hands.

"What is that?" Zoe asked.

"Cookie dough."

Her glass met the counter with a thump and Zoe's jaw dropped. "No . . . no, no . . . you can't be serious."

"It's what Miss Gina told me to cook."

Zoe was up and out of her chair in half a second. She tore off the lid and sniffed. Then the fundraising tub became a companion of the trash can. "I can't believe she's gone back to that crap."

Melanie stood back as Zoe did what Zoe did.

The pantry door opened, and out came several containers. "I've told her a thousand times. bed-and-breakfasts need fresh and organic. Not preservatives and red dye number six." A Tupperware lid met the sink and Zoe stuck her nose inside the container. "A few simple ingredients and everyone will remember the food. No wonder she's not busy all year long. Sticky cookie dough," Zoe muttered. "Grab a mixing bowl," she ordered.

Melanie found the bowl and stepped aside.

Zoe waved a container in the air. "See, she has everything she needs."

Melanie wasn't even sure what Zoe held.

"Not even expired. Why would Miss Gina buy this and not use it?"

The questions kept coming, but Melanie didn't bother answering. This was how Zoe cooked. Hands flying, fingers tasting . . . nose sniffing. She found an apron, took a swig of lemonade, and in the time it would have taken Melanie to turn on the stove and pop off the lid of the fake cookie dough, Zoe had flour, salt, sugar, and several other bits of flavor mixed and on cookie sheets.

While the cookies slid into the oven, Zoe knelt beside a deep lower cabinet and dug. She unearthed a coffee bean grinder, dusted it off, and plugged it in. "She better have . . ." From the pantry, a sealed bag of coffee beans emerged. "I don't get why she isn't using this."

Zoe continued talking to herself as the kitchen filled with the smell of fresh coffee and mouthwatering sweetness.

The screen door slammed with the sound of small feet running toward them. "Stop right there young lady. Shoes off. You and Samuel wash your hands before you come in here."

The kids turned toward the washroom without argument.

Zoe stopped her muttering and chuckled. "Ohhh, the Mom voice. You do that really well."

"It's in the guide that comes from the hospital. *Mom voice* and *Mom look* are in the second chapter."

"What's in the first?"

"*Mom worry* and *Mom smothering*."

Zoe leaned against the counter while the cookies finished baking. "It's been hard, hasn't it?"

"Yeah. You're smart to wait. Not that I planned it."

"The good things in life are never planned," Zoe said. "I didn't plan on being a chef. It just happened."

"It didn't just happen. You made it happen. You left this town before I did with half a scholarship and a beat-up pickup truck."

Zoe waved her off. "Still didn't plan it. Not all of it."

"Would you do any of it differently?" Melanie asked.

Her friend stared at the wall. "Well . . . no. I guess not."

That didn't sound convincing.

"Are you happy?"

Zoe tore her gaze away, turned toward the stove. "Yeah . . . yeah, I am."

That didn't sound convincing either.

As the cookies emerged from the oven, Hope and Samuel fled into the kitchen. Their eager faces still dirty after poor attempts at cleaning them, their hands dripping with water.

While Melanie poured milk for the kids, the screen door slammed shut again. "Someone other than Miss Gina is cooking."

Mel's heart did a quick jump in her chest before Wyatt rounded the corner. The easy smile on his lips had her biting hers. He wore the blue jeans she was used to seeing on his narrow waist. He had on a pullover shirt and a tool belt loose over his hips.

"Aunt Zoe made cookies," Hope announced, her lips smacking over the cinnamon snickerdoodles.

"Are they any good?" Wyatt asked with a wink.

Zoe scoffed and pretended offense.

When Wyatt reached for one, Melanie opened her mouth and her mother's voice came out. "Wash your hands."

Wyatt snapped his hand back and grinned. "Yes, ma'am."

Her cheeks heated. "Sorry. Habit."

Wyatt sauntered out of the kitchen and he could hear the sound of running water from the downstairs bathroom.

Melanie turned away from the kids and found Zoe watching her. "What?"

"He's cute," she said under her breath.

"Stop."

"Why?"

Footsteps stopped their conversation and Melanie pushed Zoe away.

"Mmm. Luke said you were a good cook," Wyatt said.

"He did, did he?"

"Zoe can turn macaroni and cheese into a delicacy fit for kings," Melanie praised her friend.

"I don't know about that."

"A direct quote from one of the judges of *Warring Chefs*."

"A quote used once they found out I grew up in a double-wide. It was a joke."

"It's the truth." Melanie turned back to Wyatt, his face full of another cookie. "She won her first Fourth of July chili cook-off when we were twelve. In high school, when we needed a new pole vault pit for the track team, Zoe cooked a three-course meal and sold tickets as a fundraiser. Once word got out about her culinary talents, people started driving in from forty miles away and paid forty bucks a plate."

"That's impressive," Wyatt said. "You should stick around. We could use another pole vault pit."

"We?" Melanie asked.

"I help coach at the high school," he said.

"Really? Zoe, Jo, and I were all on the track team."

Wyatt wiped cookie crumbs off his chin. Out of habit, Melanie handed him a napkin.

"I think I remember Jo mentioning that."

"Yeah, Jo was a sprinter, Zoe here did the mile, and I was the vaulter."

"Hence the pole vault pit," Zoe added.

Hope and Samuel scrambled off the kitchen stools. "We're going back outside."

"Go on."

"I keep trying to get our sheriff to coach. Lord knows she keeps bringing me kids."

Zoe and Melanie started to laugh.

"The apple didn't fall far from the tree," Zoe said.

"What do you mean?"

"Sheriff Ward, her dad . . . he did that all the time. Someone got caught doing something they shouldn't be doing . . . he gave them an option. Join track or handcuffs."

Wyatt glanced between the two of them. "And what did you two get caught doing?"

Melanie and Zoe exchanged glances.

"It wasn't us. We were there supporting our friend," Zoe offered.

It took a few seconds for Wyatt to catch on. "Jo?"

Melanie snapped her lips together. "I'll never tell."

Zoe lifted her little finger in the air, and Mel took hold with hers. The not-so-secret handshake of sorts still held.

"It's a daily education with you in town," he said.

Zoe pushed away from the counter and opened the fridge. "You kids get out of here. I have stuff to do."

"Stuff?" Melanie asked.

"Yeah . . . I need to remind Miss Gina how this is done." Zoe waved them away. "When is she coming back?"

"Dinner. She suggested I invite you over."

Zoe snorted. "I bet. Sneaky bitch."

When Zoe started muttering and filling her arms with onions, tomatoes, and some kind of cheese, Mel backed away. "I need my knives." Zoe dumped the ingredients on the counter and disappeared out the front door.

Wyatt started to say something but the words didn't articulate before Zoe marched back inside, a black bag in her hands. "What are you two still doing in here? I'd put you to work, but I don't need a hammer for dinner . . . and Melanie, bless her, is useless."

"Hey, I manage."

Zoe snorted before turning away. "And take those cookies to the parlor. I'm sure Miss Gina already has a plate ready." Another muttered *sneaky bitch* left Zoe's lips as Melanie and Wyatt left the room.

The noise generated by Hurricane Zoe drifted the farther they moved away from the kitchen.

"Is she always like that?" Wyatt asked.

"Only when she cooks," Mel told him.

In the parlor, a crystal serving tray sat empty. A small piece of paper sat to the side. Crafted in calligraphy were the words *Compliments of Chef Brown.*

"Oh, she's good." Wyatt snaked one last cookie and waved it in the air.

"What are you doing here, anyway?"

"Finishing up the roof. Bathroom still needs work."

Melanie froze. "You didn't leave the ladder—"

"I learned that lesson. The ladder is still on my truck. I smelled these before I could set up."

"Zoe's cooking is a beacon." She finished setting out the cookies, had to tilt her head to catch Wyatt's gaze. His eyes wandered to her lips.

"A beacon," he repeated.

When she bit her lip, Wyatt looked away and stepped back. "I guess I should . . ."

"You probably should," she agreed, though she enjoyed the heat he generated in her belly.

He took three steps before turning back. "I hear you're thinking of sticking around for a while."

"Is that right?"

"Small town. News travels fast." He was smiling.

She folded her arms across her chest. "I'm considering it."

He nudged the wall and changed course. "That's good." He didn't elaborate before he waved the cookie her way and walked out of the house.

That's good?

Two seconds later, she followed him out. He stood at his truck, pulling the ladder from the back.

"Why?" She yelled across the driveway.

"Why what?"

"Why is that good?" She knew, but wanted to hear him say it.

Wyatt paused in his task, offered a smirk. "You used to pole vault."

Pole vault? What the . . . "Yeah, so?"

"We haven't had a good pole vault coach since I moved here."

"Pole vault." Seriously?

His muscles worked in perfect unison as he pulled the ladder free. He leaned on it for a minute and posed. At least it looked like he posed. Like one of those guys in the calendars pretending to be carpenters. Only those men didn't wear shirts. The thought of what Wyatt looked like shirtless had Melanie biting her lip again.

"You still remember the basics, right?"

"Of course."

"So you'll consider it?"

"I . . ." Pole vault. He was interested in her track talents. Not that they did anything for her. "I guess."

Wyatt sent her a full dimpled smile, shook his hair out of his eyes.

She muttered *pole vault* under her breath and turned away.

Wyatt's laugh followed her back into the house.

Chapter Seven

All small towns across the country had a few fundamental things in common. Gossip ran like water in a stream, most teenagers left as soon as they learned to drive or graduated from high school, and they honored their heroes on the appropriate holidays and the anniversaries of their passing.

Sheriff Ward had been a River Bend hero.

So much so that the town endorsed his sometimes delinquent daughter when she finished the academy and returned home.

Jo didn't need this day as a reminder of her father, but the town did. So when her deputy lowered the flag to half-staff, she didn't suggest he not. She accepted the handshakes and pats on the back when she passed people in town without having to ask why they stopped her. This had been going on every year since his death; this year wasn't any different. Except, of course, the fact that many of the kids she grew up with were home to partake in the ritual.

Jo found herself scowling through a mental Rolodex of names. Who went out of their way to find her on this seventh anniversary of her father's death, who avoided her. Even Grant, the town drunk who spent a few nights in her lockup like that man from Mayberry, removed his hat and shook her hand.

What the town didn't know was how keenly she categorized everyone and everything on this day. Not for the desire of wallowing in her loss, but in an attempt to find her dad's killer.

The town may not remember all the details of her father's death . . . but she did. It helped that upon her return from the academy, she opened her father's files and studied the report of his death to the point of memorizing nearly every word.

Her father was murdered. She knew it, the Feds suspected it, the local townspeople thought his death was accidental.

Problem was, the FBI didn't find his case dirty enough to investigate once they found a satisfactory nonhomicidal angle.

Jo knew better.

Her daddy had been murdered. And she would, one day, find his killer and bring them to justice.

At quarter to noon, the door to the station opened. Zoe walked in beside Melanie. It was good to see her friends. She missed them both, terribly. Having them there sparked all kinds of memories.

"What are you guys doing here?"

"Miss Gina says you go to the cemetery at noon. We thought you might want company."

The world stopped in that second and emotion swam in. Emotion that Jo worked damn hard to keep away. Her eyes swelled with unshed tears and she couldn't form the words needed to tread past them.

"Uhm . . ." Damn it, she didn't cry. It wasn't something she did. Not then, not now. She blinked a few times, pushed away from her inner girl.

"I can drive," Melanie offered. "I have the van."

Jo gave a quick shake of her head. "How about you follow me. In case I get a call."

Her friends saw past her excuse and didn't press.

Zoe pressed two fingers to her forehead in a mock salute. "After you, Sheriff."

Jo pushed her friend toward the door. "Get out of here."

Before sliding behind the wheel of the squad car, Jo removed her baton and tossed it on the seat beside her. Next came her hat. She pulled out of the small parking lot, Miss Gina's flower child van following close behind. The cemetery was just outside town. Far enough to require a daily drive but close enough to see in passing several times a week. Jo always thought it was poetic that the route to R&B's passed by the cemetery, reminding people not to drink and drive. It did for her, in any event.

It was a clear summer day with only a few white clouds dotting the sky. Nothing like the day she learned of her father's death.

She shook the painful memories aside and concentrated on the familiar route to her father's final resting place.

The cemetery was maintained by the little white church, aptly named the Little White Church.

Jo left her baton in the squad car and carried her hat.

Zoe and Mel fell in step beside her. Like in a library, their voices didn't raise above soft whispers. Funny how walking among the dead made one quiet. Almost as if yelling invited a spirit to come out and play.

"I'm sorry I wasn't here for his funeral," Mel said for the hundredth time.

"Let it go, Mel."

"I just feel so bad."

Jo wrapped an arm around Mel's shoulders. "I know you do. If it makes you feel any better, I promise not to go to yours."

Mel started to laugh and the mood lifted.

They walked along the moist graves, avoiding walking right on top of them. Small town cemeteries didn't have city ordinances keeping the markers on the ground level, and here in River Bend's only resting place, the markers rose to the heavens in varying heights. The more prominent or rich the member of the community had been, the larger the stone.

Sheriff Joseph Ward's stone was somewhere in the middle. He hadn't been a rich man—no servant of the state was unless they were dipping dirty fingers into pockets they had no business being in.

The three of them stopped at the foot of his grave and Jo took in the memorized words on his stone.

Beloved Father
Honored Public Servant
Sheriff Joseph Allen Ward

The date of his birth sat beside the early date of his death. Jo accepted Zoe's arm as it snaked around her waist. She hadn't heard her father's laugh, seen her father's smile, in seven years.

"He always thought I'd end up here before him," Jo told them.

"You did give him hell." Zoe was right, she had.

They were silent for a moment.

"Do you think he sees us here?"

"He damn well better." Jo forced a laugh. "He put this badge on my chest, he better appreciate it."

"I'm sure he does."

Before Zoe and Mel could pull her anywhere close to tears again, she looked beyond the headstones. "Remember summer of our sophomore year?"

Both women followed her gaze and slow smiles started to spread. "Miss Gina's lemonade and old Mrs. Greely's grave. We got so drunk."

Jo started to laugh. "I thought we were incredibly clever drinking in a cemetery."

Zoe nudged her. "Until we swore we heard voices."

"That was you, Zoe," Mel reminded her.

"Running through the cemetery in the dark. Never a good idea."

"Nearly busted my ankle," Jo remembered.

"I ended up with poison oak," Melanie said.

"I got away with a nasty hangover and nightmares for the summer."

"Good times." Jo smiled into the memory.

"Isn't that the time your dad called you out for drinking?"

"He sure did. Said someone complained about a disturbance in the cemetery, came out the next day while I slept it off and found my school ID next to the leftover lemonade. He left my ID next to the mason jars we'd left behind on the kitchen counter. Signed me up for the summer cross-country team the next day."

"That was awful. Five miles every day in the summer."

"Smart bastard. I didn't have time or energy to drink that summer."

Zoe lifted her eyebrows. "Not much anyway."

Jo knelt down and pulled a weed that didn't need to be pulled. "I miss him," she said in a low voice. "I swear I can feel him at the strangest times. Like he's there looking over me."

Mel knelt beside her. "Sounds like a normal thing. I know if there was a way to watch over Hope if something happened to me, I'd do it."

Zoe walked along the back of the stone and paused. She lifted a single white lily from the ground and placed it on top. "Must have fallen off."

Jo narrowed her brow, a memory tried to surface but didn't make it. "That's nice."

Silence filled the space between them before Jo voiced something to her best friends she hadn't shared with anyone else. "He was murdered."

Zoe sucked in a breath.

"What? I thought it was an accident," Mel said, dumfounded.

"I know what everyone thinks. I also know what I know."

"But everyone said—"

"Accidental shooting. I know. That's what I was told. No one was more careful with his firearms than my dad."

"Jo?" Zoe held doubt in her tone.

"What are the chances of you placing your palm in a vat of hot oil, Zoe? Or you pushing Hope off a cliff?" she asked Melanie.

Both women held their breath and stared.

"I know what I know. I read the reports. I have little memories that come back to me every once in a while. They started surfacing after his death. I remember this time of year always being difficult for him."

"Kids graduating, lots of parties."

"The annual high school reunion followed by the Fourth of July and everything surrounding it. I know. But it was more than that," Jo insisted.

"Are you sure?"

Jo nodded. "Yeah. I'm sure. One of the things I learned in the academy is that criminals often return to the scene of the crime."

"And that's why you're still here. To find your dad's killer."

Jo met Zoe's gaze and moved to Mel's. "Yeah. I'll find him. Eventually."

She took in her father's tombstone and offered her pledge in silence. *I'll find him, Daddy.*

~

"Did it shrink?"

"The gym?"

Melanie looked up into the eves of the high school gym and could have sworn the room had shrunk. "Wasn't it bigger?"

"I don't think so," Zoe muttered.

"The whole town feels smaller than when we lived here." It didn't help that a few staple storefronts had closed down because of the poor economy.

"I hear ya. My old room feels like a shoe box." Zoe had spent the first night at her mom's and then decided to bunk up with Jo.

"I'm pretty sure none of us exploded . . . how is it possible everything feels smaller?"

Zoe led Melanie toward the purple and gold decorated registration table. The official reunion party wasn't for another day, but today they were asked to help sort out the list of names of attendees who were coming to the event into the clubs and activities they knew the alumni had participated in.

"I think our minds expanded, making everything else feel smaller."

Melanie could buy that. "You know what's funny . . . the inn doesn't feel smaller. Everything else . . . yeah. Even the gas station looks tiny. I know it hasn't changed. It hasn't, right?"

Zoe fell silent, her eyes locked across the room.

Melanie followed her friend's gaze and sighed.

Luke stood talking to a couple of guys who looked familiar but she couldn't place names to.

And Zoe stared.

Melanie stood beside her, silent with her own thoughts.

"Why does he have to look so damn good?" Zoe quietly asked.

"He always looked good." But he only had eyes for Zoe. Once the two of them hooked up, the town instantly assumed there would be li'l Zoes and li'l Lukes following behind in no time.

The town had been wrong.

"Just the women I've been searching for."

Melanie cringed.

"Margie."

Full of her fake bubbly self, Margie approached them with a yearbook in one hand, a pom-pom in the other. "If it isn't Zoe Brown, River Bend's claim to fame." The compliment brushed hands with sarcasm.

"Well if it isn't Margie Taylor." Zoe matched her sarcasm and added a smirk. "Still motivating the football team?" Zoe wiggled her fingers under the dangling plastic strings of their school colors.

"Once a cheerleader always a cheerleader."

"Is that so?"

Margie kept her fake grin in place as she spoke. "How is that cooking thing you're doing?"

Zoe's jaw tightened and Melanie stood back.

In the past, Zoe would light into Melanie with a snarky zinger that put the other woman back for a week.

The tight jaw lasted two breaths and Zoe shook her head. "It's doing very well, thank you. I'm happy to say my pastime in high school afforded me a living." The words she didn't say hung between them, but God help Margie, she didn't hear them.

Margie's pastime was hooking up with everyone else's boyfriend.

"That's wonderful for you."

An awkward moment of silence followed before Margie glanced at her feet, and then the yearbook in her hands. "Oh, I almost forgot. There are a few people I was hoping the two of you could identify."

The three of them moved to a table and peered at the yearbook.

Looking at the pictures of a decade past had Melanie wondering where her old yearbook ended up. She'd left it with her mom when she went off to college, but then some of her belongings went with her dad to Texas.

The pages of the track team splayed out and some of the happier times in her life surfaced.

"I'm going to break out in a sweat just looking at these pictures," Zoe said.

"Remember Coach Reynolds's punishment for showing up late to practice?"

Zoe cringed. "Running Lob Hill . . . that sucked."

Lob Hill sat beyond the track and football field on the far north of the school. There wasn't a street or anything to it other than a forty percent incline that made running up it grueling. Whenever the team had shown out or arrived late, or simply pissed off the coach by not paying attention, Lob Hill was mentioned and they all took off running.

Reynolds held a stopwatch in his hand and if you didn't return in fifteen minutes you were told to run the hill again.

Margie pointed to a face on the page. "Do you know who this is?" The image didn't strike any memories.

"I think he was only around the last year. Perry something . . . what was his last name?" Zoe squeezed her eyes as if activating her brain. "Anders . . . no, Anderson."

"Oh, that's right. Yeah, shy guy with great hair." Melanie wondered if the kid had managed to keep it.

Margie pointed to a few more alumni before gathering what she needed and walking away.

"Just as annoying as an adult as she was a kid," Zoe quietly said under her breath.

"People don't change."

"I did."

Melanie narrowed her eyes. "No. You were always wicked smart and determined to be more than what this town thought you were. You may have changed your living conditions and lifestyle, but you're still Zoe." She pointed to the open yearbook. "You're still this girl."

Zoe shook her head, her eyes darkened. "That's a prison man's daughter who lives in a double-wide on the wrong side of town. I'm no longer her."

The blood in Melanie's face drained and her lips slacked open.

With a shake of her head, Zoe mumbled something about using the bathroom and scrambled off, leaving Melanie staring after her.

Where had that come from?

Melanie started after her when Luke cut Zoe off at the door to the gym. Even from a distance, she noticed Luke's expression sharpen. It wasn't long before he put his arm around Zoe's shoulders and led her from the noisy gym. The sight of them reminded her of how much she envied their relationship in high school. How much she wanted a love like that. It wasn't a surprise she'd fallen into Nathan's hands so easily.

It was as if without the wise guidance from her true friends, she'd been vulnerable for the taking.

She meandered out of the gym and onto the field. A few joggers were taking advantage of the fair weather and running the track. In the center of the field, the football team was running drills. Up in the stands were a gaggle of cackling girls staring at the small screens of their cell phones.

Not a lot had changed in ten years. The faces were different, the dynamics . . . not so much.

The pole vault pit sat in the southwest corner of the field. A tarp covered the mass of foam and cushion that kept the vaulters from hurting themselves when they landed after their jumps. The standards framed the pit but the poles and crossbars were put away in a locked shed.

Memories of her first jump, how uncoordinated she'd felt, surfaced. It took three months before she actually landed a decent vault. It had only been five feet, but God it felt good. She remembered the senior vaulters all cheering. Zoe had given a thumbs-up, and Jo told her to aim higher or join high jump.

She aimed higher.

"Can't help yourself, can you?"

Melanie jumped and turned.

"You like sneaking up on people, Coach?"

Wyatt stood behind her with a smile. A sexy smile that warmed her.

"I didn't sneak, you weren't paying attention."

Yeah, right . . . she sat on the pit and couldn't help but bounce. The condition of the pit had deteriorated over the past decade. "Do you vault?" she asked him.

"I never got the hang of the turn. Luckily, coaching doesn't require me to break anything. Did you vault in college?"

She shook her head. "I didn't see the point. I wasn't good enough for the Olympics and no one was offering me a full scholarship."

"You cleared eleven two. That's brag worthy."

Melanie caught his eyes. "You looked up my record?"

He lifted both hands in the air. "Guilty."

"Checking out a potential coach?"

He shrugged his shoulders and said, "No. Just checking *you* out."

It took a second for his words to register and Melanie felt her cheeks warm.

He started to laugh. "You're easy to fluster, Miss Bartlett."

"I'm not flustered," she denied and removed her butt from the pit. She offered him her back and put her cool hands to her cheeks.

I'm so flustered.

You'd think no one ever flirted with her.

Or maybe those who did held little interest for her.

Truth was, she may have aged ten years, but she was relatively clueless when it came to the world of men.

Instead of admitting anything, she moved over to the giant shipping container that held all the pole vault equipment. She slid her hand between two containers and fished her fingers in the dark. She was about to give up when she found the small magnetic box she searched for.

The hide-a-key had a faded image of Hello Kitty.

While Wyatt watched she popped open the small box and removed a senior secret.

The lock hadn't changed.

"I wondered where they hid that thing," Wyatt said as he stood back and watched.

"You didn't learn it from me." She placed the key back where she found it and stepped into the dusty container. The space in front of the poles had evidence of use, but the far reaches of the container, the place where it wasn't uncommon for the team to hang out on a rainy day, had lost its luster. Cobwebs occupied the space and a forgotten, faded jersey and pair of shoes filled the corners. When Melanie had been in school, it wasn't unusual that a summer evening took place here with a game of spin the bottle along with shots provided by Jo and her hidden stash of liquor.

Instead of simmering on the high school memories, Melanie removed a pole from the tube and sighed.

"You still have it."

"They're expensive. Until they break or crack, we don't get rid of them."

She wedged the pole against the bottom of the shed and leaned into it. Where she once bent the pole with ease, she could already tell she'd lost the upper body strength to use the thing.

"You wanna try?" Wyatt asked.

"Vaulting?"

"Since breaking and entering has been mastered . . ."

Melanie shook her head with a roll of her eyes. "I know the sheriff. And besides, she had the key made."

Wyatt offered a dimpled smile. "I'm learning new things every day with you in town." He moved away from the container and over to the pit. "They say it's like riding a bike."

"They do not!"

"They do."

She planted the pole into the box and attempted to bend it again. "Who are *they* anyway?"

"Life's cheerleaders."

Melanie cringed. "Fake smiles and pom-poms . . . what do *they* know?"

"Don't be hating."

She took a few steps back and lifted the eleven-foot pole before letting the end come down with a bounce. "I'm not hating. Just not a fan."

"Yet you were on the squad."

She offered a glance over her shoulder, found his eyes snapping up from his gaze lingering on her butt. "Checking me out again?"

It was his turn to be flustered.

"Yes . . . no . . . I mean. Your friend Margie told me you were on the squad."

"Nice change of subject. And Margie is an old acquaintance, not a friend. Not to mention the reason I stopped cheer."

"Oh?"

"It was high school. Boyfriends were passed around and feelings were hurt. I'm sure it hasn't changed." Her eyes drifted to the stands where she assumed the current cheerleading team sat watching their football-playing boyfriends.

"So she broke the girl code."

Melanie leaned on the pole and smiled. "I ended up here and she had her heart stomped on. I won."

"These reunions always drag up old drama. There is seldom a year that goes by that there isn't some kind of fight."

"Really?"

"Not a fistfight . . . well, I've seen one of those, but catfights are entertaining."

"That's stupid. We're adults now."

"I'm just reporting the facts as I've seen them. It seems River Bend has a few unsolved dramas that need to be worked out."

Wyatt sat on the edge of the pit and leaned against his jean-clad thighs.

"What about you? Did you have any drama when you went to your reunion?"

"It isn't until next year. I'll let you know."

She knew it, he was younger. "Are you going to go?"

"Haven't decided. I might." He nodded toward the pit. "Now, are you going to jump on the pole or just fondle it all day?"

She glanced at her hands gripping the tape.

Wyatt laughed.

"I'm not going to get flustered," she muttered.

"Too late."

Yeah, it was too late. She returned to the shed and lifted the pole back into its home. The fit was tight and she gave it a good shove. Wyatt had moved beside her and placed his hand next to hers to push it in. For a man living in Oregon, he sure had a nice tan. Well, what she could see of it in any event. "I understand if you're too scared to try."

"I'm not scared . . ."

"If you say so."

She rolled her eyes and pushed past him to close the heavy doors. "You're a bully," she told him.

He took the lock from her hands, the heat of them shot up her arms.

"I usually get what I want," he said without shame.

"Like a bully."

"Like a coach," he countered.

He reached around her, not giving her much room to move away, and clicked the lock in place.

"I can move," she told him.

He was close enough to smell the rich pine of his skin.

"But I like you right here."

Oh, yeah . . . she enjoyed it, too, but she wasn't about to tell him so. "Like a coach?"

He shook his head. "Like a man."

There she was, all flustered and not moving away. "I think you like making me blush."

"Guilty." His voice had dropped and his eyes lingered on her lips.

Every cell inside her shivered.

She swayed a little closer, gripped the side of the shed to keep from being pulled into his gravity. "I have a kid," she blurted out.

"I know. We've met." He lifted a hand and brushed a lock of her hair away from her face.

"You're younger than me."

He offered a laugh. "Cougar material."

It was her turn to grin. "I wouldn't go that far."

Wyatt left his hand on the side of her face and forced her to meet his gaze. "Do you always talk when a man is about to kiss you?"

Great, she hadn't missed the signals.

God, he was going to kiss her. Was she ready for that?

"I talk when I'm nervous."

"I make you nervous?"

"You zap my brain cells." She hadn't meant to say that.

"A talent I didn't know I had." He moved closer.

She stiffened. "I don't know if I'm ready for this."

He stopped moving, ran his thumb along her lower lip.

Melanie's knees did that wobbly thing that only happened when her world tilted. Wyatt was doing a great job of tilting her world. Her eyes drifted to her feet.

"Melanie?"

She met his gaze again.

"I'm a patient man."

Instead of the kiss he spoke of, he eased back, letting the moment pass.

"I'm sorry," she said.

A look of confusion marred his brow. Suddenly, apologizing felt like the wrong thing to do.

"Don't be."

"I'm sorry . . . damn it." She hadn't meant to say it again. "It's just. I'm in a weird place right now. I want to." She placed a hand on his arm. "You need to know I want to."

"Melanie?" He placed a finger over her lips. "I get it."

"You do?" she asked through his finger. How did he get it when she didn't? It had been a long time since she so much as seriously flirted with the opposite sex.

"I do." His hand dropped.

"So I can have a rain check?"

He was grinning again.

Chapter Eight

Wyatt had no real need to go to the reunion. It wasn't his graduating class and he hadn't been coaching when the alumni had frequented the halls of River Bend High. Still, there wasn't a snowball's chance in hell that he was going to miss it.

That surprised him.

Flustering Melanie Bartlett and getting close enough to smell her innocence intrigued him more than he wanted. After walking away from the track the day before, he had cautioned himself. His original intentions were flighty. A little dalliance with a woman who was only visiting home. Yet when Miss Gina had told him she was going to stay on, he found himself slowing his pursuit down. No reason to rush if she wasn't going anywhere. Since when had he wanted to hook up with someone local? One with a kid, no less.

Melanie blew off like a hesitant volcano sputtering smoke before the top exploded. She came with a suitcase full of baggage that included a kid. A cute kid, but a kid nonetheless. At least there wasn't an ex in the picture.

Wyatt liked her.

His usual pursuits were attractive and available. Call him shallow, but he wasn't one for romance. Truth was, he hadn't dated in the real sense since he'd moved to River Bend. He'd flirted, and a few of the single women had that look in their eye that told him they were interested, but he wasn't. He was building a life in River Bend, and screwing around with the half a dozen single, attractive, and age appropriate women wasn't a part of that life. Not when the fallout could mean never-ending drama. Breaking up with the daughter of the bingo night emcee could remove job opportunities for months, if not years.

So why was Melanie different? And why was he breaking his own code? Was it a code, or just smart?

Didn't matter, he told himself. He fastened the last button on his dress shirt and skipped the tie. Unlike his father, Wyatt wasn't a tie kind of guy. He owned one, but it was probably holding a bundle of PVC pipes together on his truck.

The high school gym bumped with the sound of the DJ's music from a decade past. The lights were dimmed, much like a high school dance. The difference was the temporary bar set up in the corner and the lack of grinding moves that the teens of today called dancing. People gathered in clusters. From the outside, it was easy to pick out who were alumni of the school and who were the bystanding significant others obligated to escort the River Bend graduates.

A tap on his shoulder brought his attention to Luke. "I was wondering if you'd show up," Luke said over the music.

Wyatt shrugged. "Not a lot of nightlife in this town."

"Nightlife? I don't think that's the reason you're here."

"Oh?"

Luke glanced around the growing crowd before returning his attention to Wyatt. "How about a beer?"

Wyatt followed him to the bar.

Principal Mason leaned on the wall next to the bar. "Hello, Richard," Wyatt greeted him with a handshake.

"Evening, boys."

"Standing guard over the bar?" Luke asked.

Richard ran a hand over his bald head with a cocky grin. "Making sure a few of these good ol' boys buy me a drink. Some of them put me through hell. You included, Miller. You ditched school more than you showed up."

"I passed my classes."

"By a hair." Richard winked and nodded toward the bartender. "Jack and Coke, Miller. Make it a double."

Luke narrowed his eyes and bought the principal a drink.

The three of them watched the crowd for a few minutes. "Does this get old for you?" Wyatt asked Richard.

"Not at all. It's like watching a good game you have money on."

"How so?"

Richard scanned the room. "A handful of the teachers and I lay bets at the end of every year gauging who will leave town, who will stay. Then after the reunion, we wager on who is coming back."

The principal glanced between the two of them and said, "Don't judge. Vegas is a long ways from here. Take you, Luke. None of us pegged you for leaving."

Wyatt laughed at the expression on Luke's face.

"I'm not sure how to take that."

"You worked with your dad. Loved cars . . . you didn't have to leave to find yourself." Richard nodded toward the mass in the gym. "Lots of them did. Some are still searching. Some have been gone long enough to know they want what they had when they lived here, and some know a small town simply isn't big enough for them."

While Luke appeared to contemplate Richard's words, Wyatt asked, "Is there anyone here you lost money on?"

"Sure. JoAnne was a shock. I pegged her as a *leave and never come back* girl."

"I don't think she had much of a choice," Luke said.

"Everyone has a choice."

Wyatt scanned the crowd, his eyes finally finding the reason he was there.

She was wearing a little black dress, the kind that hugged a woman's curves and made a man's mouth water. From the heads she turned, his wasn't the only mouth watering. Zoe was dressed in red that offset her olive skin and drew a whistle from the man at his side. Beside the two was the third of the female musketeers. Jo skipped the dress and wore slacks. Still, she was more dressed up than Wyatt had ever seen her. If he had to guess, her friends insisted on the outfit. Still, the woman walked like a cop, her eyes darting around the room in constant motion.

"Looks like our sheriff found her posse." Richard lifted the drink to his lips, smiled over the glass.

Wyatt felt Melanie's eyes and met them. She unleashed a slow smile that illuminated the room. When Wyatt lifted his beer in salute, she nodded and pointed to Zoe and Jo.

"I think that means you're buying the ladies drinks, Wyatt."

He reached for his wallet and nudged Luke. "Next round is on you."

A couple of minutes later the two of them wiggled through the crowd, double fisted with drinks.

"Why thank you." Melanie offered a wink. "How did you know?"

Luke leaned in. "Subtle, Mel . . . real subtle."

"We wouldn't want the wrong men buying us drinks this early in the evening," Zoe said.

Jo laughed. "I don't usually have that problem."

"You have got to come visit me in Dallas. And leave your badge behind. The men will line up to pinch your ass and buy you drinks."

Jo rolled her eyes. "I'd probably put them in a choke hold and cuff them."

"They might like that," Wyatt added.

When their laughter slowed so did the music, and Wyatt moved in. "So, Melanie . . . about that dance you owe me."

She blinked a few times, a blush rose on her cheeks. "What dance?"

"My fee for rescuing little girls off rooftops."

Wyatt took the liberty of removing the beer from her hand and setting it on the high-top table before leading her away.

The curve of her hip met his hand as he faced her on the dance floor. They swayed a few times before she spoke. "Smooth, Wyatt. Using my kid to score a dance."

He turned her around and noticed Jo watching from the sidelines. "I could have used my roadside rescue skills as an excuse."

"You could have just asked."

"You could have said no." He liked his deck stacked, thank you very much.

"I could have said yes."

He leaned back slightly and looked in her eyes. Her smiling eyes.

"You could have." He turned her again, happy to feel her follow his lead. "Now that you know I won't trample your feet, you're much more likely to agree to future dances."

She kept her eyes on his. "Is that confidence or cockiness?"

"Both. I can dance, no need to pretend I can't."

"Not that you get a lot of practice in River Bend."

Wyatt turned her again, this time moving her away with a push and spinning her once before bringing her back. "You'd be surprised. Fourth of July is always a celebration. Founder's Day. Every holiday has some kind of festival . . . or have you forgotten?"

He kept her moving while they talked. He scented lemon on her skin and committed it to memory.

"And how many women in River Bend have you shown your talents to?" she asked.

"My talents?"

She blushed. "Dancing talents?" She pushed against his shoulder. "I already know you don't date the women in town."

"Is that right? How would you know that?"

When she glanced over his shoulder, he pulled her closer. The sheer fabric of her dress nothing but a thin layer between them. He had to give serious thought to their conversation.

"Jo told me."

"Oh, so you're asking your friends about me?"

"Of course. You're hitting on me. I have to make sure you're really not Jack the Ripper."

"Not a lot of prostitutes in River Bend. I'd be out of business if my name was Jack."

He took pleasure in making Melanie laugh.

The song ended, along with their dance. His hand held the small of her back as they made their way off the dance floor.

No sooner had he wrapped his hand around his beer when Zoe grabbed his arm. "So, Wyatt . . . about that dance you owe me."

"What dance?" He heard Melanie's words coming from his mouth.

"This one." Zoe dragged him away from their group. The music had turned fast, but Zoe pushed close enough to talk. "Melanie is one of my best friends," Zoe stated the obvious.

Wyatt felt the inquisition beginning and let it roll. "You seem tight."

"We are. But I have to tell ya, I kick myself all the time for not telling her what a shit her ex was."

"You met him?"

"Once. Between that and Mel's stories . . . he's a shit."

They moved beside each other, not touching, and not keeping beat with the music.

"Well—"

Zoe didn't give him time to talk.

"I won't do it again. If I see any red flags, I'm going to speak up."

"I'm sure—"

"She's sensitive." Zoe kept looking over his shoulder.

"I—"

"And vulnerable."

Instead of trying to comment, Wyatt nodded.

"I think she needs this reset, and hooking up with a guy who only wants to use her and toss her away again is going to screw her up."

Wyatt stopped dancing and Zoe's eyes met his. On some level he knew Zoe was just looking out for her friend, but she'd all but accused him of being an asshole.

"Oh, jeez, I'm being a bitch, aren't I?"

He knew better than to answer that.

"I'm sorry . . . it's just, I'm leaving in a couple of days and won't be here to kick your ass if you screw her up."

"Kick my ass?" He felt his lips lifting despite the conversation.

"I'm tougher than I look," she said in defense.

Wyatt glanced over his shoulder and caught eyes watching them. Then he moved a little closer to Zoe and said in her ear, "Melanie's stronger than she looks, too. Give the woman a little more credit."

Instead of continuing to move on the dance floor, Wyatt led Zoe away by her elbow.

This time, she leaned in and whispered, "I will come back and kick it if I have to."

~

"That shit is funny right there!" Luke stood with his hands on his hips, a wide grin over his face.

Zoe held her stomach, laughing hard.

Melanie bit her bottom lip as giggles kept erupting without her control. Every time she glanced toward the hot steam coming off Jo's face, her laughter was harder to hold back.

Morning fog blanketed the mess as the sun started a slow rise on the horizon.

As the tired houses of River Bend woke, so did the crowd surrounding Jo's home.

Squeaky brakes stopped a car and a whistle preceded the obvious comment. "That's quite a mess you have there, Sheriff."

Before Mel turned around to see who was talking, a half-used roll of toilet paper gave up its battle of hanging from a high branch of the maple tree and fell to the ground.

Zoe lost it once again and Jo grumbled.

Sheets of white toilet paper draped over every possible surface of Jo's house. The masters of TPing a house had placed rolls on the end of a broom and used it to fling tissue forty feet up into the pine and maple trees. Even Jo's squad car didn't go unscathed.

The voice from the car started to laugh.

Jo twisted and pointed. "I'm sure you have better things to do than sit here and laugh, Deputy."

Mel glanced at Deputy Emery, who leaned out the window of his squad car.

"Should I write up a report?" Deputy Emery asked, laughing.

"Don't be ridiculous." Jo was ticked, but a slight amount of admiration sat behind her eyes.

Melanie exchanged glances with Zoe and Jo with a slight nod. The three of them had done their fair share of TPing as kids and couldn't help but admire the balls of those who decked the town sheriff's house in Charmin.

Zoe lifted the forgotten broom and nudged a piece of paper off a rosebush. "Does this happen to you a lot, Jo?"

"No one would dare."

"Well someone dared. Probably several someones. I didn't hear a peep all night," Zoe said.

From the wetness of the paper, the blanketing of white happened early in the morning. The three of them had returned from the reunion and crashed at Jo's house close to one in the morning. It was just rounding on five thirty when Mel forced herself out of bed so she could help Miss Gina and get back to Hope. One glance out the front door had Melanie calling for Jo.

"I guess we should expect you a little late this morning."

Jo scowled at her deputy. "I'll be on time."

"Might wanna think twice on that, Jo," Luke said. "It's supposed to rain later today. Wouldn't want this mess to set in more than it already has."

Jo crossed her hands over her chest. "Good thing I have friends who can help me clean it up."

Luke lifted his hands in the air and Zoe pulled the edges of her bathrobe tighter. Both of them started to mumble something about a busy morning.

Jo moved on to Melanie.

"I have to get to work. Sorry."

"See you at the station." Deputy Emery drove off with a wave as Jo's neighbors started to disappear into their houses.

"I'll try and get back a little later," Melanie offered.

Jo waved her off. "Go. I've got this." With a turn of her heel, Jo disappeared inside the house.

The second she was gone, Mel and Luke both took out their cell phones and started snapping pictures.

"You two are bad," Zoe chuckled.

"I'll forward you the pictures," Mel told her.

Zoe pointed up into the tree. "Make sure you catch that."

She pointed her camera toward the sky and snapped a few more angles of the mess.

"Epic," Luke muttered.

~

As soon as Mel helped the last of the inn's guests check out, she found Miss Gina standing on the far south lawn with a can of spray paint in her hands. Miss Gina tossed back a long strand of her peppered hair with a curse and continued to lay lines in the grass.

"Do I even want to ask?"

Miss Gina didn't bother looking up as she held the can in one hand, the edges of her skirt in the other, and walked backward as she sprayed. "They don't make these things like they used to," she complained. "Stupid—" She cut herself off and shook the can in her hand before attempting to draw her line in the lawn.

"What are you doing?"

"Redecorating. What does it look like?"

"Looks like you're painting the lawn pink."

Miss Gina straightened and admired the large box she'd managed to draw.

"I think that's big enough . . . don't you?"

"What's it supposed to be?"

"A house."

Melanie blinked a few times. "A what?"

Miss Gina rested her hands on her hips. "No kitchen. I don't need a kitchen," she started to ramble. "Just a bedroom, bathroom . . . a living space with a fireplace. Simple space."

The box on the lawn took a different shape in Melanie's head.

"You're adding a guest house?"

Miss Gina lifted her hands in the air and motioned in air quotes. "Additional guest quarters."

"But the inn isn't booked up again until—"

Miss Gina waved her off. "This isn't for guests. Well, officially . . . for taxes and anyone who asks, yeah . . . guests. But it's for me."

"You have a room—"

Miss Gina pointed her can of pink spray paint back toward the ground and splattered pink everywhere. "The innkeeper's room is for the innkeeper . . . that would be you. I need my own space. I deserve my own space, don't you think?"

A chill shimmered over Melanie's spine. Equal amounts of uncertainty and unexpected pleasure clamored for space inside her head.

"Well shit . . . I forgot a closet."

"Wait . . . what if things don't work out?"

"I should probably have two closets, right? One in the bedroom and another in the living room. Something for storage?"

Clearly, Miss Gina was planning on an extended stay in her *not a guest room* guest room. But what if Melanie sucked at being an innkeeper? What if Hope became too much trouble for Miss Gina? Already Miss Gina had played surrogate grandmother, though she preferred the title of aunt to grandma. Hope already gravitated to Miss Gina's side of the room whenever she was close by.

"Mommy, look who I found." Hope bounded toward them, her hand caught in Wyatt's. "See, I told you they were out here."

Wyatt kept up with Hope's energetic stride as she tugged him toward the backyard.

"Right on time. I hope you brought a tape measure," Miss Gina said.

"I have one in my truck."

"What are you doing, Miss Gina?" Hope asked once they stopped short of the painted box on the ground.

Melanie lifted her gaze to Wyatt's and shivered. His smile caught in his eyes and warmed her belly. The image of him standing there holding her daughter's hand didn't go unnoticed. "Hi."

"Hey," he said, staring.

She should have felt the need to squirm; instead she squared her shoulders and let him look his fill. She wore blue jeans and a button-up blouse, but he still looked at her as if she were dressed in the little black dress she'd worn the night before.

"You said it was an emergency, Miss Gina."

"It is. This needs to be done before fall sets in and the rain keeps you from finishing it."

Wyatt finally looked away. "What needs to be done?"

Miss Gina waved her hands wide. "Isn't it obvious? I need a guest house."

"A guest house isn't an emergency. Broken pipes, yes . . . new construction—"

"Don't bicker with me." She pointed the spray paint at him with a shake of her wrist. "We need to jump on this and I want you to do the job."

"A guest house?"

"More guest quarters. I don't need a kitchen. Well, maybe a tiny kitchen. A refrigerator for my lemonade."

Melanie chuckled.

"Can you build a whole house?" Hope asked Wyatt.

He offered a simple nod.

Hope swung her head, her ponytail smacking Wyatt's arm. "Wow. Can I help? I'm a good helper."

"Hope, I don't think—"

"Of course you can. How about you run to my truck and bring me my pad of paper and the pencil sitting on the passenger seat."

And she was gone, running around the inn to fill his request.

"She doesn't jump that fast to help me out," Mel said.

"Your daughter loves me, what can I say?" He ran a hand through his hair with a smirk.

"If you two are done flirting, we can get on with this." Miss Gina walked to the far side of her box and started her list. "One bedroom, full bath with a closet. The walk-in kind . . ."

Hope rushed back to Wyatt's side, out of breath, and handed him his papers.

He ruffled her daughter's hair and turned his attention to Miss Gina. Instead of insisting Hope find something to do other than bug Wyatt, Melanie left her to him and walked back inside the inn.

There were rooms that needed cleaning. It was time to start making sure she was doing the job she was getting paid for. Since arriving in River Bend, Melanie had spent more time socializing than working.

As the afternoon wore on, she'd occasionally glance outside and find Wyatt placating her daughter by handing her a tape measure or something equally as safe. She couldn't help but wonder if he was entertaining her daughter as a way of working his way closer to her. Not that he needed the help. Thinking about the man had become an hourly pastime since his almost kiss on the track field. What kind of kisser would he be? The good kind, she imagined. The thought alone gave her butterflies. It had been a long time since she'd been kissed.

So why had she stopped him?

Fear.

She hated that about herself. The last time she was in River Bend fear wasn't part of her vocabulary. Then life's punches reminded her how much it hurt to get hit.

Her best friends didn't seem to suffer from the same paralyzing thoughts. Granted, neither Jo nor Zoe were involved with anyone, but it wasn't fear keeping them from it.

Jo was cursed with being the town cop. It was kinda hard to have a fling or an anything when she overpowered the single men in town.

And Zoe . . . the image of Luke staring Zoe's way most of the night before kept coming to the surface. He wasn't over her. While Zoe said she had moved on . . . Melanie wasn't so sure.

So far no one in her close circle of friends was winning in the romance category. Not even Miss Gina had found herself a lover. At least not that Mel had caught on to, in any event.

She shouldn't be thinking about Miss Gina's sex life while fishing out a towel that had been tossed under one of the guest room's beds.

"There you are."

The sound of Wyatt's voice had Mel tossing her head up too fast. The back of it caught the edge of the bed.

"Ouch!" She wasn't sure what was more unflattering . . . her ass sticking in the air as she retrieved someone else's castoffs or her clumsy move that made a few stars sparkle in her head.

With a quick twist, she plopped on the floor, her ass no longer flying, and grasped her head. "That hurt." And it did. Right down to her toes.

"Sorry. I didn't mean to—"

When she opened her eyes, Wyatt was kneeling, his hand over hers holding the back of her skull.

"Are you okay?"

Melanie grumbled and rolled her eyes. "A little warning next time, Mr. Ripper."

Wyatt smiled at her dig and sighed.

She couldn't stop the smile any more than she could ignore the man who stood close.

"You're beautiful."

Melanie didn't do speechless often, but the compliment was so unexpected she didn't know how to respond.

Wyatt removed his hand from hers and slowly pushed a lock of hair from her eyes.

Her gaze moved from his eyes to his lips and he drew in a sharp breath.

Without warning, without an open invitation . . . he was there.

His lips were soft, warm, and electric. Everything inside her tensed, and those butterflies that appeared with the thought of his kiss turned into majestic birds in full flight.

She moaned. The sound surprised her nearly as much as his kiss. Her breath caught and her eyes closed. And for the first time in forever . . . Melanie just felt.

Wyatt's lips, his tongue seeking acceptance . . . his hand as it rested on the side of her face, tilting it up to reach his . . . it was wonderful. *Knock her out of her panties* wonderful.

For a brief moment, she felt Wyatt move away.

She dug her fingers into his shoulder and didn't let him move. He may have started the kiss, but she'd be damned if he ended it. A woman had to hold some power, after all.

The slight laugh under his kiss prompted her hand down his chest.

His laughter ended and she wasn't the only one moaning.

"Melanie!"

Her name, like nails on a chalkboard, irrevocably pulled her from the single best moment in her life.

The kiss ended as abruptly as it began, but Melanie didn't let go.

Instead, she held tight as if Wyatt was a shield against the dark magic of a known enemy.

Her eyes shot open and landed on the one person she never wanted to see ever again in her life.

"Nathan."

Chapter Nine

The dark suit hanging off Nathan's shoulders was as out of place as the man himself.

Melanie scrambled to her feet, her hand grasping ahold of Wyatt's. "What are you doing here?"

A practiced smile lifted the corner of Nathan's lips. "It's good to see you, too, precious."

The pet name he'd used for her back when made her cringe now. "Don't . . . just don't."

"Who is this guy?" Wyatt took the space in front of her, keeping Nathan at a distance. This close, he threatened the very air in the room.

Nathan stared Wyatt down. "I'm Hope's father."

She wanted to deny him the title, but couldn't.

"And Melanie's husband."

"No! You're not. I am not . . ." She dug her fingernails into Wyatt's arm tighter. "We didn't." Good God, why was she babbling? "What are you doing here, Nathan?"

"I'm here to see—"

"Mommy?"

Oh, God, Hope.

There were times when she and Nathan had been together when he'd turn his head in just the right way, grin ever so much, and she knew trouble sat behind his eyes.

Melanie heard Hope's feet running up the stairs and she pushed past both the men in the room. She lifted a hand in the air.

"Don't you even think about it, Nathan. She doesn't know you."

"She's mine, too."

Every muscle in her tensed and heat rose in her head. "I don't know why you're here, but you aren't going to mess up *my* daughter with whatever game you're playing."

"Mommy?" Hope was just a few feet away.

"Don't follow me, Nathan." She wasn't sure he'd follow her command, but she turned her back on him and headed Hope off before she could reach the men.

"There's a car in the driveway," Hope said as she reached the top step.

Melanie glanced behind her and grasped Hope's arm. "Really? Let's go find the driver."

"I looked and looked."

She all but dragged Hope down the stairs and out the front door.

According to the sticker in the window, Nathan had rented a town car in Eugene.

What the hell was he up to? It had been close to six years since she'd seen him. Last she'd heard he was off to some fancy law school and struggling to stay in.

"Maybe they're around back?" Melanie pulled Hope to where she'd last seen Miss Gina.

"I don't think so."

"C'mon."

Miss Gina sat on the back porch, a glass of lemonade in her hand, a cigarette in the other. "Did you find our guest?"

Hope shook her head.

Melanie stopped short and knelt to Miss Gina's level. "I need you to keep Hope out here with you," she whispered in her ear.

Miss Gina offered a slow smile. "Wyatt, eh?"

Melanie squeezed her eyes shut. "No . . . just please. I'll explain later."

Miss Gina narrowed her eyes. "You okay?"

She said yes, and shook her head no.

The older woman took the hint and patted the swinging chair beside her. "Hope, hon . . . what do you say we try and sweet-talk Wyatt into building a tree fort?"

"Like a tree house? Really?"

"Yeah, like a tree house."

"Do you think I can have a puppy? I've always wanted a puppy."

"One thing at a time," Miss Gina said.

Melanie disappeared through the back door and ran up the back stairs that led from the kitchen.

Wyatt and Nathan were standing exactly where she'd left them. Nathan with a shitty grin, Wyatt wore an angry frown.

She pointed at Nathan. "You. Out."

"I'm here to see Hope."

"You're not going to see her. Not today." Not ever if Melanie could manage that.

"Melanie . . ."

His tone set her off even more than his presence. "Don't *Melanie* me." She shook a hand in his face. "You have no right to interrupt my life."

His smile fell and he moved forward.

She stiffened and Wyatt stepped between them.

"I have every right."

If it wasn't for Wyatt's hand holding her back, she might have slapped the smug look off Nathan's face. "Don't make me call the sheriff and have you arrested for trespassing."

Nathan had the balls to smile. "This is an inn, a public place. I'm looking for a room."

It was time for Melanie to smile. "I'm the innkeeper, and I have the right to refuse service to anyone."

He rocked back on his heels and sighed. "I just want to see my daughter."

She didn't want to remind him the last time they spoke he accused her of sleeping around and questioned Hope's DNA. One thing was for sure, Nathan wasn't here for Hope. He had another agenda. He hadn't wanted to be a dad before, and she didn't think for a second he wanted to be a dad now.

"I can get a court order, Melanie."

For the first time since Nathan walked in the room, Wyatt attempted to intervene with words. "It's safe to say your presence isn't expected," he told Nathan. "Maybe you two should talk outside of the inn, away from Hope, and come to some kind of agreement."

Melanie wanted to scream, argue, throw really heavy objects that hit her target with a thud! "Fine."

"I saw a diner in town. How about noon tomorrow?" Nathan asked.

"I can't. I'm working."

Nathan narrowed his eyes. "Then the evening."

"Still working."

"Melanie?" His placating look of disbelief took over his face.

The urge to slap him was huge.

"Tuesday, eleven o'clock, at Sam's."

"That's two days away."

"Next time call before you pop into my life." It felt good to take control.

His smirk unnerved her as his eyes traveled down her frame. "Always did like your feistiness."

Wyatt took a step in front of her, cutting off Nathan's view. "I think you need to leave."

"I'll show myself out."

"I wouldn't want you to get lost," Wyatt said with a sweep of his hand toward the door.

As much as she wanted to stay behind and crumble on the half-made bed, she followed them down the stairs and split away when Wyatt walked Nathan out the front door. Melanie detoured toward the back until she heard her daughter's conversation with Miss Gina. The sound of a car starting, and the kicking up of the gravel in the drive, gave her pause.

He was gone.

She leaned against the wall between the kitchen and the sitting room and held her head with one hand. She didn't look up until Wyatt's boots stood beside her.

"I'm sorry for the drama," she said without looking up.

"You didn't invite it."

"What is he doing here? Why now?" Why when she was finally making positive decisions in her life instead of just letting life lead her in whatever direction it wanted to?

"Maybe he just wants to see his daughter."

No, she didn't believe it. Why would he use the old line about her being his wife? He used it when they first met to lay claim . . . to offer legitimacy to their illegitimate daughter. To placate his parents. "It's more than that."

"I'm not sure I can help since I don't have all the details. My guess is your girlfriends do."

Melanie actually groaned. Jo would just shoot him, and Zoe would sauté what was left in butter and garlic. But Wyatt had a point. Between Nathan's bullying and her embarrassment, Mel hadn't called on her friends the first time around, and look where it had gotten her.

She groaned again.

Wyatt placed a finger under her chin and forced her eyes to meet his. "I'm just sorry he soiled our first kiss."

She smiled and pushed back the images of Nathan and laid a hand to Wyatt's cheek. "Me, too."

"I'll make sure he's not around to mess up the second one."

The fact that Wyatt was already thinking about kissing her again brightened the dark spot Nathan had left.

"I'd like that."

Sam's diner sat on a corner of the main street in town. At one point Sam had changed the decor to resemble fifties rockabilly. As the years went on and the decay of use took its toll on the restaurant, the fifties gave way to a hodgepodge of seventies orange retro and nineties modern lines. In the end, it was a typical small town diner that made enough money to stay in business but not enough to warrant a redesign every decade.

Melanie showed up at eleven sharp and waited outside in Miss Gina's van. Nathan sat in one of the booths in the front window and kept looking at his watch.

"Make him wait a few minutes," Zoe said from the passenger seat.

Melanie had to grip the steering wheel to keep her hands from visibly shaking. "Him being here is a bad sign."

"You've been muttering that for two days, Mel. Snap out of it and deal."

"I don't want to deal. I just want him to go away."

"Maybe he's ready to start paying child support."

Melanie couldn't help it, she laughed.

"Yeah," Zoe said with a slight laugh. "That didn't sound right coming out of my mouth either."

Melanie grasped the handle on the door and shoved. "There's only one way I'm going to find out what his game is."

She jogged across the street to avoid a passing car and sucked in a fortifying breath as she pushed the glass door of Sam's open. A bell above her head brought a few faces swiveling her way. She returned a couple of smiles and a wave from the waitress before forcing her attention on her ex.

"Three-piece suits have no place in River Bend," she said the second she slid into the booth opposite him.

His eyes snapped to hers, then glanced at his watch. "Didn't we say eleven?"

"Traffic."

He narrowed his eyes and said nothing.

Just when she felt the need to squirm she remembered this intimidating quality he'd always played when they were together. His quiet, confident stares continually had her caving to whatever his demand was. It wasn't until she'd broken away that she had realized he intimidated her with silence.

Melanie held his gaze, sat back in the broken-down booth, and lifted one corner of her mouth.

He broke first. "You've changed."

She let her eyes sweep his frame in a very deliberate fashion and said nothing. He hadn't, but she'd be damned if she was going to engage in small talk with the most disappointing person in her life.

"I know I haven't been there for you and Hope."

She huffed out a breath.

Nathan tilted his head and paused before he asked, "Aren't you going to say anything?"

"Yeah," she said. Melanie met the eyes of the waitress. "Hey, Brenda . . . can I have a cup of coffee?"

"Sure, Mel."

The bell sounded on the door and Melanie caught Luke out of the corner of her eye.

"Hey, Mel." Luke didn't offer a greeting to Nathan.

"Hey."

Luke slid up to the counter and grabbed a menu.

He never grabbed a menu. The thing hadn't changed in fifteen years. It was only when Zoe cooked in the back that the patrons of Sam's were in for something new and exciting.

Brenda brought her coffee and cream from the back. "You need anything, I'm here."

Nathan lifted a hand. "I'll take a—"

Brenda turned away from him without giving him the time to finish his sentence.

Melanie kept in her smile. If Nathan thought he was going to come to River Bend with a welcome, he'd been mistaken.

Nathan had this tick under his left eye that always gave away his emotions before he voiced them. That tick started a slow twitch as he watched Brenda walk away.

"Why are you here?"

"I went to Bakersfield. You weren't there."

Leave it to him to avoid her questions. After a sip of the coffee she set the cup down and stared. "You didn't fly all the way here to tell me I've changed and remind me that you've been the biggest deadbeat dad there is."

"You took her away."

"You left!" Her voice rose and Luke swiveled in his seat.

"You wanted me out."

Yeah, she didn't want the man any longer, but that didn't mean he had to abandon his daughter. The old argument sat on her lips and stayed there. *What's the point, he'll only deny everything like he always does.*

Outside the diner, Jo pulled along the curb in her squad car and got out. All dolled up in her uniform, she placed her hat low on her head and walked into the diner.

"Hey, Mel."

Instead of asking what Jo was doing there, Mel just smiled and waved.

If Nathan recognized Jo, he didn't say anything.

". . . another chance." Nathan was talking, but Mel wasn't listening. Her focus was now on Zoe, who slid in the back door before taking a seat at the counter with Luke and Jo.

"Another chance at what?" Mel asked, turning her focus on her ex and not the posse that was starting to form in the diner.

"Us. I want to give us another chance."

She sat speechless for the space of two breaths. "You can't be serious."

"I am. I'm in a better place now. I think we should—"

She cut him off with a wave of her hand. "Stop . . . just stop. That ship sailed a long time ago, Nathan."

That tick kept twitching now, faster with every word. "Hope deserves a father."

"Hope? You want to tell me what my daughter needs?"

"Our daughter," he corrected.

She placed her hand on the table to avoid balling it into a fist. "You were the sperm donor, Nathan. You didn't want to be a father."

His eyes skirted over to the counter. "Melanie, keep your voice down."

"Don't tell me to keep my voice down. You have no right."

"Melanie!"

"Don't *Melanie* me." God, how she hated that when they were together.

Nathan took a deep breath and turned his back to the others in the restaurant and lowered his voice.

"I didn't come here to fight," he told her.

"Did you think you could come here and we not fight?"

"I want to work things out."

Her eyes caught Zoe's before moving back to his. "And I want you to leave."

"Hope deserves a father." His words caught in her chest.

"She deserves someone who isn't going to leave the second things get hard."

He nodded and his face softened. If it wasn't for his telling tick, she might believe he was actually listening to her. "I'm an attorney now, Melanie. In a much better place . . ."

Of course he was. He didn't have a child or a family to worry over while he finished his education. She would love to be happy for him, but all she could feel was envy. He'd fulfilled his dreams while she was eating noodle soup and driving around in crappy cars. Or better yet, bumming a ride from her friends in their cars.

She shook the negative thoughts from her head and thought of Hope.

She had Hope, and she wouldn't trade that for an education or a title.

"It's great that you continued with your life, Nathan."

He grinned as if she'd given him a gift.

"But I don't need you."

That grin fell.

"I want to be a part of Hope's life."

"That's going to be a little hard to do, living in California."

"When you come back—"

"We're not coming back," she cut him off.

He glanced around the diner and scowled. "What do you mean?"

"Hope and I are staying here. I've already enrolled her in school for the fall."

"My God, Melanie. You're better than this place."

She laughed. "But not better than Bakersfield?"

Nathan flicked a crumb left by another patron off the table as if it were an ant.

"You ran away to Bakersfield. If I had known you were there, I would have . . ." his words trailed off.

"Would have what, Nathan? Come galloping in on your trusty steed and rescued us from my crumbling apartment and shitty school?"

"Yes. All that."

He kept glancing at their audience, who were doing a great job of keeping their backs to them while remaining silent enough to hear most of the conversation.

"Well you're too late. And unless you plan on sticking around, there is no reason for you to see Hope and mess her up. She doesn't need you. We don't need you."

The bell over the door rang again.

Wyatt's frame filled the door.

His smile filled her heart.

Wyatt offered a single nod and moved toward the growing crowd. When Melanie turned her attention back to Nathan, that tick was going full steam.

"He's not her father."

Was that jealousy? "No, and unlike you, he's not pretending to be either."

"I don't have to pretend."

She tried to put an end to this once and for all. "Go home, Nathan. I'm giving you a free pass. Go live your life and leave us to live ours."

His snarky smile started to replace his tick, and that had Melanie's heart beating too fast in her chest.

"That's not how this is going to play out, Melanie."

She didn't care for the conviction in his tone. "And how is this going to play out?"

His silence unnerved her this time.

Jo stepped up to the table, the sound of the belt holding all her cop toys clapping along the way. "You're okay here, Mel?"

"She's just fine," Nathan said.

"Mel?"

The fact that Nathan didn't bother looking at Jo gave a twist to her stomach. He was up to something . . . had need of something. He just wasn't giving her any clue as to what.

"I'm going home to clear my calendar for a while, then I'll be back."

Melanie swallowed hard. "You don't have to—"

"I'm not leaving my wife and child here forever."

Again with the wife thing. "I'm not your—"

Nathan reached over to pat her hand.

Melanie pulled back as if stung.

Jo placed her hand on the table and leaned in front of them. "I think you should leave."

It was then Nathan looked up to see every set of eyes in the diner on him.

He lifted both hands in the air before scooting out of the booth.

Once on his feet, he looked down at Jo and smirked.

His parting words were directed at Melanie. "I'll be back."

Then he was gone.

Chapter Ten

Melanie's ex slithered out the front door of the diner after a sneer that should have been illegal. The door no sooner shut than Zoe moved in beside Melanie and put her arm around her. As much as Wyatt wanted to be the one to comfort her, he had other things he was much better at doing.

He leaned toward Luke and kept his voice low. "I'm going to follow him."

Luke offered a nod while Wyatt moved out the back door.

The dark sedan Nathan drove belonged in a B movie filled with espionage and spies . . . not in the sleepy town of River Bend.

It wasn't as if Wyatt could blend in with traffic, and he wouldn't know how to do it if there were any. He pulled up behind Nathan's rental and kept an appropriate distance while they inched through town.

It wasn't until they passed Miller's and the gas station that Nathan started to stare through the rearview mirror.

Wyatt kept an empty look on his face and tailed the man.

As soon as they passed the last speed limit sign stating thirty miles per hour, Nathan sped up.

Wyatt kept pace without getting too close. The two-way road had several blind corners and more than a few four-legged critters that crossed the thing.

When Wyatt had to take a corner a good fifteen miles per hour faster than he'd ever done before, he started to mutter, "Why are you in such a hurry?"

They passed the cemetery, rounded another corner before the long stretch of road leading to R&B's. Instead of blowing past the bar, Nathan skidded the car into the gravel and pulled to a stop.

He sat behind the wheel with the engine running for several minutes, giving Wyatt the impression he was going to rip out of the parking lot just as quickly as he'd pulled in.

Nathan pushed out of the car, dark sunglasses over his eyes, and started for the door to R&B's . . . then, as if it was a second thought, he twisted in Wyatt's direction and marched across the gravel lot.

Wyatt jumped from his truck, shut the door, and leaned against it with his arms crossed over his chest.

"What the fuck do you think you're doing?"

"Out for a Sunday drive," Wyatt replied.

"Screw you."

The words *you're not my type* sat on his tongue unsaid.

"Messing with another man's family is always a mistake," Nathan told him.

"Is that some kind of threat, Counselor?"

Nathan was only a couple of inches shorter than Wyatt; his build told Wyatt that Melanie's ex didn't spend all his time behind a desk pushing papers.

"Just a statement, Redneck. Melanie and Hope are mine. You'd do well to remember that."

The man thought he was insulting him. Instead, the compliment made Wyatt smile.

"I'm not sure how the rules are in your county, but here in Redneckville a man takes care of his family, provides for them. If he doesn't, he leaves that role open for another to take over."

Nathan shuffled his feet and Wyatt kept going. "In case you haven't noticed, Melanie has a family here that doesn't include you. And family in Redneckville take it personally when you screw with one of their own." Wyatt ended with a nod.

"Is that a threat?"

Wyatt grinned. "Just stating facts, Counselor."

Nathan clenched his fists several times before taking a deep breath. Wyatt didn't bother to unfold his hands and waited.

"You don't scare me."

That was unfortunate. The fact the man was lying to himself was a terrible quality.

Nathan turned on his polished heel and took long strides to his car. Once there, he turned and waved a finger in the air. "Stop following me."

"Call the sheriff," Wyatt muttered to himself before sliding behind the wheel and pulling in behind Nathan as he drove away.

Nathan pulled into the parking lot of a motel several miles outside of town.

Wyatt took pleasure in every glare the man tossed his way.

Wyatt sat in his truck for about an hour before Nathan reappeared with a suitcase in hand. He took note of Wyatt's presence, tossed the case in the trunk, and drove away.

By the time Wyatt returned to River Bend, the town had all but closed up for the day, only the diner and R&B's still showed signs of life.

He took the liberty of showing up at Luke's uninvited.

Luke didn't question his presence, just opened the door wide and let him in.

"Wanna beer?" Luke asked, turning his back and heading into his kitchen.

"Have anything stronger?"

"Ohh, that bad?"

Wyatt let the door slam behind him. "Long day."

Luke removed a bottle of Jack from the cabinet above his fridge and placed it on the kitchen table before searching for a clean glass.

Wyatt swung the forgotten pizza box toward him and opened it in hopes of a few scraps. Without asking, he grabbed a slice and bit off a cold end with a moan.

"It's like college all over again," he said between bites.

"I wouldn't know," Luke said.

Straddling a chair, Luke took a pull on a beer and waited a few seconds while Wyatt took the edge off his hunger and washed it down with a shot of whiskey.

The burn in the back of his throat warmed him with a shiver.

"Well?"

Wyatt shoved the last bite into his mouth and reached for another piece before talking. "Followed him to the airport in Eugene."

"So he's gone."

Wyatt spoke around the pizza. Why did cold pizza on an empty stomach taste so good? One of life's questions, to be sure. "Not for long."

"You spoke with him?"

"Briefly."

Luke reached for one of Wyatt's fists, glanced at his knuckles. "Care to elaborate?"

Before relaying the conversation he'd had with the man, it was time to hear a few facts from Luke. "Tell me what you know about him."

Luke shrugged. "Just what I've heard from Jo over the years. Melanie met him in college, before long she was pregnant and dropped out. Not sure what came first, now that I think about it. Jo wasn't living close when all that happened and my ties to Zoe had been cut. Everything I heard was long past it happening."

"Were they married?"

Luke shook his head with a shrug. "Couldn't tell you. Everyone said yes a couple of years ago. It's only been in the past few weeks that Melanie claimed all that was a lie."

Wyatt poured another couple of fingers of Jack and kicked it back. "Does Melanie make a habit of lying?" He hated to ask but wanted to know for many reasons.

Luke laughed. "No. She sucked at lying in high school. People change, I guess, but I don't know. I would think she would have been straight with her best friends."

"What did Jo and Zoe say about all that?"

"Don't really know. I don't think they care. Neither of them approve of the man so his status, divorced or just an ex, doesn't mean crap to them."

Staring at the white wall on the opposite side of the kitchen kept Wyatt's attention as he finished the second slice of pizza.

"Does it matter to you?"

"Lying?"

Luke waved him off. "Lying sucks . . . I'm talking about her single or divorced status."

Wyatt wiped his hand over his face and removed any evidence of the pizza before answering. "We all have a past."

Luke seemed to sit on that for a few minutes. "So what did the man say to you?"

"That I was stepping on his family."

Luke ran a hand through his hair. "That's just bullshit. If there is one fact, it's that Melanie and Hope haven't been a priority to that man. You saw her car."

"Yeah, I get that. So why is the man all hell-bent on making everyone think he's sticking around this time?"

"Maybe he woke up and realized he's a dad."

"It's more than that. He's talking about Melanie as if she belongs to him."

"That's what Zoe told me. Makes me wonder about the man's head. What kind of man goes out of his way to make strangers think he is something he's not?"

Wyatt finished his drink, poured another, and vowed to walk home.

". . . and they all lived happily ever after." Melanie leaned against the headboard with her daughter nestled in the crook of her arm.

Hope released a contented sigh and snuggled closer. "I wanna be a princess when I grow up," she exclaimed.

"A noble goal."

Melanie lifted the book from her lap and put it on the side table. With the inn lacking in guests, they'd placed Hope in the room they'd first shared alone, while Mel took the room across the hall.

"Princesses wear pretty clothes."

"You like your jeans and T-shirts."

"Yeah. And they have a prince who takes care of them."

Melanie's hand hesitated over the book of fairy tales that Hope loved her to read from. "Sometimes the prince doesn't do such a great job of taking care of his princess. It's always better for the princess to learn to take care of herself."

Hope seemed to chew on that for a few seconds. "But isn't it easier if a prince helps her?"

"Some things might be easier."

Hope twisted in her lap and blinked wide eyes. "If you had a prince, you wouldn't have to scrub floors or make all the beds here."

She placed a hand on the side of her daughter's face. "In the real world, a mommy is always scrubbing floors and making beds, sweetie.

And I like working here. It's not like in the books. Not a lot of life is like what you read in a book."

"I know it's pretend." Hope rolled her eyes. "But it would be cool to be a princess."

Melanie slid from the bed and helped Hope under the covers. "You can be a princess, but I want you to marry a knight, not a prince."

"Who is the knight?"

"He's the warrior who fights for the princess. He's the one who can protect her."

"Is he rich?"

Melanie sat on the edge of the bed and brushed Hope's hair from her face. "No. He has something money can't buy."

Hope's eyes were drifting closed. "What's that?"

"The princess's heart." Melanie tapped her chest.

Hope smiled.

Melanie kissed her daughter's forehead. "Good night, princess."

"Night, Mommy."

The phone rang as Melanie left Hope's room. She took the steps faster in an effort to answer it before the caller hung up.

Miss Gina beat her to it. "No, she's right here."

Miss Gina's words stopped Melanie from walking by.

With a hand over the receiver, Miss Gina pointed the phone at Melanie. "It's Wyatt."

With the phone in hand, Melanie smiled at Miss Gina and felt her cheeks warm. "I'll just take this outside."

"I'm sure you will."

When she reached the screen door, she put the phone to her ear. "Hey."

"Hi. I hope it's okay that I called."

It was dark on the back porch, the twinkly lights under the eves drawing any flying bugs away as she sat.

"Of course. I was wondering what happened after you left Sam's."

"Well . . . in his defense, it wasn't a fair fight."

Melanie felt her smile freeze on her face. "You're kidding." Her heart leapt in her chest and started pounding to the beat of Metallica. "Oh, God, Wyatt . . . he's a lawyer, please tell me—"

"Relax. I just followed him out of town."

Melanie closed her eyes and tried to slow her anxiety down. "I'd hit you. If you were here, I'd hit you right now."

Wyatt laughed.

"There wasn't a fight?" She had to ask and clarify.

"No fight."

She imagined the two of them side by side. It wouldn't be a fair match.

"Did you just get home?"

"I went to Luke's for a while, but yeah, about an hour ago."

"The edge of town isn't that far, Mr. Ripper. You sure there isn't more to your story?" She hated to ask, but couldn't help but want to know exactly what transpired between her ex and her new . . . was he her new? She thought of their kiss, the butterflies.

"I followed him to the airport."

"Eugene?"

"That would be the one."

"Jeez, Wyatt, that's a long way." Still, the relief of knowing Nathan had left town was a weight lifted.

"I didn't want to miss him doubling back if he was bluffing."

"And what exactly would you have done if he had?"

She recognized Wyatt's soft laugh as one filled with mischief. "How is Hope? She doesn't suspect anything, does she?"

"She's fine. And you're changing the subject."

"How are you? You seemed upset when I left the diner."

"I've had better days. Nathan is the last person I thought would show up on my doorstep. He's just as infuriating now as he was when we were together."

Wyatt took an audible breath over the phone. "Can I ask you something?"

"We are talking."

"If he was infuriating, why did you stay with him?"

Melanie tucked her feet under her while she attempted to answer the question without appearing like a complete bitch. "He was charming in the beginning. I was just a kid and traversing the landscape of college, dating, my parents' divorce. When it became apparent that I wasn't going to be able to continue at the university, he was there. Not completely supportive, but there. If that makes any sense."

"I think it does."

"Then Hope came and I tried harder. He didn't have an ounce of patience for his daughter, for me." She shook her head, remembered him screaming at her to stop Hope's crying. "Things eventually shifted and I felt safer on my own." Those were dark days. Days she didn't want to repeat.

"Safer?"

"What?"

"You said safer. Were you scared of him, Melanie?" His question came in an even, controlled voice.

She hesitated. He'd never been abusive with her . . . so why couldn't she jump on a quick *no* for an answer?

"Melanie?"

"Sorry . . . no. Things were blurry in the end. I remember thinking how much he'd changed. How stress closed him off. It was unnerving."

"Scary?"

"Yeah, I guess." She shifted in her seat and switched the phone to her other ear. "I'm sorry. Talking about an ex is a classic mistake."

He laughed. "Everyone in this town is talking about you and your ex, so cut yourself a break."

She rested her head in her hand. "When I lived here before, all that talking would drive me crazy. Now it just feels like support."

Wyatt started laughing. "Luke and I were betting that Brenda was going to dump coffee in his lap."

And the look on Nathan's face when Brenda walked away had been priceless.

"I'm going to change the subject," he told her.

"You seem good at that," she said with a chuckle. "Go for it."

"They are setting up for a carnival and strawberry festival in Waterville next weekend."

She waited for the question with a Cheshire cat grin on her face.

"Would you and Hope like to go?"

"With you?"

"That would be the general plan." There was a slight edge to his voice, which made her grin wider.

"Like a date?"

"Is it a date when you bring a kid?"

"It's not a date?" It was time for her voice to carry a sharp edge.

"We can call it a date if that makes you feel better."

"I don't have to call something a date to feel better . . . I just . . . what are you calling it?"

When he didn't reply quickly, she unfolded from her chair and started to pace. "Wyatt?"

He huffed out a laugh. "A date."

"You!" She pointed a finger in the air as if he could see her. "You did that on purpose."

"I like pushing your buttons."

"One of these days I'm going to figure out what your buttons are and pushing them will become my pastime."

"Aw shucks, darlin' . . . I've never been someone's pastime before."

"You're incorrigible."

"I'll take that as a compliment."

"It wasn't."

He laughed.

Chapter Eleven

Zoe barked orders from the inn's kitchen as if she were on set. She couldn't help herself; the kitchen had an energizing effect on her that few understood. "The smaller the cut, the more flavor throughout the salad, Mel."

"Yes, ma'am."

Zoe tossed a tomato at her friends before wiping her hands on a towel.

"There's enough food here for an army."

"We do it big in Texas."

From outside, the smell of ribs on the barbeque drifted through the inn.

"Is Zane coming?"

Zoe shrugged. "I couldn't tell you. Mom says he has a job up in Waterville. I'm afraid to ask what kind of job."

The youngest of the Brown children had never moved out of his mother's house. Then again, her sister was back with her mom after a failed relationship that took her to Eugene and back.

"Is he still on parole?"

"Mom said no, but I'm not sure."

Between his temper and his drinking, Zane had landed in jail more times than a kid at twenty-one should. "Is it too much to want him to grow up?"

Mel offered a smile from across the kitchen. "You can't force people to do the right thing, Zoe."

"It's frustrating. I can't help but wonder if I was around more if things would be different."

Melanie slid closer and placed the knife on the counter. "You can't live your life for your family. The three of you all had the same deck of cards handed out to you. You found your path and ran with it . . . they will find theirs."

"And if it's the wrong path?"

"What if it is? What can you do, Zoe? You give Zane money and you enable him to keep doing stupid shit. You preach, he tunes you out. He knows right from wrong."

Mel was right . . . it just sucked to see someone she loved falling down the wrong rabbit hole. "Since when did you become so wise?"

"A few years at the school of hard knocks."

Zanya, Zoe's sister, walked into the kitchen holding a six-month pregnant belly. "Mel, please tell me you have Tums somewhere in this place."

"Tums? You haven't even eaten yet!" Zoe exclaimed.

"Oh, baby . . . come with me," Mel said as she pulled Zanya into a half hug and walked her from the kitchen. "I bet he comes out with a full head of hair."

Zoe watched as her BFF left the kitchen with her sister and future nephew. At least Zanya could rely on Zoe's friends. There was some comfort in that.

Voices from the back door brought an even bigger smile to her face.

"Mrs. Miller." Seeing Luke's mom always made Zoe's insides turn to mush. The woman was everything a happy stay-at-home mom should be. She loved to bake, loved to can fresh preserves in the summer . . . and craft a few silly things for the rummage sale hosted by the Little White Church in spring and again at Christmas.

"I hope you have room in that fridge, Zoe."

She stood double fisted with pie, Mr. Miller followed with two more.

"Looks like you've been busy."

"You said pie. I bring pie. Apple, strawberry rhubarb, chocolate, and banana cream."

There was nothing better than Mrs. Miller's banana cream. "I love you."

"I know, baby. Now make room in that massive tin box. It's too hot for these to sit out."

Mr. Miller left the apple pie on the counter and waited until Mrs. Miller took the remaining pie from his hands before turning to Zoe. After a kiss to the cheek, he left the kitchen as quickly as he entered.

Zoe looked beyond Mr. Miller.

"He's on his way."

"What . . . who?"

Mrs. Miller pinched her lips and tilted her head. "You might have gotten older, but you haven't changed."

The fact that Mrs. Miller called her out about searching for her son, without truly calling her out, was a testament to their relationship. The woman never sat in judgment nor did she question Zoe's decision to leave River Bend to find herself.

Instead of saying anything, Zoe returned to the finishing touches of the tiny feast she was preparing as her own going-away party. She was leaving in the morning, bringing to a close her brief hiatus from her daily life.

"What can I do?" Mrs. Miller asked.

"How about tossing the salad?"

Luke's mom moved to the sink and washed her hands as the sound of a motorcycle drowned out the voices from the back of the house.

Luke was there.

She knew that, and her heart sped up, which gave her equal parts of happiness and sorrow.

It was breaking again.

Like it did every time she saw the man and knew she was leaving.

She was trying so hard to be his friend . . . only his friend.

Her dreams, however, weren't allowing her to remain platonic. Memories and reality were mixing every damn night, making it impossible to sleep.

"Hey, Zoe?" Wyatt called from outside.

"Coming."

Wyatt manned the barbeque with a strict set of instructions, though he tried hard to convince her he knew his way around the grill. He'd have to prove himself before she let loose the reins of her meal.

The sun decided to cooperate on her last day in River Bend, giving them all a chance to play and enjoy the outside.

Miss Gina had an old badminton set that Jo and Mel had set up earlier in the day. Miss Gina was lofting a birdy over the net to Hope, while Zoe's mom watched from the shade of the porch.

"Can I help with something?" her mom asked.

"I got it."

"Almost done," Wyatt told her as he pushed the barbeque fork into the center of the meat.

"Not bad, Mr. Gibson." She closed the lid to the grill, turned off one burner, and lowered the others to a small roar. "Five minutes."

She blew past him and back into the kitchen.

She stumbled over her own feet at the first sight of Luke. "Just in time," she said as she blew past him without a hello. "Dinner's ready."

Luke simply laughed while Mrs. Miller shoved a massive bowl of salad into his hands.

Mel and Zanya returned and helped parade food to the back porch.

Mel had done a great job of setting the perfect table on the covered porch. Flowers sat in vases on the long expanse of wood, and a hodge-podge of white and blue plates offset old mason jars that were either filled with spiked lemonade or tea. Mr. Miller held the long neck of a beer, as did his son.

The food was simple . . . perfect, but simple.

And Zoe took pride in every moan as her friends and family consumed each mouthful.

"Remind me to visit Texas," Mr. Miller said between bites.

"If there is one thing I have learned from living there . . . it's that Texans take their barbeque seriously. This is the best I can do without a smoker."

"It gets better than this?" Wyatt asked.

"It's really good, sis." Zanya had gotten over her bellyache and was plowing through her plate like a linebacker.

Jo pointed the end of her corn on the cob in Zoe's direction. "It better not be another decade before you visit again."

"It's been less than ten years since I visited," Zoe defended her absence.

"A real visit," Miss Gina added. "Not a hit and run. Those are fine for a one-night stand, not for us."

"Miss Gina!" Mel chastised, eyes wide as she shifted her gaze to her daughter.

Zoe's mom laughed and Mrs. Miller tried not to.

As the laughter died out, Zoe caught Luke's piercing gaze.

And she knew, in that moment, that she couldn't promise anything. As much joy as everyone at the table brought her, she knew the fall was going to suck.

"Hey? Where is everybody?"

Zane.

The voice of her brother interrupted the meal.

He walked around the side of the inn, his footsteps less than steady. He smiled and waved. "Am I late?"

"Only by an hour," Luke said.

The second Zane tripped on the first step, Zoe knew he was drunk. Or something else. If the table were filled with people from her life in Dallas, she'd want to hide. There wasn't one person at Miss Gina's table who didn't know her brother.

"Can't blame a man for not wanting to break bread with a cop."

Zoe exchanged glances with Jo. "Knock it off, Zane."

Zane was the spitting image of their dad. All dark hair, dark skin, muscle, and attitude. When he drank too much his temper wasn't easily controlled and his mouth ran like a faucet stuck on high.

"Sit down before you fall down," their mom told him as she pulled out the empty seat beside her.

"Who's that?" Zoe overheard Hope asking Mel.

"That's Zoe's brother." Mel ruffled her daughter's hair.

"Oh."

Zane must have heard the question from the other end of the table. "I'm the black sheep. You know what a black sheep is?"

"Zane!" Zoe yelled.

"Knock it off!" Zanya shook a finger in her brother's direction.

"Mommy?"

"I'll talk about it later," Mel whispered.

"Sheryl says you have a job up in Waterville," Mr. Miller changed the subject.

Zane glanced at their mom. "Yeah. Part-time."

Several people started back on their plates while Zane reached around to fill his up.

"What do you do?" Wyatt asked.

"A little of this, a little of that."

Zoe found Jo's concerned gaze again.

"I've had jobs like that," Mel said.

Zane muttered something under his breath that only their mother heard. She elbowed him in the ribs.

The last thing she wanted on her last day in town was a scene. The itch on the back of her neck told her that no amount of hoping was going to do a damn bit of good.

"So, Zoe . . . are we going to see you on the TV this year?" Mrs. Miller asked.

"There is some talk about a holiday special. I should know by August if it's going to happen."

"Did you film the last holiday gig in September?"

"Yes. It was awful. They had me dressed in sweaters for the promotional stuff when it was ninety degrees and dripping with humidity."

"The price of fame," Jo teased.

"Could be worse."

Zane snorted and once again their mom elbowed him.

"Knock it off." He jerked away from her with a glare. "She's bitching about cooking." He stood and searched out a cooler that held chilled beer.

Like he needed another drink.

"You know, Zane, I'm glad you saw it fit to come here to say goodbye before I leave. Would it be too much to ask for you to bring it down a notch?"

"What's the matter, sis? I don't fit in your world?" He twisted off the top of the beer and tilted it back.

"You're being an asshole," Luke put it the way it was.

Zane glared. "Who the fuck asked you?"

"Hey!" Wyatt pushed his plate aside. "Language."

Zane's gaze moved to Hope.

"I'm sure she's heard worse."

Sheryl pushed away from the table and tossed her napkin from her lap. "C'mon, Zane, I'm taking you home."

"The hell you are. I just got here."

"Mom's right. You're in a mood and no one wants to hear it." Zanya rested a hand on her belly.

As if to add an exclamation point, Zane flopped in his chair and grabbed a fork.

When their mom placed a hand on his shoulder he shoved it away, knocking her off balance.

Every man at the table was up in a heartbeat.

Jo practically flew across the table.

"I'm okay," Sheryl said once she balanced herself.

"Time for you to go." Luke loomed over him.

Zane glared at him, then moved that pointed anger to Jo, who pinned his hand holding his steak knife to the table.

"Get off me!"

"You drive here, Zane?" Jo asked in the coldest voice Zoe had ever heard coming from her friend.

Her brother let a slow smile spread over his face. "Sure did, Sheriff. Drank half a fifth in the driveway before walking back here."

There wasn't one person who believed him, but if there was one thing every criminal understood, it was the law.

Zoe pulled in a shallow breath and swallowed the tears that threatened to spill. "Please leave, Zane."

Mr. Miller rounded the table and flanked her brother. "I'll take you, son. Wouldn't want anyone getting hurt."

Zane shoved from his chair, leaving it to tumble behind him. "I can manage."

"The hell you can," Jo said. "Don't make me arrest you."

The line in Zane's jaw started to pulse. "I'd like to see you try."

Miss Gina slapped her hand on the table, making everything within a foot of her plate shake. "Enough! This is my home and we will *not* do this here!"

Zoe was on her feet.

Mel had taken Hope from her chair and moved away from the men.

Mrs. Miller placed an arm over Zanya's shoulder.

A voice from inside the inn drew everyone's attention from the table.

"Uhm, excuse me . . . but do you have a room for the night?"

Several faces swiveled to the stranger in the door.

Zane attempted to break free of Jo's hold with a buck while Mr. Miller and Luke took him by the shoulders and walked him down the back steps.

Zoe's mom slumped in her chair. "Son of a bitch."

Hope clung to Mel's side and Zanya was in tears.

"About that room?"

Miss Gina marched back into the inn, past the stranger, and barked, "Follow me."

"Our guest is settled," Miss Gina said when she returned.

Mr. Miller and Luke had forced Zane into a car and left.

Mel busied herself around the table, putting to rights the mess caused by Zane's outburst. Her attention kept traveling to Zoe. The steam coming from her eyes said it all. She'd pushed her food aside and sat drinking Miss Gina's lemonade in silence.

Sheryl kept apologizing to Mrs. Miller, who shook her head and reminded Sheryl that Zane was a grown man who was no longer someone she needed to apologize for. Mel wasn't sure Sheryl heard her.

"You okay, Zoe?" Jo asked from the other side of the table.

Zoe attempted a half smile and pushed her hair behind her back.

"I'm all right. Ticked . . . but Mrs. Miller is right. Zane's a grown man and is making his own choices."

"Even if they're bad ones," Zanya added.

"Jo, I need you to know . . . if you ever have to put Zane in his place, do it. Our friendship will never come into question. Isn't that right, Mama?"

Sheryl offered a single nod and looked down at her plate.

"I never thought it would."

Melanie really hoped it wouldn't come to that, but from the way Zane reacted to Jo, she couldn't help but wonder how many times Jo had let him slide away when she shouldn't have.

Wyatt interrupted her thoughts with a tap on the shoulder. "How about a walk?"

Hope still sat in Melanie's lap, her tiny arms still wrapped around her waist. "I should probably help with the dishes."

Miss Gina picked up a few plates. "You go. There will be plenty to do after all that pie."

"C'mon, Mommy." Hope slid from her knees and tugged on her hand.

Wyatt nodded toward the back of the house.

It wasn't until they'd walked far enough away from the inn, and out of earshot of those still sitting on the porch, when Melanie released a deep breath.

"That was intense." Wyatt kept pace beside her while Hope ran ahead.

"Is he always like that?"

Wyatt shrugged. "I don't really know the guy. Luke might be a better one to ask."

"He was just Zoe's kid brother . . . annoying, but not crazed like he was today."

"He reminds me of a kid searching for himself."

They followed Hope on a path that led through a patch of trees. "I really hope he isn't violent with Sheryl. I don't think she'd do much about it if he was."

"Have you ever met Zoe's dad?"

"No. I know Sheryl used to drag them all to visit him in prison a couple times a year. When Zoe started high school, she always gave an excuse as to why she couldn't join them."

They were silent for a while before Wyatt said, "It must have been hard for them to grow up without a father."

Melanie couldn't help but look at Hope with Wyatt. "According to Zoe, he used to hit Sheryl all the time. I'm guessing it's better the man was locked up than teaching his children that behavior."

"True. I just can't imagine not having a dad. Mine has always been there."

"Hope doesn't seem to miss it at all."

"She's a girl," he said as if estrogen explained everything. "It would probably be harder for her without a mom."

Now it was time for Melanie to think about Jo. She'd grown up without her mom, bucking her father . . . "Yeah, I guess."

"Mommy! Uncle Wyatt . . . c'mere."

"Uncle?" Wyatt asked with a grin.

"She's been calling Zoe 'Aunt Zoe' and Jo 'Auntie Jo.' I told her it was okay." Melanie took his smile as acceptance and didn't correct her daughter when she met up with her a few yards later.

Hope had climbed five feet up into a pine tree. "Look what I found."

Wyatt stood at the base of the tree and looked up. "What is it with you and climbing a tree?"

"Mommy told me she used to climb them all the time when she was my age." Hope took another branch up with a firm grip.

Melanie felt herself cringe but didn't say a thing.

"You climbed trees?"

She narrowed her gaze to Wyatt. "Don't sound so surprised."

He shook his head. "I can't see it."

She placed a hand to his chest and pushed him aside before reaching for the first branch.

Within three feet, Melanie knew the sap wouldn't come off her hands for a week. But as she closed the gap between her and Hope a familiar sense of awesome washed over her.

Hope sat perched on a sturdy branch with a silly grin. "This is so cool."

"Be sure and hold on tight," Melanie instructed. "And don't get freaked out by bugs or flying insects."

Hope wiggled her nose and did a little search of her personal space as if she were being swarmed.

"Even bees?"

"A bee sting is better than a broken arm."

Hope shrugged and reached for a higher branch. The two of them climbed in tandem for a few more feet.

"Hey, ladies . . . how high are you planning on climbing?"

Melanie glanced down to find Wyatt standing with his hands on his hips, his neck stretched to keep an eye on them.

"You'll learn not to challenge the Bartlett girls."

Hope giggled. "Yeah, Uncle Wyatt . . . are you coming?"

Apparently, all he needed was an invitation.

He looked a little like Spider-Man without the red costume and mask. He was less careful of where he placed his hands and didn't pay attention to the branches brushing against his face. Wyatt hung on to a sturdy branch at the base of the tree, near their feet.

"Why are we climbing a tree again?" he asked.

"Because it's fun!" Melanie said.

Hope pointed to a tree across from them. "Look at that."

A nest the size of a grown man's fist held a single bird that intently watched them.

Melanie was about to tell Hope to hold on when her daughter used her free hand to brush off a few ants that were walking along her arm. "This is awesome." Hope went ahead and pushed farther up.

Melanie followed, Wyatt trailing behind until the branches started to thin. "That's far enough," she told her daughter.

They were in the thick of the trees, a good thirty feet off the forest floor. The smell of pine would probably stay in her hair for as long as the sap stuck to her palms . . . but Melanie didn't care. "You can't do this in Bakersfield."

"I don't wanna go back there again ever. I like it here."

Melanie glanced down at Wyatt, who had heard her daughter's words. "I like it here, too."

They listened to the wind in the treetops for a few minutes, and pointed out things they couldn't see from the ground. "We should probably get back and help with the dishes."

Hope offered a small protest but didn't whine for long.

Climbing down from the tree was a little harder for Hope than ascending.

Wyatt guided her from under, and Melanie stayed a foot above.

Wyatt reached the ground first and lifted Hope from the last few branches before setting her on her feet.

With her daughter safe, Melanie stopped watching the activity on the ground and concentrated on her own descent. The feel of Wyatt's hand on her ankle made her grin and look.

Watching the mischief behind his eyes, she took another step and felt his other hand reach her thigh. "I think I have—"

"Gotta keep the Bartlett girls safe," he said.

And then both his hands were on her ass and sliding to her waist, where he plucked her off the tree as if she were a fly.

"There you are." Only he didn't let go.

When Melanie turned around, he was snug inside her personal space, reminding her how lonely it was without him there.

For a minute, she thought maybe he'd lean in a little closer. His eyes were already traveling to her lips.

A small voice stole the moment. "We should climb trees every day."

Wyatt lifted one eyebrow without breaking eye contact with her.

"Mommy?"

Melanie had to turn away from the tractor beams of Wyatt's gaze. "Yeah?"

Hope was studying the two of them . . . her eyes shifting back and forth.

Melanie took a tiny step back and Wyatt let go.

Hope pushed in between them and grasped one of their hands in each of hers. "Can we climb another one?"

"Sure, sweetie. But not today."

Melanie noticed the shadow of the three of them once they left the crush of trees. The song in Hope's voice as she talked Wyatt's ear off about tree climbing and sticky fingers followed them all the way back to the inn.

Chapter Twelve

Wyatt opened his refrigerator door, took one sniff, and shut it. He really should do something about the smell in the icebox, but not tonight.

Exhaustion wasn't going to allow him the chore of cleaning out the fuzz growing in the vegetable drawer or the unmentionables tucked in rubber containers.

Hunger drove him to his pantry, which wasn't better than an oversize cupboard with canned and boxed food. The standby go-to box of mac and cheese sat beside a jar of peanut butter.

He reached for the peanut butter and made sure there wasn't any green growing on the bread sitting on the counter before making himself a quick sandwich. He wasn't halfway through the first one and he was making a second.

He leaned against the kitchen counter and hummed.

Nothing better than a PB&J.

The past week had been a blur. Between the drama at Miss Gina's and the week of reunion chaos . . . and Melanie, Wyatt was beat.

It didn't help that when he finally closed his eyes at night, his thoughts of Melanie kept him tossing and turning. And if he was honest with himself, he'd acknowledge the soreness in his shoulders after climbing up after her and Hope in the tree.

He might climb on a house a couple of times a week, but tree climbing used a few muscles his body forgot he had.

Wyatt took his second half-eaten sandwich into his living room and sank into his couch.

The coffee table was nothing more than two milk crates holding up a piece of glass, but it worked to suit his needs. He'd started the remodel on his own house the minute he'd moved into the place five years before. Once each room was completely redone he would go through the effort of furnishing it before moving on to the next. To date he had his bedroom and master bathroom along with the kitchen completed. The living room was still a shell that needed masonry work around the fireplace, completed flooring—hardwood was his preference—and new lighting throughout. That didn't mean he didn't have a big screen hung on a half-finished wall and a couch . . . but he drew the line at tables and occasional chairs. The only real visitors he had were friends like Luke, and they couldn't give two shits about the decor in his home. They would continue to crack jokes about the plumber's faucet leaking . . . or in his case, his half-finished house when he could fix just about anything.

Problem was, he'd been working continually since he moved to River Bend. Between the odd-end jobs and handyman needs of the widowed and divorced . . . and the full-time needs of the businesses in town, Gibson Construction was booming. On occasion he would hire a few men to help with bigger jobs, like the one Miss Gina wanted him to do. There was no way he was going to be able to do that solo with the timeline she'd measured out. Why the woman wanted a guest house when the inn sat half full at best most of the year was the question. He wondered if Melanie had given her the excuse to go into an early retirement. The woman had always been eccentric and outspoken, but she was like a comet lighting up the northern sky since the reunion.

He flipped through the channels and kicked his feet up on his hillbilly coffee table and managed maybe three deep breaths before his phone rang. Thankfully the handset was sitting next to his feet and he didn't need to pick his sore ass up off the couch to answer it.

"Yeah," he said without checking the number.

Loud voices and music in the background met his ear, which prompted Wyatt to turn the volume down on his TV.

"Wyatt!"

One word was all it took to know Luke was toasted. "Luke, that you?"

"I-I'm gonna need a ride, buddy."

"Where are you?"

"Jo would kill m-me if I drove. Probably toss the key in the high school time capsule."

Wyatt switched off the set. No use pretending there'd be any stationary time in front of it with his friend slurring his words.

"Luke, it's not even eight." And it wasn't like his friend to get cooked, let alone midweek.

"And bring your truck so I can get my bike back home."

"All I own is a truck," Wyatt reminded him.

"R-right! Thanks, Wyatt. I owe ya." And then he hung up.

Good thing there was only one real bar in town. The beer and wine served at Sam's wouldn't do the bang-up job Luke had apparently managed.

For an early Thursday night, R&B's was tight with people. Sure enough, Luke's motorcycle sat parked in the lot along with several others.

Wyatt shoved his keys in the front pocket of his jeans as he walked inside.

The jukebox was pumping out a seriously heavy metal tune with an ear-piercing volume, and patrons were overly loud and intoxicated for such an early hour.

Apparently the post-reunion party wasn't over yet.

Luke caught sight of him from across the room and waved him over.

"Is this place crazy or what?" Luke asked.

"I thought it would thin out after everyone left."

Luke held his glass of amber liquid and waved it around. "Not everyone left. Some people actually like it here." There was bitterness in Luke's tone.

Josie slid by their table and nodded toward Wyatt. "You driving this one home?"

"That's the plan."

Josie patted her hand on the table. "Then I guess I can get you another drink."

From the glossy eyes and less than steady hand, Wyatt considered suggesting Luke switch to coffee, but he held in his words. There was only one thing that drove a man to this level of drunkenness.

Women.

He wasn't sure if he should bring up the elephant in the room or leave the fact that Zoe had flown out the day before unsaid.

Wyatt asked Josie for a beer . . . something to nurse while he listened to what he was sure was going to be a slurred, enlightening conversation about the opposite sex.

"What is up with all the bikers in here tonight?" Wyatt asked after taking a seat.

"Couldn't tell ya. Maybe some kind of rally up the coast."

That sounded about right, only those usually happened closer to the end of summer when the weather in California became unbearable and the north looked more appealing for those driving with two wheels and no doors.

Most of the time, the bike rallies consisted of middle-aged businessmen wearing black leather and revisiting their younger days. This crowed looked a little less like lawyers and doctors and a little more like the real thing. Hence the out of place timing for the up the coast drive. Then again, who knew?

Josie brought their drinks and put a big glass of water next to Luke's whiskey. "In case you think hydration might be a good idea for the morning," she said with a wink.

"Oh, baby . . . you're so thoughtful."

Josie rolled her eyes. "I just don't wanna hear about your puking in Wyatt's truck." She glanced at Wyatt. "It is a nice truck."

Wyatt laughed. "Thanks, Josie."

"Hey, lady . . . we need another round," one of the leather wearing strangers called over the music to capture Josie's attention.

She rolled her eyes. "It's going to be a long night."

Before Wyatt could process the energy in the room, Luke started in. "The problem with women . . ." His words trailed off.

"Boobs?" Wyatt joked in an effort to keep the conversation light.

Luke lost his train of thought, Wyatt could tell by the sliding up of the edges of his mouth. "She has the best rack. And that red dress." He again pointed with his drink. "She knows I loved her in red."

"So we're clear . . . tonight's lack of sobriety is about Zoe."

There was a sigh and a sip of his drink. "She left again. I thought maybe, with Mel coming home . . . maybe. Damn it."

Wyatt let Luke linger in his depression for a few minutes. "Seems like there is a lot of drama here for her. Her family . . ."

"I wanna kick Zane's ass."

Good thing Luke's father had ridden with them that day. No telling what shape Zane and Luke would have been in had he not. "We all wanted to kick his ass."

"He wasn't like that. Jo says he's been in and out of trouble. Petty shit mostly, but damn. Sheryl doesn't need that."

"She can kick him out."

Luke shook his head. "Never gonna happen. Zoe always said her mom was afraid to live alone. That's why she always put up with her daddy's shit. I don't think any of that has changed."

"Well maybe that's why Zoe needs to live somewhere other than River Bend."

Luke narrowed his eyes. "I'm not following you."

"Maybe living alone is Zoe's rebellion. To avoid falling into her mom's life." And since when did Wyatt become a family therapist? He tilted back his beer and glanced around the bar.

"You know somethin', Wyatt . . . you might be right."

"Or you might be drunk."

Luke let his dimples show. "Oh, I'm wasted . . . but Zoe avoiding her mom's life. That . . . that makes sense."

"Considering how many of her friends are here, I'd think there has to be something equally powerful keeping her away. Doesn't seem like her life in Texas sucks, but she didn't exactly brag about it either."

"No. She's doing great. Really great."

Even in Luke's drunken self-pity, Wyatt could see the respect he had for the woman that drove him to the bar early on a Thursday night.

A loud noise interrupted their pause in conversation.

Apparently Luke wasn't the only one in the bar overindulging. From the placating smile on Josie's face as she passed the loud party next to the jukebox, she was earning her tips the hard way.

"There's a weird vibe in here tonight." Wyatt returned his attention to Luke.

Luke ignored his comment. "Ever been to Texas? With a name like Wyatt . . ."

He nodded. "It's flat and hot."

"Humid."

"You've been?"

"Once," Luke said, without elaborating. Lost in his thoughts, Luke finished his drink and looked around.

"How about the water? Save my truck." Wyatt nudged his friend's arm with his.

"Yeah."

Luke drank the water slower. "Any word from Melanie's ex?"

Wyatt shook his head. "Not that I've heard."

"Not sure if that's good."

"You think he's going to cause her trouble?"

"I think he's already caused her trouble and I don't think people change all that much." Even drunk, Luke made sense.

The next track on the jukebox screamed off the walls of the bar. Someone had found the volume control and was doing their best to have a rock concert in the small space. When Luke caught his head in his hands Wyatt suggested they leave.

"You stay here, I'll settle up with Josie."

Luke pointed two fingers in the air and offered a drunken grin.

"You guys are leaving?" Josie asked instead of telling Wyatt what they owed.

"Gotta get him home before he passes out."

Josie stood on her tiptoes and glanced around the bar. "Can you just give me like ten minutes? I think I'm gonna call Jo, have her swing by."

"Any trouble?"

"No. Well . . . just a little crazy and not enough locals to keep it sane . . . ya know?"

"I hear ya. We'll hang out until Jo gets here."

"Thanks, Wyatt. Melanie's a lucky girl."

It took Wyatt a full second to move his feet. Where had that come from?

Small town, he reminded himself.

"Ready?" Luke asked when he returned to his side.

"Not yet." Wyatt went on to explain Josie's worry, which resulted in a bobblehead nod from Luke.

Luke attempted to hold in a burp and failed, then waved his thumb toward the bathroom. "I'm gonna . . ."

"You do that."

Luke swiveled off the high stool, steadied himself, and then found his path to the john.

Wyatt turned back to his lone beer and played with the bottle.

Over the music he heard a shout, turned in time to see Luke stumble, then saw the first fist thrown.

Wyatt was out of his seat and across the room in two breaths, but not before Luke's ass took out one of the tables.

Somewhere a woman screamed and several men started shouting. Wyatt pushed in between Luke and the stranger in an attempt to stop the fight.

Before he could, a hand gripped his shoulder, spun him around, and a fist connected with his jaw.

There weren't too many things that shot his adrenaline through the roof, but a punch to the face did it every time. He saw red and came up swinging.

He punched and blocked and took a hit from the opposite side. A warm trickle of blood ran down his cheek, the feeling hardly registered.

Luke had managed to gain his feet and everything was a blur of fists, screams, and pain.

He couldn't even calculate time until he spun toward another hand on his shoulder and damn near dislocated his shoulder to stop his punch from connecting with Jo's face.

"What the fuck, Wyatt?"

Someone had the good sense to unplug the jukebox, abruptly ending the majority of noise. A couple of men were still tossing punches and stopped only when Deputy Emery broke them up.

Wyatt wiped his forehead with the back of his hand, grimaced at the blood he found. That's when he saw the destruction.

"What the hell is going on?" Jo twisted in a circle.

Wyatt couldn't tell if it was the uniform or the woman under it that caused several grown men to study their shoes.

"Well?"

Josie tossed a towel on a broken stool.

Noise from outside told him a few of the bikers who managed to slip out were driving away. There were still three shaking out bruised fists and glaring at Wyatt and Luke.

"I said stick around and help, not bust the place up." Josie placed both hands on her waist and glared.

"I can explain," Wyatt said.

"I'm listening." Jo waited.

Wyatt glanced at Luke. "I tried to break up a fight."

Jo swiveled toward Luke. "Who started it?"

Luke pointed to the stranger. "He punched me."

"You knocked me over," his nemesis yelled. "No one knocks D-Man over."

Luke started yelling, followed by D-Man pushing closer.

Jo stood between the two of them.

"Enough!" Josie did the yelling that time.

"Damn it." Jo reached for her handcuffs. "Turn around," she ordered the stranger.

"What the fuck!"

"Turn around!" Jo's *don't screw with me* voice had the grown man turning around.

D-Man spread his hands on a table as if he'd been in the position before. After a quick frisk and the removal of a pocket knife, Jo cuffed him and turned to another biker and did the same thing.

When she was done, there were three strangers with their hands tied behind their backs. Luke, Wyatt, and a local by the name of Matt stood in a broken bar that had been vacated by everyone other than those involved in the fight and the employees.

"I don't even have room for all you shits in my squad car."

One of the bikers laughed.

She turned on him, pointed. "Emery, get them back to the station."

D-Man lifted his chin toward Wyatt. "What the fuck about them? Playing favorites, Sheriff?"

One of the other bikers muttered, "Probably fucking them."

Luke started toward the cuffed man.

Wyatt stopped Luke from moving.

Jo took one look at them and narrowed her gaze. "You drive him to the station and wait for me," she ordered Wyatt. "Matt, you've been drinking?"

"Uhm . . . yeah."

She nodded toward Wyatt. "You ride with them." She took Luke by the shoulders with a shake. "When you get there, you pour yourself a big cup of black coffee, sit the hell down, and don't plan on getting up until I say . . . got it?"

"Jesus, Jo—"

"It's Sheriff Ward right now, Mr. Miller."

"C'mon, Luke. Do as Jo says," Wyatt said, taking Luke by the elbow.

"Sheriff Ward, Mr. Gibson. And I expect the same of you. No one goes anywhere until I figure this mess out."

"Got it."

Before Wyatt could take a step, Jo asked, "You been drinking, Wyatt?"

"Half a beer," he told her.

Jo glanced at Josie, who nodded.

"Get out of here," she said before turning back toward the others.

Wyatt didn't make her say it twice.

Chapter Thirteen

"A bar fight." Melanie stood with her hands perched on her hips, her gaze shifting from one bruised face to another. Luke looked like he'd had a one-on-one with a prizefighter. The red, angry welts would prove to be every color of the rainbow by morning. He nursed a split lip with a bag of ice that he alternated between his face and the top of his head. The man was still drunk a good hour after Jo had forced them back to the station. Wyatt had a cut above his right eye and bruising on the left side of his jaw. At least he looked sober.

Jo called Melanie to help with the triage of the deviant testosterone-charged men.

Matt sat in the corner, his head in his hands, an angry wife at his side.

"A bar fight," she said a second time for good measure.

Melanie had ignored the drunken comments as she walked into the back room, but took note of the unfamiliar faces as she passed them by.

She opened the first aid kit Jo had handed her before pointing her toward the men.

She removed a jar of Betadine and poured a generous portion onto a gauze pad and pushed Luke's hand away from his face before mopping up some of the mess.

"Ouch!"

"You can't feel too much with the amount of alcohol swimming in your veins."

Luke pulled away and winced as his back hit the wall.

Melanie moved to his side and pushed up the edge of his shirt. Sure enough, there was a scratch taking up the left side of his back, complete with what looked like a couple of decent size splinters from a broken table.

"Good Lord. Poor Josie. I bet her place is jacked."

"Poor Josie, what about me?" Luke asked.

Melanie rolled her eyes and helped Luke out of his shirt.

She fumbled through the first aid kit and found a pair of tweezers. With more than a little bit of pleasure, she poured hydrogen peroxide over Luke's back and watched a grown man whimper. "And Jo . . . you know how hard it is for her to police this town. The last thing she needs to do is pull your sorry ass in here."

"They started it," Wyatt said from his quiet corner in the room.

Melanie stopped picking at the wood in Luke's back and glared. "You sound like a teenager."

"It's true," Luke said.

"I don't think it matters to Jo. Everyone throwing punches gets hauled in. That's what she said on the phone."

"Jeez, Mel . . . be careful back there," Luke whined.

"Suck it up." She was less than gentle but managed to get the splinters out before placing a generous amount of medicated cream on his back, along with a bandage.

She moved to Wyatt.

"I'm okay."

"Yeah, that's why you're bleeding."

"It's stopped." He pulled the gauze away from the cut above his eye to prove it.

It looked like he could use a stitch or two.

"Needs to be cleaned," she told him.

He hissed but didn't pull away when she saturated the cut with hydrogen peroxide. Wyatt kept watch with his one good eye as she removed the clotted blood and cleaned him. "I think this needs a stitch."

"I'm sure there's a butterfly in there," Wyatt said.

"I don't know."

"It's fine, Mel."

She dug again, found a fancy bandage to hold the edges of his eyebrow together. When she finished, she placed a large Band-Aid over the whole thing. "Anything else?" she asked, poking his shoulders and glancing at his back.

"If you want to take my shirt off, go ahead. But I think I'm good." He was smiling at her.

"Brat."

He managed a wink with his bad eye.

Jo strode into their room a few minutes later, words tumbling out of her mouth. "Next time take the fight outside. Did you see the damage to R&B's?"

"They started it, Jo!" Luke took one look at Jo and added, "Sheriff."

"Yeah, well, several people saw you fall into that jackass. Ty's friends said you rushed him."

"That's crap—"

She waved off Wyatt's comment. "Doesn't matter. They're screaming self-defense and you yourself said you tried to stop the fight, Wyatt. Putting your hands on someone first."

"But—"

She stopped him with a hand in the air. "It's all a 'he said, he said' game. Comes down to one thing . . . are you pressing charges?" Jo looked between them. "And before you answer, know that if you press charges, they will press charges, and Josie will have to go that route as well. Right now she's willing to let it rest as long as you guys promise to repair the damage."

"Even those yahoos out there?" Matt asked.

Jo shrugged her shoulders. "Everyone is booked, or no one is booked."

Wyatt hedged his arm toward Luke, nodded at Matt. "We'll make sure Josie's taken care of."

"Good choice," Jo said before twisting around and marching out of the room.

It took ten minutes for Jo to clear out the bikers and return to them. Matt's wife promptly stormed out of the station, her husband in tow.

When it was just the four of them in the room alone, Jo shook her finger at both of them. "Don't ever make me fucking arrest you. Damn, Luke . . . what were you thinking?"

"I'm blaming the liquor."

"It's not even midnight," Jo pointed out.

"Yeah. It won't happen again, Jo."

Melanie saw a cloud pass over Luke's eyes and she knew the reason behind the alcohol.

"And you," Jo pointed at Wyatt.

Wyatt didn't offer a liquor excuse. "Can't watch a friend take a beating, Jo. If you need to cuff me, do it. I won't hold it against you."

Jo's chest heaved with every breath she took. "Take them home, Mel."

Then she was gone.

Melanie dropped Luke off first since he lived close, then drove Wyatt to R&B's to retrieve his truck.

A sign on the door said the bar was closed until further notice.

Mel parked next to Wyatt's truck. "Is it that bad in there?" she asked.

"It didn't look good."

Wyatt didn't rush to leave Miss Gina's van.

"Luke was torn up about Zoe, wasn't he?"

Wyatt shrugged. "Man code."

She grinned. "I'll take that as a yes."

"Take it however you need to, darlin'."

"I guess it's probably good you were here then."

"Tell my head that in the morning."

"Is it bad?"

A mischievous smile spread over his face. "Might have a concussion."

She regarded him with caution. "A concussion."

"Yeah, the kind that needs someone to keep me awake all night."

"Holy . . . you did not just say that."

He laughed and opened the door. "C'mon, give me a hand with Luke's bike."

She followed him out in the cool night, let the headlights of Miss Gina's van light the parking lot.

Wyatt removed a ladder from the side of his truck and used it as a ramp for Luke's motorcycle.

Melanie helped with the straps to keep it in place before Wyatt closed the tailgate. "That should do it."

She wiped the dust from her hands. "You're okay from here?" she asked.

Wyatt leaned against his truck and crooked his finger his way. "C'mere."

She took a step closer, felt the energy change between them. When she was close enough, he reached out and tucked a strand of hair behind her ear. "Thanks for coming."

"Jo's my best friend," she offered.

His grin spread. "Right."

Melanie leaned her head into the palm of his hand that lingered on her face. When he stepped closer, she met him halfway and lifted on her toes to reach his kiss.

Who knew the swelling in her belly could explode with such a simple touch. But Wyatt's kiss unleashed a crash of feeling she couldn't describe. With a moan, she closed her eyes and pressed her tongue against the edge of his lips.

Wyatt opened for her and took control. He spread his hands along her back and pulled her flush against his body. From knees to lips, he was everywhere. His hands took their time caressing her waist before finding the edges of her breasts.

Her knees buckled and Wyatt turned and sandwiched her between him and the truck. The hardness of him pressed against her stomach, giving all the evidence she needed of her effect on him. And she liked it. Only when she filled her palm with the globe of his firm butt did Wyatt pull away from her lips with a groan. "Come home with me," he whispered.

She wanted to . . .

"The inn has guests. Hope . . . Miss Gina."

Wyatt leaned his forehead against hers and winced.

"Poor baby," she said, giggling.

For a moment he just held her and didn't attempt to kiss her again. "We should probably go."

He gave one more lingering kiss before releasing his hold.

With weak knees and a speeding heart, Melanie slid behind the wheel of the van and let Wyatt close the door behind her.

"Thanks again," he said.

"You're welcome."

He tapped the side of the van as she drove away.

∼

"I suddenly don't feel so bad." Wyatt took one look at Luke and winced. Purple was the predominant color of his face with a bright bluish-red spot on the left of his head. If you didn't know Luke, you might not catch the extent of swelling, but you'd definitely know he didn't look right.

"I can't tell how much of this is hangover or broken crap underneath."

The hour rounded on noon, removing some of the hangover time Luke suggested.

R&B's would normally hold a handful of people at this hour but today held only a small crew destined to serve their community service for a night of crime. At least that was how Wyatt painted the picture in his brain.

"There you are." Josie walked from the bar, hands on hips, attitude in her stride. "I thought I was going to have to call Jo."

While Josie's words were stern, her smile was anything but.

"Cut the crap, Josie," Luke told her as he made his way up the steps to the bar and pulled her into a half hug.

"You look like someone drug you behind their truck on a rope for a good ten miles."

"That's about how I feel."

Josie nudged his hip with her own. "I probably should have cut you off."

"I doubt that would have helped," Wyatt said. "The place was charged last night."

Josie had her long brown hair twisted into a braid. Her jean shorts shouldn't look as good as they did on a woman in her midforties, but Wyatt had to admit, they did. "Matt's inside cleaning up."

"I'm going to make a run to the Eugene hardware store when I leave here. Try and get you back up and running by tomorrow night."

Luke was already inside, Wyatt right behind him.

Matt stood in the center of the room with a broom. Some of the tables that still had all their legs had been placed to rights. Those that couldn't be salvaged were still where last night's fight had left them. A big pile of glass had been mounded up on the floor, the smell of stale beer more pungent than on any given Saturday night.

Luke let out a long-winded whistle. "I didn't remember it being this bad."

"You were drunk," Josie reminded him.

Wyatt placed a hand on Josie's back. "I'm really sorry."

"No, I'm sorry . . . if I hadn't asked you to stick around until Jo got here, this might not have happened."

Wyatt had already considered that. "It is what it is, darlin'."

Josie offered a smile. "I've already ordered replacement glassware. There's a restaurant and bar warehouse in Eugene that supplies my tables and I've already given them a call. If you can go and pick them up, that would be great."

For the next hour, Wyatt, Matt, and Luke cleared out the dozen tables and chairs that were unsavable, cleaned the room, and mopped up the liquor that had fallen in sheets on the walls and stuck.

Wyatt took note of a couple of holes in the walls. A little drywall and paint would show up the rest of the bar. It was really hard for him to do anything halfway, but since Josie was already paying for the broken glassware and helping with the tables and chairs, it was the right thing to do. He already knew Luke would be on board with helping with the manual labor.

Outside, the gravel kicked up from the parking lot, which prompted Josie to step out while they finished the cleanup.

"Lunch is here," Josie said when she walked back in.

Melanie had her hair pulled into a tight ponytail, and her short shorts hid enough of her ass to keep him guessing, but not enough to think she was trying to hide something.

He licked his lips and leaned the broom in his hands against the wall.

Hope ran in behind her mom and wrapped an arm around Wyatt's waist before he could say hello. Her tiny arms felt strange and strangely comforting. "Mommy said you were hurt."

He knelt down and leveled his face with hers. "I'm okay."

Hope's tiny smile fell and her hand reached to touch the tender spot above his eye. Wyatt held his breath, hoping she wouldn't push too hard and make him wince.

He didn't need to worry.

"That looks bad."

He glanced at Melanie, who was watching the exchange. "Your mom took good care of me."

Hope leaned in, lowered her voice. "Did she put that stingy stuff on you?"

Wyatt made a silly face and nodded.

"We should probably take that away from her, huh?"

Holding back his laugh at the seriousness of Hope's face was the most difficult thing he'd ever done.

After swallowing hard, he bit his lip and said, "I think the stingy stuff helps clean cuts and stuff."

Hope pushed out her lower lip. "But it hurts."

"Yeah. It sure does."

There was an argument stuck between Hope's brain and her mouth, but she held it in and pressed her lips to Wyatt's forehead.

"Kissing it better."

The tiny punch in his heart was unexpected.

He patted her head as he stood, left an arm on her shoulder as they both faced Melanie.

"I thought you might need food."

"Food never sucks, Mel." Luke was the first one across the room. "My stomach finally feels like it can eat."

"Considering last night's indulgence, I'm surprised."

Luke wiped his hands on his jeans and pulled up an operable chair to a sturdy table.

Melanie had brought several sandwiches, potato salad, and a full container of cut up summer fruits. Considering the slim delights in his refrigerator, Wyatt was happy to fill his stomach with someone else's idea of lunch. He made a mental note to buy some groceries on his way home from Eugene.

"How are you feeling this morning?" Melanie asked him as the others gathered around the table to dish out a portion of food.

"Like I've been in a bar fight."

"So you've been in them before?" she asked.

He shrugged, knew there was a fine line for a woman when it came to fighting. "I've blocked a punch or two before. A couple in high school, usually over a girl."

"Humph." She regarded him from the corner of her eye before walking behind the bar.

"Not bad, Mel," Luke told her from across the room.

"You better offer a deeper compliment than that if you ever wanna free meal off me again," she told him.

"You women are never satisfied." Luke waved his sandwich as he spoke.

"Says the man who is going to be very hungry if he doesn't start shoveling out the sugar!" Melanie teased.

Luke started to hum and licked his lips. "Oh, Mel-Bel, this is the best damn sandwich I have had all summer. My mom needs to take notes."

Melanie rolled her eyes as she walked around the bar with several cups filled with ice on a tray. "Your compliments suck."

Luke winked and bit off half his sandwich with one bite.

"I like your sandwiches, Mommy." Hope was in the process of removing the crust from hers and nibbling on the inside.

"Thanks, sweetie."

Wyatt was about to add his thanks when Hope added, "But Aunt Zoe's cookies are waaaay better than yours."

The mention of Zoe's name had a couple of heads turning toward Luke. The man was brushing crumbs off his shirt while speaking with a full mouth. "She has a point, Mel-Bel."

"Yes, yes I know. Good thing sugar is bad for you or I might have to bake more and make you eat my mess."

"No need to eat bad sugar when there is good sugar out there," Josie said, and Matt agreed.

Wyatt enjoyed the friendly banter from the sidelines until the conversation found a break. He walked up beside Melanie and placed a hand on the side of her neck and kissed her surprised lips. "It was delicious."

Her cheeks turned pink when he stepped away. "It was just a sandwich."

Then, to tease, he added quietly, "I wasn't talking about the food." Her jaw dropped.

Wyatt waved his soda in the air and walked away. "I have my list. If you think of anything else we need, call or text. I'll be back in a couple of hours."

He felt Melanie's eyes follow him out the door.

"Mommy, Uncle Wyatt just kissed you!"

"He's not your uncle, honey."

"Ewehhhh."

The smile he'd managed since he'd met the woman accompanied him all the way into Eugene.

Chapter Fourteen

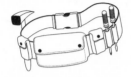

The drive from R&B's to Miss Gina's inn only took about ten minutes. The constant questions and comments coming from her daughter kept the drive lively.

"Why did Wyatt kiss you?" The first question played inside Melanie's head for a good minute before answering.

"I think he likes me."

"Likes you like, like you like you? Like a boyfriend?"

Boyfriend felt a little deep considering their early stages of getting to know each other, but for her daughter's sake, it was probably best to keep it simple.

"Yeah, kinda like a boyfriend."

"So you have a boyfriend." It wasn't a question.

"I'm . . . yeah . . . I guess you can say that." She might need to explain that to Wyatt before the seven-year-old inquisition happened to him.

"My friend Kimmie told me that sometimes boyfriends turn into daddies. Is Wyatt going to be my daddy?"

"Oh, honey, let's not go there. Wyatt and I hardly know each other. Being a dad takes a long time to figure out."

"Hmmm." Hope stared out the window, her fingers tapped on the edge of the door in thought. "I think Uncle Wyatt could be a good dad."

Melanie wondered if Wyatt had any clue as to what his simple kiss had started.

She pulled into the driveway of the inn, noticed a rental car that hadn't been there when she'd left. *Nathan?*

She felt her pulse jump, hoped he wasn't the one behind the car. Her head scrambled for an excuse to keep Hope from following her inside. "Sweetie, take the leftovers to the kitchen for me."

Hope shrugged and pushed out of the car.

When Hope stepped in place beside her, Melanie clarified what she wanted. "Around back, honey."

"But I can go through the front."

"The fruit container is dripping. I don't want to mess up the floor." It was a complete lie, but Hope took it and walked around the back.

Melanie squeezed her hands into fists and released them before stepping inside.

Her breath released in a happy rush. "Mr. Lewis."

The man who had stayed one night on the evening of Zane's craziness stood at the front desk with Miss Gina.

"Hello again." Mr. Lewis was ten years her senior and had recently started some kind of business that brought him through River Bend.

Melanie's relief that Nathan wasn't behind the rental car kept a smile on her face as she approached the desk.

"That was a quick trip," she said to him.

"I have another one next week."

Miss Gina handed him his room key. "Might need to get a punch card or something."

"My boss takes care of it," Mr. Lewis told them. "He doesn't complain about the price."

"Then maybe we should charge you double," Miss Gina suggested.

Mr. Lewis laughed and tapped the counter before reaching for his bag.

"Should I show you your room?" Melanie asked.

"No, I remember where it is."

The sound of feet running through the hall accompanied Hope's happy voice. "Oh, hi, Mr. Lewis."

"Hello, beautiful." Mr. Lewis placed a hand on Hope's shoulder and left it there. "You're not running through the house, are you?"

Hope snapped her lips shut and looked between the three of them. "Uhm . . ."

"I didn't think so," he said.

Hope had the three of them laughing when she offered an animated smile full of teeth and mischief before walking slowly out the front door.

"Guest reception is at five, Mr. Lewis."

"I'll be there."

"Nice man," Melanie said after he made it halfway up the stairs.

Miss Gina offered a shrug without words.

"You don't think so?"

"Nice enough, I guess. Wyatt is more your speed."

Melanie rolled her eyes. "I didn't mean it that way."

"Good. Now, how is Josie's place?"

"A mess. According to Luke, he and Wyatt are going to be up all night painting the place."

"How does a bar fight involve new paint?"

Melanie shook her head. "It doesn't. But patching a wall isn't Wyatt's style without a complete upgrade . . . at least according to Luke."

Miss Gina looked around the reception area. "Maybe we need to start a fight here."

Mel nudged Miss Gina aside and stepped around her. "You're bad."

"Sounds like a big job for just two men."

"It is. I was wondering if you'd mind keeping an ear out for Hope tonight so I can lend a hand."

"Of course, love. Hope is easy. And if painting results in an overnight stay, that's fine, too."

Melanie's jaw dropped for the second time that day. "Miss Gina!"

"I'm just sayin'."

"You're suggesting."

They kept the conversation going as they entered the kitchen. "You're young, honey. You should be knockin' boots with someone while you can find them."

She laughed. "Do you have any idea how long it's been since I've knocked anything with anyone?"

Miss Gina pulled her special lemonade from the refrigerator before turning over two glasses that were drying on a towel by the sink. "That's a damn shame. When I was your age I didn't go a week without sex."

"Those were the sixties."

Miss Gina stopped pouring and stared longingly out the back window. "Indeed they were. Best time ever."

Melanie accepted the lemonade and leaned against the counter. "Why is it there isn't a Mr. Gina around?"

A visible shiver actually ran down Miss Gina's body. "Good God no. Commitment? I never could go that route."

"I'm sure there had to be someone, somewhere who made you consider it . . ."

A play of emotions danced over her face as if she were rewinding the tape of her life and watching it a second time. "Nope. Not really. When I was your age, the men were everywhere. The last thing I wanted was to pick just one."

"What about later?"

"Later happened in my thirties. I had a few men pass through town once I started the inn, but they weren't the sticking type, and I wasn't one to ask to change their minds. I understand a free spirit."

"Yet you've had the inn for decades and almost never leave town."

"Doesn't mean I haven't wanted to."

That's where Melanie found herself stuck. "Then why didn't you? Why not find someone to help with the inn and tap into that free spirit of yours?"

Miss Gina sent her a devil of a smile. "That's a really good idea. Maybe I should pack my bags and go to Europe for the rest of the summer."

Melanie choked on her drink, started coughing until tears welled behind her eyes. "W-wait . . ." She looked around the kitchen as if it were an unfamiliar space. "I didn't mean . . . I don't know."

Miss Gina replaced the devil with innocence and chuckled. "Relax, sweetie. You're not ready to take over quite yet. But by the fall, things should settle into place."

Trepidation and pride in Miss Gina's words left warmth in Melanie's heart. The fact that the woman she'd felt closer to than her own mother was confident enough to leave her baby for Melanie to run did something more than a paycheck could.

"Maybe by fall," Melanie found herself saying.

"It's paint!" If Melanie had a romantic thought in her brain about how the night was going to go . . . it was all but gone after an hour under Wyatt's direction. *Direction* being the completely wrong word for how he ordered everyone around.

Everyone consisted of Jo, Luke, Mel, and Josie.

"It's really hard to screw up paint," Luke added to Melanie's previous words.

"You tell that to Josie in the morning after it's dry and half of it looks like five-year-olds tossed this on the wall." Wyatt stood with a roller in one hand, his other pointing at the wall that looked less than perfect.

"I think five-year-olds might have done it the last time." Josie tipped back a beer that was free for everyone to drink during the all-night paint party.

"Well it's not being done by five-year-olds this time." Wyatt placed his roller on the wall with conviction. "Make sure you cover every inch. And Jo," he said with a shake of his free hand. "If you're not going to use the tape around the molding, don't slop it on. Be more careful."

Jo saluted him with a wet paintbrush, which brought laughter from the others in the room.

Josie placed the digital jukebox on free play and had a few tunes pumping into the room while they worked.

"I swear this bar wasn't this big when we walked in," Luke said less than ten minutes later.

"Just keep moving," Wyatt said from the corner of his mouth.

Jo leaned close to Melanie. "He's a paint Nazi."

"I heard that!" Wyatt said over the music.

Melanie laughed. "You know what this reminds me of?"

Paint dripped from the end of Jo's brush and ended up on her shirt. "No, what?"

Melanie reached out to try and remove some of the mess Jo was making. "Why I don't do home improvement projects."

"Amen," Luke said.

"It's just paint." Wyatt moved faster than all of them combined. He was clearly on a mission and focused on his work.

Luke reloaded his roller and stepped back up to reach the top third of the wall. "Says the man whose own home is in a constant state of unfinished projects."

Melanie stopped smearing the paint over Jo's clothing and focused on Wyatt. "What's this?"

"Nothing."

Luke laughed.

"No, wait . . . what is Luke talking about?"

"It's nothing." Only Wyatt glared at Luke.

"Wyatt has a hard time completing his own projects within any reasonable time frame," Jo told her.

"But this is what you do."

"I'm busy. And since it doesn't affect anyone but me, I can take my time."

"Nothing like living on milk crates and walking on plastic to make you feel at home."

"Screw you, Luke." Apparently Wyatt didn't like his imperfection vocalized for everyone to hear.

"Grrr," Luke teased.

"Living the cliché, eh, Wyatt?" Josie asked.

"Every cliché holds truth or it wouldn't have made it to cliché status."

"Paint Nazi and philosopher. You're a man of many talents." Jo paused and tilted back her beer.

"Are we going to talk or get this shit finished?"

"Someone is sensitive," Luke said.

"Just keep painting."

The hour rounded on two before they lowered the last brush and surveyed their work.

"Wow."

"It's awesome." Josie wore a huge grin.

"I can't believe how big this place feels now," Luke said.

"The last time it was painted was before we banned smoking in here. I guess I should have painted sooner." The fresh paint, even in a soft beige color, lightened up the room.

"It's a bar, Josie. No one really cared."

"We'll see about that when people come in tomorrow night." Josie did a full turn and took in the room. "The floors could use an upgrade."

Wyatt groaned.

"If you don't want the job, I can find someone else."

"Bite your tongue." Wyatt drew in a full breath and met Melanie's eyes. "See why my house never gets done?"

"Well I'm shot. C'mon, Jo . . . you can give me a ride home," Luke offered.

"The brushes need to be cleaned," Wyatt said.

"And you can clean them. My head is killing me."

"And I have to work in the morning," Jo said.

Melanie stayed back while the others prepared to leave. "I'll help."

"There is a faucet out back," Josie told them. "I'll turn a light on."

After Jo and Luke drove off, Josie stayed inside and cleaned up.

A few bugs buzzed around them as they started pulling paint from the brushes. "Don't they make these in a disposable variety?"

"The cheap ones. I don't like them."

"A perfectionist."

"I'm nowhere close to perfect," he said.

Water-coated paint ran from her hand to the ground, where it splattered on her bare legs. Wearing an old pair of shorts to paint in had been a great idea considering how much of the stuff she managed to accumulate on her skin.

"Imperfect house . . . I heard."

He grumbled.

"Why did Luke talking about your house bother you so much?"

He ran his hands through the brush with more vigor. "I don't know."

She knelt closer to the ground to keep the splatter to a minimum. "Yes you do. Out with it."

"You're bossy."

"Says the paint Nazi."

"Humph!"

"So why?"

Wyatt was quiet for a minute. "Letting a woman discover my faults isn't the best way to impress her."

The comfortable warmth that Wyatt always managed to put in her belly snuck inside again.

"A woman?"

He glanced at her. "You."

She knew that, but enjoyed the unease vocalizing it gave him. He'd been so confident since they met; it was nice to know he was knocked back a little with her presence.

"You think I'd be less interested if I learned your house isn't a castle?"

He shrugged.

"Oh, my God, you do."

He stayed quiet.

"Wyatt?"

"Yeah, I . . ." He ran the back of his hand along the side of his face before leveling his gaze on her.

Melanie stood slowly and brushed her thumb along the smudge of paint he'd left on his forehead. "I'm already impressed. Your house isn't going to change that."

He captured her hand and pressed it into his cheek before kissing her palm.

She melted. His soft smile and tiny insecurity empowered something inside her and made her want him all the more. Melanie dropped her paintbrush and pressed her lips to his.

She heard his brush hit the ground and felt his hand reach around her waist to pull her close.

He warmed the chill the outside brought to her skin and deepened their kiss. The familiar swipe of his tongue against her lips had her opening. He tasted like hops and barley and felt like home.

As her eyes closed and he tilted her head back, she knew this night was going to end in satisfaction instead of frustration.

Melanie ran a hand down his hips and pressed as close as she could.

Wyatt moaned and pulled away. "You're killing me."

She giggled and lifted her knee to run against his leg. "You dropped your paintbrush."

"Fuck the paintbrush."

His lips found hers again with hot, impatient kisses. Wyatt lifted her offered leg and wrapped it around his waist as he backed her up against the back of Josie's bar. His hips pushed against her, the heat and friction of him made her stomach spasm. Made her want.

Wyatt pulled away, then changed his mind and returned with a force that made her breath catch in the back of her throat.

He held her against the wall, his hands rounded on her ass, kept her pinned, and seemed content to kiss her until she wept for air. Only her body wanted more than air, she wanted more.

It was her turn to pull away. "Take me to your castle, Wyatt."

He hesitated, his lips hovering over hers, his breath short and hot. "What about the inn?"

She shook her head. "One guest. Miss Gina said . . ." Melanie didn't elaborate. "It's fine."

He kissed her again, sucked her lip between his teeth and gave a tiny bite. "You're sure?"

"Are you going to make me beg?"

His eyes grew wide, his grin even wider before he released her and wrapped his fingers around hers. Wyatt started toward his truck, then detoured to the back door of the bar. He poked his head inside and yelled. "We'll be back in the morning, Josie."

Laughter followed them as they drove away.

Chapter Fifteen

Wyatt's home sat on the opposite side of town from R&B's. The single-story ranch sat on a little bit of land, as did most of the homes in the area. As a kid she'd passed this place continually en route to her family home, which sat on a hill behind his.

The house was dark with the exception of a single porch light.

They'd driven to his house with only a few words.

Are you sure about this?

More than sure.

It was the holding of her hand the entire trip to his home that turned her to mush. The cab of Wyatt's truck wasn't exactly small, and his reach had to be uncomfortable . . . but he held it anyway.

He pulled into the driveway, then lifted a finger in the air when she reached for the door. "Hold up."

She let go of the handle and waited for him to run around the truck to open the door for her.

"You're crazy."

"A little," he agreed as he grasped her hand and tucked her into his side. "The house isn't as bad as Luke led you to believe."

The second her foot stepped through the front door, she thought Luke had it completely right. The bare living room held a couch, a hillbilly coffee table, and a TV.

"Do you want something to drink?" he asked as he led her to his kitchen. Obviously this was one of the finished rooms. Granite countertops and modern appliances were the cornerstone of the warm and inviting space. Brushed nickel pulls on the aged maple cabinets matched the longneck faucet over the sink. Melanie was innately happy Wyatt wasn't into a cold, modern style of living with hard edges and uninviting surfaces.

"I'm good," she told him. After turning a full circle, she asked for a bathroom.

"I have two, but the one in my bedroom is the only one working."

She pointed down the hall. "That way?"

"End of the hall, double doors."

She passed a couple of closed doors before making her way into Wyatt's bedroom. Rustic wood furniture filled in the generous space. Dark colors adorned his unmade bed and a copy of Lee Child's latest novel sat on the side table. One rustic red wall accented the room and drew her eye to a single piece of art. The Oregon coast with sea cliffs and crashing waves was captured in the same muted tones of the room, blending perfectly with the decor. To say she was impressed would have been an understatement.

When she stepped into the bathroom and switched on the light, she let out a tiny gasp.

The space was huge compared to most of the homes in River Bend. A deep vessel bathtub sat in front of a large window, the double vanity had glass sinks and a furniture base that she would never have thought would work together, but they did. It was the shower that was the most impressive, however. She couldn't help but duck inside the space and gawk. A rain showerhead hovered on the ceiling with a fixed head on one side and a removable one on the other. The glass enclosure kept the space bright and cheery despite the dark tiles that covered the wall. It was stunning . . . all of it.

She caught her reflection in the mirror while she was washing her hands a couple of minutes later.

What a mess. Paint was everywhere, her eyes held tiny circles from many late nights and not enough sleep. How could Wyatt look at her and do anything but cringe?

She removed the band from her hair and attempted to run her fingers through it and untangle some of the mess a labor-filled day caused.

It only looked worse.

She undid one of the buttons on her blouse and pushed her breasts a little higher in her bra before letting her hands drop to her sides. There wasn't anything remotely sexy about her at two in the morning, she decided.

Second and third thoughts about being with Wyatt started to seep in. Not that she didn't want the next step, but that he might realize that a woman like her might not measure up. Then the most disturbing thought of all came from nowhere . . . had Wyatt ever slept with a woman who had a child before? Melanie lifted her shirt and patted her mostly flat stomach.

A soft knock on the door had her tugging her shirt back down.

"You get lost in there?"

"Ah, no." She scrambled with nerves leading her actions. She turned on the water and let it run for a second before turning it off. The reflection in the mirror laughed at her before she stopped watching it and walked away.

Wyatt stood outside the door, a cocky grin lingering on his face. "I was starting to worry."

Melanie ran a hand over her hair, knew it was useless. "It's a nice bathroom." She wasn't usually a nervous laughter kinda girl, but that was starting to change. "I'm a mess."

"You're beautiful."

She leaned against the door frame and tried to feel the smile. "I look about as sexy as a wet cat."

Wyatt's eyes did a slow dance down her frame and took their time moving back up. A warm shiver had her catching her breath.

He took a step toward her and pulled her back into the bathroom. He sat her on the edge of the tub and turned toward the shower. He had the water flowing and the bright lights in the room dimmed to a romantic glow that made Melanie smile.

He leaned down and pulled her shoes off one at a time. All the while she watched him. Wyatt ran the edge of his thumb on her instep once her sock left her foot, and moved to the next. With her shoes to the side, he placed both hands on her bare knees and smiled up at her. Then, without notice, he grasped her hips and lifted her off the tub and carried her to the shower.

"I'm still dressed," she offered a protest.

"So am I." But he took them both into the warm spray of water anyway.

She giggled when he set her back on her feet.

He pushed her hair out of her face and tilted it so the spray could saturate each strand. And when she opened her eyes, Wyatt was staring with a hooded gaze that made her feel beautiful.

Melanie ran her hands up his chest and grasped the edges of his T-shirt. He ducked and helped her remove it. She allowed her hands to run over the smooth muscles of his chest. "Nice," she mumbled.

"Your turn," he said before reaching for the buttons of her shirt. The water made slipping the buttons through the holes difficult, but he managed and brushed the shirt away as if it were an annoyance. Strong hands cupped the sides of her breasts through her bra, and Wyatt's lips replaced his gaze. The graze of his teeth made a path from the top of one breast to the other before he slipped one strap down her shoulder and kissed her there. She felt her knees give out just a little and Wyatt steadied her. "None of that," he whispered.

"Can't help it," she said.

He lifted his kiss and turned her away from him.

He filled his palm with shampoo and ran his hands through her hair and followed the suds down her shoulders and back. He ran a finger between her bra and skin before snapping apart the clasp and tossing the garment over the top of the glass door.

She glanced at him over her shoulder with a smile. He found soap and lathered his hands before running them over her back and slipping around to follow the curve of her chest. Even in the heated water, her nipples tightened with his touch as she pushed into his palms. He didn't linger there; instead he kept moving his soap filled palms over every inch of her exposed skin.

Her shorts proved a little difficult with wet denim, so she helped with the snap and the zipper and let him draw them down along with her panties, her back still to him.

Wyatt kept her from slipping as he brought one leg out of her shorts at a time. The two met her bra outside the shower. When he returned, his hands started at her thighs and explored. Slow movements cleaned the less private areas, leaving her breathless with only a touch.

He leaned into her, the feel of his jeans rough on her skin, and kissed the side of her neck. "I've thought about you in here, like this," he told her.

Melanie rested the back of her head on his shoulder and let the water cascade over her. "I like your shower."

He turned her around, captured her lips, and pressed her into the cool tiles. The heat, his kiss . . . the chill of the wall, all of it made her shiver and reach for him. When her hands slid past his waist, she fumbled with the button of his jeans and pulled.

They didn't give. She tugged harder and failed.

Wyatt smiled through his kiss and helped her. Once the snap was off, the zipper was down; she pushed his hands away and broke their kiss for air. Instead of turning him around, she offered a sly smile and forced her palms between his ass and his jeans and slid them down his hips. Like him, she removed his underwear with his pants and tried not to stare at his erection when she knelt to help him safely remove one foot at a time. Taking his lead, she tossed the soggy clothes outside the shower and continued her exploration. She found soap, lathered her palms, and took her time scrubbing his tight muscles. From knee to hip, up his chest and over his shoulders she lathered and scrubbed. When her fingers slid over the globes of his ass, he hissed and she smiled.

His hands rested on both sides of her against the wall, his attempt, she knew, to keep this slow. When her hand rounded to the front of him and brushed against his erection, he broke.

Hands were everywhere, his lips took hers and weren't letting go. Between the water and the pleasurable assault of his tongue, she was captured. He lifted her knee, pushed dangerously close.

Melanie felt herself slide and caught his shoulders to keep from falling.

"We've got to get out of here before someone gets hurt," she told him.

He nodded. "And we need a condom."

Her thoughts exactly.

He shut the water off, stepped out of the shower, and returned with a huge towel to wrap her in. When she attempted to take over the chore of removing the water from her skin, he moved faster, then lifted her in his arms and carried her into his bedroom. "I can walk," she giggled.

"I've got you."

He placed her on the bed and removed the towel. With a quick brush against his skin, he tossed it to the floor and crawled up beside her.

"Hi," he said with a smile.

She ran her foot over his thigh. "Hi."

The chill of the room didn't last long. His kiss returned where it had left off, only without a threat of slipping and falling, and Melanie closed her eyes to enjoy it. All of it.

He moved down her body, gave her nipple a quick pinch before comforting the tiny sting with his lips and teeth. Had there been a time in her life when she'd been so sexually charged? She couldn't remember.

She opened for him, felt his fingers spread between her thighs, and when he finally touched her, she moaned. Tiny stars floated in her head as she pushed against his hand. There was no shyness now, no insecurity of how she looked, of her being a mother . . . nothing. It was just her and Wyatt and this incredible moment.

"So wet," he said before replacing his finger with his tongue.

"Oh, God." She sighed, caught her breath, and ran a hand through his wet hair as he tasted his fill. And when she was close, so close she felt the rush of the wind on her thighs, he pulled away.

She whimpered.

When he returned, he was covering his erection and teasing her again.

A look in her eyes and a smile was apparently all the encouragement he needed. When he filled her, she wrapped her legs around his waist and met him with every push and pull. When he kissed her, she tasted herself and his smile. When she came for him, he eased his pace, rolled over, and kept going. She clenched every muscle she had and watched his face until she felt a second orgasm forcing her eyes closed.

Then there were stars and Wyatt was calling her name in his release.

~

They cooked eggs after only a handful of hours of sleep, and sipped coffee. All the while Wyatt kept a hand on her in some way. When they were eating, she rested her feet in his lap and he ate with one hand and rubbed her with the other.

It was incredibly sweet and comforting in a way that the actual act of making love wasn't. He talked about his vision for his living room and what he wanted it to look like when he was finished.

He asked her about what she liked when it came to design. Melanie didn't have too many strong opinions, based on the fact that she had never owned a place of her own to give it much thought. "I don't even have my own bed, Wyatt."

"It's okay," he told her. "You can share mine," he said with a grin.

Sometime in the night Wyatt had put their clothes in the dryer, making the morning walk of shame a little less damp.

They piled into his truck, and once again he held her hand all the way back to the inn. It was after nine, but Melanie had already sent a text to Miss Gina making sure everything was okay with her absence that morning.

Miss Gina sent her a cartoonish picture of a pair of boots lying beside a bed with a caption saying everything was fine.

Wyatt walked her inside, pinched her butt as she walked up the stairs.

She batted his hand away. "You're awful."

He wrapped an arm around her waist and snuggled as they walked inside. It was quiet with only a faint hint of music coming from the back of the house.

"We have muffins," Melanie said.

"I'd kill for a muffin."

That had her rolling her eyes and smiling when she greeted Miss Gina in the kitchen.

"Well, well, well . . ."

Melanie kissed Miss Gina's cheek. "Good morning."

The older woman simply smiled.

Then Wyatt kissed her cheek. "Good morning, Miss Gina."

She started to laugh. "Well, you two should get laid more often."

Melanie's jaw dropped. "Miss Gina!"

"What?" There wasn't an ounce of remorse on the woman's face.

The warmth Wyatt had placed inside her the night before refused to go away, and Melanie wasn't going to let it go anytime soon.

Melanie found the muffins and put one on a plate before setting it in front of him. She moved to the coffee pot and lifted it in offering. When he nodded, she found two cups and poured them both a portion. "I see Mr. Lewis's car is still here."

"Yeah, he said he'd be leaving by noon."

Melanie found the creamer, poured a generous portion inside her cup before letting the hot caffeine do its job. "Where's Hope?"

Miss Gina glanced out the kitchen window. "Outside."

When Melanie looked, she didn't see any sign of her. With coffee cup in hand, Melanie slid beside Wyatt, took a bite of his muffin, and went in search of her daughter.

The screen door slapped against the back door with a familiar twang. The slightly cool morning felt good on her skin . . . or maybe it was the sex from the night before.

Melanie smiled as she walked off the back porch and around the house. The tire swing Wyatt had managed to place in the maple tree sat abandoned. It swayed slightly, as if her daughter had recently sat on it playing. The dirt pile, otherwise known as a garden, sat empty . . . no sign of Hope. Melanie called out her name with no reply. When she entered the house again, she set her coffee cup aside and climbed the stairs to their room. Hope's nightgown was tossed to the side, a clothing drawer opened halfway in what looked like a typical haste to get on with her summer day.

Still no Hope.

A tiny bit of concern started to weaken the euphoria Wyatt had given her.

Melanie found Wyatt and Miss Gina in deep conversation when she walked back into the kitchen. "She's not out there."

Miss Gina tilted her head. "Hope?"

"Yeah, she's not in her room either."

"That's strange, she was just in here not twenty, thirty minutes before you walked in."

The three of them stopped what they were doing and all headed out back. "You check the garage," Melanie instructed Wyatt. "I'll see if she's by the climbing tree."

Even though she'd been given strict instructions to never climb a tree without another person with her, anything could have happened.

Melanie called Hope's name several times en route to the tree the three of them had climbed only a few days before.

When there wasn't any evidence of her there, that little tickle of worry started to blossom, and the hair on her neck stood on end.

Melanie ran the path back to the inn, fully expecting to find Hope standing beside Miss Gina and Wyatt.

Melanie's feet faltered when she caught sight of Wyatt and Miss Gina walking in separate directions calling Hope's name.

She started to tremble. "Hope!" Her voice lifted above the treetops, her cry anything but sane. "Hope!"

Chapter Sixteen

By the time Jo arrived, Melanie was a babbling mess.

Wyatt stood aside and watched as Jo jumped from her squad car and engulfed her friend.

"I can't find her, Jo."

Jo took Melanie's head in her hands and stared her friend down. "We *will* find her."

"But she was . . . damn it . . . where is she?" Melanie's tears kept coming.

"Mel! Stop. Stop! Dry up those damn tears and focus. You're no good to Hope like this."

Jo's words must have sunk in. Melanie visibly shook as she sucked in a quick breath and let it out slowly.

"Okay."

A second squad car drove up, lights blazing.

Jo moved past Melanie and walked to Miss Gina's side. "Tell me again, from the beginning. Where did you last see her?"

Wyatt heard the recall of Hope's last known moments for the third time. The need to move, the need to stop talking and search the woods crawled under his skin. He held Melanie's hand in a tight squeeze.

"And who are you?" Jo turned her attention to the one guest at the inn.

"Patrick Lewis."

Jo stared at the man. "When was the last time you saw Hope?"

"She ran through when I was eating breakfast."

Miss Gina placed a hand on Jo's arm. "Mr. Lewis heard us yelling for Hope and came down from upstairs."

Deputy Emery joined Jo on the porch.

"Why aren't we looking for her?" Melanie asked Wyatt.

"We will, baby." He kissed the top of her head.

Gravel kicked up again, this time with a cloud of smoke that indicated cavalry arriving.

Jo turned around. "What the . . ."

"I called in some help," Wyatt told her.

Luke jumped off his bike; behind him his parents arrived in their truck. Josie arrived with her bartender and a couple of other employees. Sam and Brenda, Principal Mason, and half a dozen teachers.

Beside him, Melanie started to suck in tight breaths. "Keep it together, honey. We'll find her."

Mel could only nod and blink her eyes repeatedly to keep the tears from falling.

Wyatt left Melanie's side when Josie came to take her in her arms. "She's probably just turned around in the woods."

"What's going on?" Luke asked.

"We came home half an hour ago. Miss Gina said she saw Hope

out in the backyard less than a half hour before. When we looked, Hope was gone."

"No chance she's just playing?"

Wyatt shook his head. "She doesn't leave sight of the house unless someone is with her."

Luke looked at the time on his phone. "So it's been an hour?"

It sounded worse when Luke said it out loud. "Yeah."

Deputy Emery walked into the inn with Mr. Lewis and Miss Gina as Jo joined them.

Jo tossed her hat on the bed of the truck. "Thank you all for coming."

"What can we do, Jo?" Sam wasn't a young man, but he seemed more than eager to move.

Wyatt and Luke flanked Melanie before Jo started giving instructions.

"We need to spread out until we have more people to help. Hope was wearing a pair of jeans, a purple shirt, and a white sweater. She likes to climb trees. She may have simply climbed too high and can't get down." Jo passed a glance to Melanie and added, "Or she might have fallen and can't walk home."

Melanie grasped Wyatt's hand but didn't cry. "I told her that if she was lost in the woods to find a tree and wait for help."

Jo offered a smile. "That's good, Mel . . . real good. She's a smart girl."

"She's adventurous," Jo told the others.

"And fearless," Wyatt added.

Jo broke down their search party into groups of three and moved to the back of her squad car and popped the trunk. She removed two-way handheld radios and tuned them all in to the same channel before passing them out.

Wyatt took notice of Mr. Lewis shaking the hand of Deputy Emery as he closed the trunk of his car.

"I don't have to tell you all that finding Hope before sunset is our priority."

"We'll find her, Jo," Luke said.

As the search party broke apart, Wyatt caught Jo's attention. "She's never gone this long," he said close to her ear.

"I know."

He glanced at the retreating car of Mr. Lewis. "Where's he going?"

"Has a flight to catch. I have his information, Wyatt."

"This sucks."

"Yeah. Keep Mel sane. I'm going to hold back and search the house."

Wyatt glanced up at the three-story inn. "You think she might be in there?"

Jo's words were hardly heard. "I hope not."

"Jesus." The memory of a high-profile case swam in his head . . . the outcome less than favorable for the missing child.

Melanie jogged up beside them. "Let's go."

Wyatt let himself be led away.

"I'm right behind you," Jo told her.

~

Every five minutes felt like thirty.

Every ten felt like an hour.

And every hour felt like a lifetime.

While she choked back the tears, her fear was a tsunami inside her head. They were past the three-hour mark. Every ten minutes Melanie called back to the inn and asked the same question. "Anything?"

Deputy Emery stayed at the house with Miss Gina and instructed the new sets of volunteers on where to search. By now, River Bend was all but closed down and the townspeople combed the woods outside the inn in groups of five and ten.

"Hope!"

Her daughter's name was called out continually.

Still nothing.

"Melanie, you there?"

Jo's voice had her fumbling for the radio, her heart racing. She pressed the button and stopped walking as she talked. "Did you find her?"

"No. I need you back at the house."

She tried not to feel the crushing disappointment of the call. "No. I'm staying out here until we find her."

"Mel, I've called in reinforcements. K-9 units are here. I just need you to do a few things here and you can go back out."

Wyatt saw her standing still and ran to her side. "Did they find her?"

Melanie shook her head, returned to the radio. "I'm on my way."

She turned toward the inn and started to jog.

Wyatt kept pace beside her. "What's going on?"

"Jo brought in the dogs."

Sweat rolled down her back as she hit the inn's deck completely out of breath.

The barking of dogs kept her jogging until she rounded the front of the inn.

Cars were everywhere. Two more squad cars, both from neighboring towns, were tossed into the mix. The sheer mass of them brought home the magnitude of her missing daughter.

Miss Gina saw them first and called into the house for Jo.

"How you holding up?" Miss Gina asked.

Melanie didn't trust herself to speak.

Miss Gina lowered her head. "I should have kept a better eye on her."

Melanie shot a hand in the air. "No. This is not your fault."

"If I had—"

She jumped right up into her friend's face. "This is *not* your fault!"

Melanie pushed past Miss Gina, saw Wyatt from the corner of her eye.

It's my fault.

"Mel?"

Jo stood with two other uniformed officers, people Mel didn't recognize.

"That was quick." Jo wasted little time introducing the dog handlers.

"What we need is something of Hope's that has her scent on it."

"Like a sweater?"

"Only if it's seldom washed. Stuffed animals, favorite blanket . . . that kind of thing is better."

She ran upstairs and dived for the bed, found a favored stuffed toy, then searched a drawer for a ratty baby blanket that Hope often slept with, but always put away in the morning. Someone had teased her about it the year before when they lived in Bakersfield, and now Hope hid the thing and didn't talk about it.

Melanie buried her face in it and sucked in a deep breath. It smelled like her daughter.

She shook her head and jogged to Jo's side before shoving the items into her friend's hands.

Jo turned and gave them to the men at her side.

"Perfect."

Both officers had to be in their forties, one a little thicker than the other. They both had kind smiles and faces that didn't tell her a thing. "We'll find her, Mrs. Bartlett."

"It's Miss."

The officer on her right—she'd already forgotten his name—nodded and walked from the room.

Wyatt walked in, a bottle of water in his hand. "Here."

She started to shake her head.

"Melanie." He thrust it into her hand.

"Fine." She took it from him and swallowed half the bottle in one gulp before putting the lid back on.

"I should go with them," Melanie told Jo.

"You should rest for a minute, catch your breath."

Melanie ignored her friend and turned to leave. She wasn't going to rest until Hope was back in her arms.

"Mel!" Jo attempted to stop her.

Melanie lifted her hand, middle finger in the air, and continued out the door.

Wyatt fell into step beside her.

"Are you going to tell me to rest?" she asked.

"Nope."

She offered him a passing glance. "Good."

"Officer Maaco?" Wyatt called out to the man pushing Hope's blanket into the nose of a German shepherd.

Maaco passed a look between the two of them with understanding.

"Bella is one of the best, Miss Bartlett. Since your daughter lives here, she might explore the grounds for a little bit, but she'll catch Hope's recent scent."

"Okay." *Not okay . . . none of this is okay.* The desperation of the day started to weigh in as Bella sniffed around the places Hope usually played. It seemed the dog chased her tail and spun in circles.

Melanie clenched her hands into tight fists and tried to wait.

Bella, and her counterpart, Fisher, both headed off in the same direction at nearly the same time.

The direction they headed was entirely opposite of what Melanie expected.

The dogs went north, leaving behind the south woods they had been searching.

"Where are they going?"

"Following a scent, ma'am."

It was time for Melanie to turn a full circle. "We never walk this way."

Bella ran and Maaco followed. "She did today, Miss Bartlett."

Melanie and Wyatt jogged to keep up.

Maaco called into his radio, "The dogs found a scent, northwest."

Jo's voice screeched over the line. "Damn, all right . . . moving reinforcements your direction."

"Copy."

Wyatt kept pace beside her. His eyes scanned the landscape in silence, his jaw tight.

They had to be a half a mile from the inn when the dogs split in two directions.

"What the—?"

"They might double back."

Melanie stared into Wyatt's understanding eyes. "I'll go with him," he said, nodding toward the second K-9.

She bit her lip, nodded, and followed Bella.

Fifteen minutes later, a call came in to the radio.

"We have something."

Maaco stopped midstride and Melanie held her handset tight. "What?"

"Her sweater. We found Hope's sweater."

"Is she in it?" There was a pause. Pain gripped her heart. "Is she in it?"

Wyatt's voice replied. "No, baby . . . she's not. We're still looking."

Chapter Seventeen

It was an hour until dusk. The media had shown up once the Amber Alert had been issued, and according to Jo, Nathan had been notified of Hope's disappearance.

Melanie never felt so hopeless in all her life.

The search concentrated on the area where they'd found Hope's sweater. Faces she hadn't seen in years popped in front of her, encouraging her . . . then took their posts to search.

Even Zane showed up with Zoe's mom to help. Zanya stayed behind at the inn preparing food for the volunteers who checked in every couple of hours for food and water.

The FBI was en route, which made Melanie feel equal parts crazed and hopeful. Much as she loved and trusted Jo, her exposure to missing persons wasn't vast.

Still the search was impressive.

Wyatt never left her side. Never suggested she slow down or stop.

He'd hand her water, shove something in her hands to eat during the search . . . but he didn't falter one step.

Once it was apparent that Hope's sweater wasn't anywhere near her daughter, Melanie started back in the direction she'd been searching with Bella before they'd been called away. Search parties tightened up to look for any signs of Hope's recent presence, and not just the girl.

It never occurred to Melanie that they'd find a piece of her. Even a sweater. Now the possibilities of finding something other than her entire daughter threatened her sanity.

She was cold, shivering under the oversize coat Wyatt had placed over her shoulders at some point in the cool day. Every muscle in her body ached, and her head felt as if it were splitting in two under the weight of it all.

Melanie did what any mother would . . . she pushed on.

The sun kept a steady pace toward the horizon no matter how much Melanie willed it to stay high.

"This is about where we were when they found the sweater."

Maaco agreed with a nod.

The handler knelt next to Bella for the hundredth time that day, said a few things to his dog while holding Hope's baby blanket.

"C'mon, Bella," Melanie heard Wyatt say at her side.

A half a dozen volunteers stood beside them, all focused on the K-9.

Bella ran in a couple of circles before heading in a western direction.

"Isn't that the way we came the first time?" Melanie asked.

Wyatt was the only one listening to her. "Maybe Hope turned around."

By now, Jo was beside them, no longer able to stay behind and direct traffic. "Spread out," she told those around her. "Same procedure. Anything, no matter how small."

A mumbling of voices agreed and the group took spaces beside each other, some twenty to thirty feet apart, all of them headed in the same general direction of Bella's lead.

It wasn't until the hillside started a steep descent that the team slowed its pace.

Melanie knew the hill would eventually find its way to a cliff, which was why this route was off-limits for Hope to explore. At the bottom of the cliff was a ravine, but it was far too dangerous for those with only two legs to traverse. Hope, being the rule follower that she was, would never have ventured here on her own.

And that scared Melanie even more.

While the others held back, she followed Bella, Maaco, and Jo down the hill. Wyatt held her hand to keep her from falling. At some point, Bella disappeared and Melanie panicked.

When the dog started to bark and Maaco took that as a sign to move faster, Melanie followed. At some point, she shook off Wyatt's hand and damn near crawled on all fours to keep herself upright.

Maaco reached Bella behind a rock that protruded from the side of the cliff. The obsessive barking shot Melanie's heart rate higher.

She scrambled faster, felt a sharp rock cut the palm of her hand when the ground beneath her feet let loose and had her gripping the side of the hill to keep from tumbling down.

"Oh, God!" Maaco shouted over the bark.

Melanie froze.

"She's here!"

Every nerve ending in Melanie's body stood at sharp attention, waiting for his next words.

"Alive."

Tears were close, but she didn't acknowledge them as she followed Maaco's voice. Once she caught sight of Bella, Maaco looked uphill, waved both hands in the air. "Stop . . . stop!"

She couldn't see her. Couldn't see her daughter behind the rock.

"It's unstable."

"Hope?" Melanie called out.

"She's out cold. Breathing. Nice and steady. Looks like she hit her head. Maybe a broken arm."

Jo rushed up beside Melanie and Wyatt, heard the last of Maaco's words.

"I need to see her." Despite Maaco's warning, Melanie started down the hill.

Wyatt grasped her arm. "Don't be reckless now. We found her, she's safe."

Melanie looked to where her daughter lay and knew he was right.

Jo called into the radio, "We found her. I repeat, we found her. We need medical. Head trauma . . . I want a helicopter."

"Late in the day for a chopper, Sheriff."

Melanie caught Jo's eyes.

"I don't care. Make it happen."

It felt like forever to be so close and yet not see her daughter.

Search and rescue were on them in minutes with pulleys and ropes. Everyone was moved to higher ground to keep them safe while the crew secured Hope into a basket and hoisted her to the top.

Once there, Melanie rushed to her side.

"Oh, sweetie. What happened to you?"

Hope was still unconscious, a nasty bruise already had five shades of color on her forehead.

Melanie leaned close, felt her daughter's breath on her cheek, and kissed her. "Wake up, baby."

"We need to move her, Miss Bartlett," one of the medics told her.

Melanie gripped the side of the basket and didn't let go. She'd never let go again.

A helicopter was on standby in the center of the clearest point of Miss Gina's lawn.

Melanie vaguely caught the mass of people who watched from the side as someone pushed her into the helicopter and wrapped a seat belt across her lap.

The blades of the chopper started to turn, the noise drowned out everything.

Medics worked in frantic haste beside her daughter.

Melanie felt the eyes of someone and lifted her head to see Wyatt staring.

He lifted a hand as the helicopter pulled away from the ground.

~

His fingers gripped the steering wheel with white knuckles.

He'd controlled it . . . the urge . . . the need. After all, he was a professional now. People paid him to take care of their problems.

Perhaps he shouldn't have taken things as far as he had, but he had to prove to himself that he was in control.

One deep, satisfying breath helped him release the wheel and run his hands over his thighs.

He was in control.

~

The police escort to the hospital in Eugene reduced the normally two-hour drive down to an hour and fifteen minutes.

He'd attempted to text Melanie in hopes of an update, but didn't receive a reply.

The stress, pain, and yes, even guilt of the day should have made him want to fall into a heap on the floor of his truck, but instead, he drove behind Jo's flashing lights as they pulled into the emergency room parking lot.

"I'm going through the back," Jo yelled as she ran from the car. "I'll call you in the minute I can."

Jo disappeared through the glass doors of the ambulance bay.

Wyatt ran a hand through his hair and proceeded into the busy lobby. It was after ten, children were everywhere, people sleeping in uncomfortable chairs with their knees tucked under them, heads rested against shoulders and walls. It smelled of illness and antiseptic.

Ten minutes passed before Jo poked her head through a door he assumed led to the heart of the ER and waved him in.

"How is she?"

"Responding, according to Mel. Broken arm. The head scan showed a small bleed behind her ear, which probably kept her unconscious."

"That doesn't sound good."

Jo shook her head. "She's lucky we found her when we did. Her temperature was dropping, which wouldn't have ended well."

"What was she doing out there, Jo?"

Jo's jaw physically tightened. "I don't know. Between you and me, I don't like it. Something feels completely off about this whole thing."

A nurse brushed past them with an armload of IV solutions.

Wyatt moved out of her way and glanced around. "Where are they?"

Jo nodded in the direction she started to walk. "Mel's a wreck."

"I know."

Jo captured his arm. "No, she's feeling guilty about being gone last night."

Yeah, he understood the feeling. As irrational as he knew it was . . . guilt weighed on him, too. "I know," he repeated.

The private glass doors of the bay opened and Wyatt felt as if someone punched him in the gut.

Hope looked like a tiny wrapped bundle with wires and tubes running all over her little body. Melanie sat at her side, her hand holding Hope's, her head lowered on the side of the bed.

"Hey, darlin'," he whispered.

Melanie lifted her red, tear-filled gaze to his.

He waited for an invitation, wasn't sure there would be one.

When she lifted her free hand to him, he stepped inside the room, knelt at her side, and wrapped her in his arms.

And she cried.

Soft, quiet tears until he felt her shaking with the effort to hold back the noise he knew was deep inside her soul.

The scuffle of shoes had Wyatt glancing toward the door, where he saw Jo step outside the room.

"It's okay. She's safe now."

Melanie kept sniffling as if attempting to hold back. "I've never been so scared."

"I know, honey . . . I know." And he did. He leaned back and ran his thumb under her eyes to catch some of the moisture and tried to smile.

"I should have come home. If I hadn't spent the night—"

"Darlin', stop. You can't blame yourself."

"But—"

The agony in her eyes spoke volumes. If he looked deep enough, he'd probably see the same depth of guilt in his own. "Shhh." He placed his thumb over her lips and attempted a soft smile of understanding and support.

Melanie offered half an attempt at a grin and returned her gaze toward her daughter.

"What did the doctors say?" he asked as he pulled a second chair close to Hope's side.

"They called in a pediatric neurologist. But he isn't here yet."

"Jo said something about bleeding."

Melanie nodded, kept her voice low. "Yeah, but they said it isn't moving anything around inside, which is a good thing. When Hope woke up right after we got here, she didn't make a lot of sense. The doctor said it wasn't abnormal after the knock she's suffered and the amount of time she's been unconscious."

Hope twitched in her sleep but didn't wake up.

"Do they think she's been out all this time?"

"They can't tell. We won't know until she wakes up and makes sense. Even then we have to base the timeline on her memory, which might take some time to come back."

Wyatt covered the hand Melanie used to hold Hope's.

Their silence was interrupted by one of the nursing staff walking into the room. Her genuine smile and kind eyes gave him a passing feeling of comfort.

She set some supplies down on a rolling table and moved about the room. "The orthopedic doctor is here to set and splint her arm," she told them.

"Is it gonna hurt her?" Melanie asked.

The nurse squinted and sighed. "A little. The doctor will inject some pain meds in her arm, and with any luck, she won't feel much after that."

"All right." Melanie stood when a man wearing a suit walked into the room.

"Mrs. Bartlett?"

Melanie corrected the man, like Wyatt had noticed her doing repeatedly throughout the day. "It's Miss."

He smiled. "I'm Doctor Johnson."

The doctor glanced between the two of them as he explained what he was going to do.

As he spoke, he turned on a lighted box used to view X-rays and slid in what Wyatt assumed were Hope's films. The break was clearly visible in her forearm, both bones crossed over each other in the wrong places.

That had to hurt.

"Once I line up the bones, it's just a matter of time for it to fuse together again. In six weeks we'll take the cast off. I don't anticipate any problems."

Another set of hands came in the room and started adjusting the bed to a higher level. Wyatt stood back and watched.

Hope stirred on the bed.

"Hope, sweetie, Mommy's here."

Hope moaned and blinked her eyes a few times. For Wyatt, it was the best thing he'd seen all day.

"Miss Gina's gonna be mad." These were the first words out of Hope's mouth.

Melanie laid a gentle hand to Hope's forehead as the staff in the room opened different packages of what Wyatt assumed was the splinting material for Hope's arm.

"Miss Gina's not mad," Melanie told her daughter.

"Mommy?" The question and tone of Hope's voice made Wyatt pause.

"That's right, sweetie. I'm right here."

"Something's not right." Hope looked beyond Melanie to those around the room.

"You're in the hospital, honey. You fell."

"Mommy . . . Miss Gina's going to be mad." Hope tried to move on the bed and cried out.

"Don't move, baby."

Hope opened her eyes again and stared at Melanie as if seeing her for the first time. "Mommy, is that you?"

Melanie started to tear up again. "Why does she keep asking me that?" she asked the doctor.

"Repetitive questions after a head injury are common. Most of the time they go away."

Wyatt placed a hand on Melanie's shoulder, she gripped it with one of hers. "Most of the time?"

"She's already making more sense than when she first arrived. I know it's hard, but just answer her questions and keep her calm."

"Mommy, where am I?" Hope kept staring around the room until her eyes finally connected with his. "Uncle Wyatt?"

"Hey, princess."

Hope gave him a strangled smile. "Miss Gina is mad."

"We're about to get started, Miss Bartlett. Do you want to stay here while we do this?"

"I'm not going anywhere." Melanie sat on the edge of the bed as if proving a point.

The nurse eyed Wyatt. "We need a little more room. Would you mind stepping outside?"

Wyatt turned to Melanie. "You gonna be okay?"

"Yep."

No . . . she wasn't, but she was putting on a good face.

Wyatt kissed the top of her head and stepped to the doorway. Jo stood just outside, her head tilted toward her cell phone. "No, don't," he heard her say. "Tell them to wait until I get back. There are a few things I want them to check out before we shut this case."

The noise of a curtain closing and the voices inside Hope's room carried into the hall, equally distracting from the conversation Jo was having.

He heard Hope whimper and cry and Melanie console her daughter, telling her it would all be better soon.

"One night. They've flown all this way. Hide their car keys . . . just keep them there."

"Ouch, ouch . . . ouch."

"Just do it, Emery." Jo hung up the phone and tucked it into her front shirt pocket of her uniform.

"What was that all about?" Wyatt asked.

Jo released a frustrated breath. "Nothing . . . nothing. How is she?"

"They're setting her arm."

They stood with an ear toward the glass door, the hustling emergency room in full swing around them.

Hope let out another cry before the doctor's voice stated the worst was over.

From there, Jo and Wyatt listened, and waited.

"See, Hope. It feels better now, doesn't it?"

Wyatt leaned against the wall and started to feel some of the day seep into his bones. "I could sleep for a week," he said under his breath.

"We all can," Jo chimed in.

One of the nurses left the room and told them it was clear for them to go back in.

Wyatt pushed the curtain back and saw a bright purple cast holding Hope's arm in a perfect L. She'd been crying, but Melanie was whispering in her ear while the staff cleaned up the room.

"I'm going to send her to X-ray again, make sure everything looks like it should, and then I'll check on her during rounds tomorrow."

"Thank you, Doctor." Melanie shook the man's hand.

"Mommy?"

"Yeah, baby?"

"Where's the puppy?"

Melanie closed her eyes and shook her head. "There isn't a puppy, honey."

"He's going to get hurt if we don't find him."

Jo leaned closer to Wyatt. "What's she talking about?"

"A lot of questions, not all of them make sense."

"Miss Gina's going to be mad."

When Hope started to repeat what he'd already heard a few times, Wyatt knew it was going to be an even longer night than the day had been.

"Miss Gina is happy you're okay, sweetie."

"No!" Hope's voice rose with conviction. "Miss Gina is going to be mad if we don't find the puppy!"

To Wyatt's side, he saw Jo's frame freeze.

She took a step closer to the bed. "Hope, honey?"

"Auntie Jo . . . can you find him?"

Melanie sighed again. "Hope, there isn't any—"

Jo placed a hand on Mel's shoulder and shook her head.

"Where's the puppy, Hope? Did you see it?"

Hope closed her eyes as if searching behind her lids for the answer. "No. I heard it. And Miss Gina won't be mad if we find him."

It was then some of the pieces fell into place. Hope moving far away from the house in search of a puppy . . . down a ravine.

Hope started to close her eyes. "We should find the puppy."

"We'll look, honey."

That seemed to quiet her down.

Just when they thought Hope was done talking, her next words brought the temperature in the room down twenty degrees.

"Maybe Mr. Lewis found the puppy. He's good at finding animals."

Chapter Eighteen

"Who is Mr. Lewis?"

Melanie didn't think her head, her heart, or her adrenaline could pump any faster. Then she turned to see who asked the question and realized it could all double with the presence of one man.

"Nathan."

Jo took a step in front of the man, blocking his view. "I told you to call me when you got off the plane," Jo scolded with her tone.

Nathan placed a hand on Jo's arm and attempted to push her aside. "I'm here to see my daughter."

Melanie cringed and snapped a glance to Hope.

Hope was looking around the room as if seeing it for the first time. "Mommy, where am I?"

"Out of my way." Nathan's voice bordered on violent as he pushed past Jo. "Good God, what happened to her?"

"Keep your voice down, Nathan," Melanie tried to calm him.

"Don't tell me to keep it down. Is this what you call protecting our daughter?"

Once again, Melanie cringed.

"Mommy, who's that?"

"I'm your daddy, Hope. And I'm going to protect you from now on."

"Hey!" Jo shoved in between the bed and Nathan.

"Please, Nathan. Not now!"

Hope started to cry. "Mommy . . . where am I?"

"You're either going to arrest me or get the hell out of my way, woman!" Nathan all but spat in Jo's face.

"Don't tempt me."

"Mommy . . . why is that man yelling at Aunt Jo?"

"You know, Nathan . . . now might not be the best time to upset the patient." Wyatt's words brought Nathan's gaze across the bed.

"Who the hell are you to tell me what to do?"

Melanie felt the charge in the air crack when the nurse walked into the room. "I don't know what's going on in here, but it stops now!" She pushed past Jo, Nathan, and Wyatt and moved to the monitor above the bed. "Everyone out!"

"Mommy!"

"Except Mom. Everyone else, solve your issues outside."

"Let's go," Jo said, placing her hand on Nathan's arm with a nudge toward the door.

He shook her off. "She's my daughter, too."

The monitor started to ping.

The nurse placed both hands on her hips. "Out!"

"I have rights." Nathan lowered his tone and glared at the nurse.

"And we have rules. One visitor at a time. Out!"

Melanie felt Hope squeeze her hand as Nathan looked at everyone but his daughter before storming out of the room.

"We'll be right outside." Wyatt kissed the top of Melanie's head and smiled at Hope.

The nurse closed the door after they left and pulled the curtain around the bed. She pressed a few things on the monitor and checked Hope's IV. "How are you feeling, honey?"

"Who are you?" Hope's tears were already drying up.

"I'm Clarisse, one of the nurses. You're at the hospital."

Hope looked down at her arm. "I broke my arm."

"Yes, you did. Do you remember falling?"

Hope shook her head.

"It's okay."

Clarisse turned her attention to Melanie. "We should try and keep her calm. The bed in ICU will be ready in about an hour, until then I'm going to keep visitors away."

Melanie looked at the monitor. "What happened?"

"Her pulse shot up. Then I heard the yelling. She's had enough stress."

"I'm tired," Hope said, closing her eyes.

"You sleep, sweetie. I'm right here."

Melanie nodded toward the door and slipped away from the bed with the nurse. In hushed tones, she explained the situation.

"Hope doesn't know her father. He's just reentered the picture and seems determined to cause chaos."

Clarisse frowned. "I'll notify risk management and the nursing director. Maybe they can talk with him and let him see how his impact isn't helping the situation right now."

"Thank you."

Clarisse left the room, and when Melanie turned back, Hope was already asleep.

Jo started into Nathan the minute the three of them were clear of the lobby doors.

"How stupid can you be? Hope has a head injury, you asshat. The last thing she needs is her sperm donor coming in to screw things up more inside her head."

"Fuck you, JoAnne. She's my kid. I have rights."

"You have squat. You gave up your rights when you walked away."

Wyatt didn't want to yell at the man, he simply wanted to punch him. Maybe bruise up his left fist to go with his right.

"You don't know what you're talking about."

"I know exactly what I'm talking about. And if you try a stunt like that again, I'll slap handcuffs on you so fast your cocky grin will slide right into hell where you belong."

Nathan took a step way too close to Jo for Wyatt's comfort.

"Just try it. False arrest, false imprisonment."

"Obstructing justice, threatening a peace officer, interfering with police proceedings."

"All right, enough." How the hell did Wyatt become the calm one? "Much as I'd love to kick your ass right now for what you pulled in there, the last thing Melanie needs is this."

Nathan put both hands in the air and waved Wyatt toward him. "Let's go, Redneck. You just throw the first punch."

Wyatt clenched his fists, his jaw tight. It would be so nice to see blood on Nathan's three-piece suit. He heard his father's voice inside his head . . . "Don't throw the first punch, son; throw the last."

He forced his fists to unwind and turned his attention toward Jo. Without turning his back on Nathan, he said to her, "I think Mr. Lewis has a few questions to answer."

"Damn it." She waved a hand in the air at Nathan. "We're not done."

"Not by a long shot."

Then Jo ran toward her squad car, leaving the two of them behind.

Wyatt took one last look at Nathan, turned on his heel, and walked to his truck.

His mother answered on the second ring. "Well, if it isn't our long lost son calling, even if it's close to eleven."

He hadn't even thought of the time when he dialed their number. "Yeah, sorry. I should call more."

"And visit more." His mom was the quintessential housewife during Wyatt's youth and still took the role seriously while heading up a dozen charity organizations and causes that helped define her as something other than the wife of William Gibson, otherwise known as the defense attorney to some of the most prominent people in the country, the man you called when you knew damn well you were guilty but had enough money to pay your way out of jail time.

Wyatt was the polar opposite of his father, but unlike most of the kids he grew up with who were all but bullied into the family firm, big companies, or startups that dotted Silicon Valley, William always encouraged Wyatt to take his own path.

He remembered once, when he was a kid, the road trip that took them up the coasts of Northern California, Oregon, and into Washington State. The three of them had stopped in a town a lot like River Bend, and he and his father tried to toss poles into a stream to fish. They didn't catch anything, probably because of all the talking they had done. William had confessed that if he were to do it all different, he'd trade his life for something simple . . . like a small town in a nowhere place where people were kind to each other. Where defending property lines and lot usage would way outnumber violent crimes and the nasty people who did them.

Wyatt knew, deep down, that was why he'd chosen the life he had. And his parents had always encouraged him to do it.

"I need to make the time," he told her.

"I'm glad to hear you say that. Your father was saying the same thing the other day."

"Yeah, uhm, about Dad . . . is he there?"

"Of course." She paused. "Is everything all right? You don't sound yourself."

"I've had a long day and I need to talk to Dad."

"All right, I'll go get him." He knew his mother was tuned in to his problem.

He heard the muffling of the phone, his mother speaking to his father, but not the words that were spoken.

"What's the matter, son?" William skipped *hello* and *how are you*.

"Have you watched the news today?"

"I've been in court all day. Why? Are you in trouble?"

"No, Dad. I'm not. C'mon." Wyatt took a deep breath. "I met this woman . . ." For the next ten minutes Wyatt told his father briefly about Melanie, about Hope . . . about the past twenty-four hours.

And he told him about Nathan. "He's a weasel, Dad. He doesn't give a crap about his daughter."

William chuckled. "Most lawyers are weasels, son."

"Yeah, you've told me that before. But this guy. He's going to cause trouble. I feel it. The thing is, I don't know why. It wasn't like Mel was going after him for a dime."

"Have you considered him having a change of heart about his kid?"

"He caused chaos in the ER, stressed out Hope, made a scene. Does that sound like a man caring about the health of his kid?"

"No. Sounds like a man trying to make a scene and gathering witnesses."

Wyatt hated that he'd picked up on that.

"You told me once that half your job was being a private investigator. Can you look into him for me?"

"Consider it done. What else can you tell me about him?"

He told his father what he knew, which wasn't a lot. "I know a few people that know a little more. I'll e-mail you the details I can find in the morning."

"Sounds good."

"Thanks, Dad."

"Oh, and Wyatt?"

"Yeah?"

"This Melanie . . . is she someone your mother and I might meet someday?"

Wyatt read through the lines of the question and smiled.

"Yeah . . . I think maybe you will."

"Mommy?"

Melanie had fallen asleep in the recliner chair that sat beside Hope's ICU bed and woke with a start when she heard Hope calling.

"Right here, baby." She wiped the sleep from her eyes and scrambled to her daughter's side.

"I'm hungry."

Two words.

Two perfect words.

It was four in the morning, but that didn't hold a lot of concern for a little girl who had last eaten the morning before.

"I'll get the nurse, see if we can get you something."

Hope looked around the room. "I'm in the hospital?"

"Yes, baby."

"And I fell and broke my arm."

"You did." The fact that Hope told her instead of asking was a huge improvement. Her little girl was living up to her name.

"I'll be right back."

"'Kay."

The ICU was in the shape of a U, with rooms surrounding a central nursing station that had a half dozen nurses working behind it. She found the night nurse in charge of her daughter's care and told him Hope was asking for food.

Phillip put the chart he was writing in aside and stood. "Let's go talk to her."

They walked back into the room and found Hope smiling. "Hi, Hope. Do you remember me?"

She squinted her eyes then smiled. "Phillip."

"That's right."

Instant tears sprang to Melanie's eyes. The doctor had told her that Hope's scrambled head was temporary, but she had a hard time believing it.

Until now.

"You okay, Mommy?"

"I'm fine, sweetie." She wiped her eyes and turned away. "I need to find a bathroom. Are you all right here without me for a few minutes?"

"I'm okay."

Melanie looked at Phillip. "I'll be right back."

"Take your time," Phillip said with a knowing smile.

Yeah, that wasn't going to happen. She just needed a few minutes to remove the emotion from her face.

When Melanie walked outside the double doors of the ICU, several familiar faces were in various positions on the couches and cushioned chairs.

Miss Gina noticed her first and shook the blanket from her lap.

Then Wyatt opened his eyes and caught hers. It took a second for the smile to come. When it did, both Miss Gina and Wyatt released a deep collective sigh.

"She's awake, making sense."

"Oh, hon." Miss Gina took a few steps and pulled Melanie into her arms.

Wyatt ran both hands through his hair before he stood and took his turn hugging her.

Luke woke next and placed a hand on Zoe's shoulder.

When did she show up?

Zoe jumped, saw Melanie, and scrambled off the couch. There weren't any words . . . just Zoe taking both hands and holding Melanie's eyes with a stare.

Then she hugged her . . . hard.

"You didn't need to come."

Zoe pounded on her back. "Bite me."

The one face missing from the room was Jo's.

"Where's—"

"Back in River Bend with the FBI. Investigating," Zoe told her. "Has Hope said any more about Mr. Lewis?"

"Nothing. I haven't asked her." The last thing she wanted to do was upset her when she did open her eyes. "She hasn't mentioned Nathan either." Another glance around the room proved Nathan wasn't among the concerned. Then again, maybe he didn't feel welcome with so many people in her world setting up camp. "Is he—"

"He hasn't shown his face since the ER," Wyatt told her.

That news brought some relief. "I should get back in there," Melanie said, pointing to the door with her thumb. "You guys really don't need to stay. The nurses say she's stable for an ICU patient."

"That doesn't sound right," Luke said.

"I know. The knock on her head is why she's in this unit. In case something went wrong." It didn't appear that was going to happen, thank God.

"Really. I'm sure sleeping in here isn't the most comfortable. I'll call you if I need anything."

Miss Gina let her gaze sweep down Melanie's frame. "Like a change of clothes?"

The shorts she'd been painting in two nights before were still on her body. The only addition to that evening's clothing she had with her was a coat Wyatt had placed over her shoulders during the search.

"What about some food? When was the last time you ate?" Zoe chided.

Melanie glanced at the ceiling as if it held the answer. Then decided to divert. "I'm sure the hospital has a cafeteria that opens soon."

"But will you leave Hope's side long enough to find it?" Miss Gina asked.

"I'm okay. Really."

Zoe glanced around the group of them before turning her attention to Melanie. "So are we. You take care of Hope, we'll take care of you."

It wouldn't be any different if the situation were reversed.

She kissed and hugged each of them, lingered a little longer with Wyatt and whispered in his ear, "Thank you for being here."

"Anytime," he whispered back.

Chapter Nineteen

Sometime before dawn, Zoe and Miss Gina left the hospital to gather a change of clothes for Melanie and to retrieve Hope's favorite stuffed something. Wyatt was new to the world of kids, but it wasn't hard to figure out what a little girl might like. In the hospital gift shop he found a plush purple teddy bear with a pink bow and added a bright silver balloon saying "Get Well Soon." Because the ICU was extremely limited as to when they could come in and visit, he and Luke camped out in the lobby for the first half of the day. By noon, Zoe, Miss Gina, and Jo returned with a basket full of food and provisions.

Jo appeared to have taken a shower, but the color under her eyes suggested she hadn't slept much, if at all, the night before. She wore her uniform and a frown. Beside her was a woman in dark blue slacks and a crisp white shirt. She had short, dark hair and an easy smile. "This is Agent Burton," Jo told him when it was clear the woman was with them. "She needs to ask Hope a few questions."

He saw that coming, he supposed.

"Is she awake?"

"Off and on all morning," Wyatt told her.

Jo didn't seem pleased with her position. "No time like the present," she said before reaching for the phone that called into the nurses' station inside the ICU. A brief conversation had the two of them being buzzed in. Wyatt didn't ask, he just took his teddy bear offering and walked alongside them.

Jo nodded with a smile and followed his lead.

The ICU was much busier than it had been during the night. Doctors in white coats and a handful of radiology and respiratory technicians joined the busy ward.

Jo stopped by the nurses' station while Wyatt detoured directly into Hope's room.

She was sitting up, her broken arm resting on a pillow while she attempted to eat what looked like soup from a rolling table pulled up over the bed. "Hey, princess?"

Hope looked up and offered the most precious smile. She skipped *hi* and *hello* and went straight to the point. "Is that for me?"

Melanie released a long-suffering sigh when she noticed him standing there.

He stepped into the room and handed the stuffed toy to Hope before he ruffled the top of her head with two fingers. "You're looking better."

"My arm hurts, my head hurts, and my butt hurts!"

Wyatt laughed as he walked around the bed and greeted Melanie with a kiss to the top of her head. He leaned over so only she could hear his words. "Jo is here with an FBI agent to ask her questions."

She sucked in a tiny breath and the smile on her face suddenly looked forced.

"You okay?"

She nodded.

He wasn't convinced.

A few seconds later Jo and Agent Burton stepped into the room. Hope greeted her with an enthusiastic *Auntie Jo!* welcome, with Jo kissing Hope's cheek. "So good to see you awake and eating."

"They made me drink broth for breakfast." Hope made a squishy face.

"She's progressed to soft food," Melanie told them. "By dinner she'll be asking for a hamburger."

Jo pulled up a chair along with Agent Burton. "Hope, this is my friend Mrs. Burton. She and I are working together to make sure we know exactly what happened when you were asleep yesterday."

Hope scanned the four of them. "Am I in trouble?"

"No, baby!" Melanie patted her leg. "You're not in trouble."

"'Kay."

Agent Burton started with a simple smile. "Hope, honey . . . do you remember what happened yesterday?"

"I fell and broke my arm. Mommy said I hit my head hard, too."

"Right. What about before you fell? You were really far from the inn. Do you remember why you left home?"

Hope bit her lip and looked around the four of them again.

Melanie once again patted Hope's leg through the blankets. "Honey, you're not in trouble. Just tell us the truth."

"M'kay . . . I was playing outside, in the backyard where Miss Gina could see me. I heard a dog barking. It sounded like it came from the front yard so I looked. I didn't see a dog."

Wyatt kept a hand on Melanie's shoulder, which she covered with one of hers.

"Then what happened?" Jo asked.

"Uhm, I was going back when I heard it again. Then I saw Mr. Lewis by the trees on the other side of the road."

Melanie gripped his hand. Both of them knew instantly how wrong this was going. Mr. Lewis had hustled from his room, or so they thought, and was outside when Melanie started screaming Hope's name. Then he told them he hadn't seen her since breakfast.

"Did Mr. Lewis say anything to you?"

"He went like this." She made a waving motion toward herself. "I ran across the street. Mr. Lewis said he saw a puppy running off in the woods without its mother." A pained look crossed Hope's eyes. "I told him I wasn't supposed to leave the inn. He said it was okay and that Miss Gina wouldn't be mad cuz I was with him." Hope stared at Melanie.

"It's all right, baby. No one is mad at you."

Jo pushed out a long breath. "Then what happened?"

"Mr. Lewis and I ran in the trees. He said he saw the puppy go down the hill. It was really steep. I was scared."

"I bet," Agent Burton said in a soft voice. "Did you go down the hill?"

Hope started to shake her head. "I-I didn't want to go down. Mr. Lewis said I should find the puppy and maybe my mommy would let me keep it."

"Did Mr. Lewis go down the hill?"

"No, he said he was too big."

Wyatt felt Melanie start to tremble under his hand. His feet itched to move. Find Mr. Lewis and beat him within an inch of his life.

Instead, Wyatt did his best to keep all emotion from his face and listen while Agent Burton and Jo asked questions.

"So you went down the hill?"

Hope shook her head faster. "I didn't. I guess I tripped or something. I don't remember falling."

"Did you see the puppy?"

"No. Mr. Lewis saw the puppy," Hope told them.

"Do you remember anything else, Hope? Anything about Mr. Lewis that didn't feel right?"

Hope sat in silence for a several seconds, then opened her eyes wide. "He had a tattoo on his arm."

Jo leaned forward. "And that didn't feel right?"

"Well, Mr. Lewis is always so nice, but the picture on his arm was like a scary Halloween."

"Mel, have you seen this tattoo?"

"No. He was always in a full dress shirt when I saw him."

Agent Burton lifted both of her arms to Hope. "Can you point on me where you saw Mr. Lewis's tattoo?"

She pointed to the agent's left forearm, right below her elbow. Wyatt tried to remember if he'd seen the man with short sleeves. Like Mel, he only remembered a suit.

"Was it his left arm?"

Hope shrugged. "I don't remember."

"What does a scary Halloween mean?"

"Dark and squiggly. And kinda like the picture the doctor put on that thing." Hope pointed to a light box on the wall of the room.

"Like an X-ray?"

Hope nodded.

"An X-ray of your arm?" Jo asked.

Hope pointed to her head. "An X-ray of my head."

Jo glanced at Agent Burton. "A skull."

"Yeah," Hope added. "I saw a few of them. They were mean and ugly."

Jo patted Hope's leg. "You've been really helpful, honey. I'm going to talk to your mom outside for a few minutes."

"M'kay."

Melanie kept it together until the four of them walked out the double doors of the ICU. Then she lost it.

"He hurt my baby!" She turned toward Jo, grabbed both her friend's shoulders, and shook them. "He did this!"

The River Bend posse jumped to their feet and moved by Mel's side, all asking questions.

"What happened?"

"This is about Mr. Lewis, isn't it?" Miss Gina asked.

"Okay, okay . . . everyone needs to settle down," Agent Burton attempted to calm the room.

"The man lured my daughter into the woods and left her there to die. I'll kill him. I swear—"

"Mel, stop, please. You need to stay focused again. Okay?"

Luke slid next to Wyatt. "Is this for real?"

"Hope said he told her he saw a puppy running in the woods and they went to find it."

"That bastard!" Miss Gina muttered. "If I get my hands around his neck—"

"Get in line," Zoe added.

"Guys, enough with the death threats. Jeez, I am a cop and Burton here is a Fed."

Agent Burton offered a little shake of her head. "Emotions are high. But Jo is right. If this bastard ends up dead, I don't want to have to stand witness. Keep that among yourselves. I'm going to check in with my partner." She looked around the faces. "Then I'm going to have to interview each of you . . . see if we can gather any more information about our Mr. Lewis."

"His address and credit card are all at the inn," Miss Gina told them.

Agent Burton released a drawn-out sigh. "All of which are bogus. Along with his name."

"But I saw his ID," Miss Gina said.

"When was the last time you saw a fake ID?" Jo asked.

"The sixties."

Jo patted her arm.

Wyatt realized that Melanie had gone silent.

"You all right?" He placed his arm over her shoulders.

She shook her head. "Do you think he pushed her?"

"I don't know."

"The doctor said Hope might not ever remember falling. You saw her, she knew she didn't go down the hill willingly. Why would he want to hurt my baby?"

Everyone stopped talking and focused on Melanie.

"Why would a grown man want to kill my child?" She started to tear up. "Hope wouldn't step on a spider."

"We're going to find out, Mel."

When she started to shake again, Zoe stepped forward and wrapped her arms around her. Wyatt moved away and watched.

"C'mon, Mel. You heard Jo, hold it together. We'll find the bastard."

"He hurt my baby, Zoe."

"I know. C'mon . . . let's find a ladies' room and clean you up a little. Splash some water on your face so you don't scare Hope when you go back in."

Wyatt watched as Zoe grabbed her bag and led Melanie away.

"Why would he toss her down a hill?" Luke asked the moment Mel was out of the lobby.

"God only knows. Sociopath? Child molester?"

"Oh, hell no!" Miss Gina cussed.

Jo lifted both hands. "Hold up, Hope isn't giving any indication that anything like that happened."

"Could be an offender trying to avoid the crime. We don't know yet," Agent Burton said.

"Kill the kid so you won't touch them? Damn, that's sick." Luke turned away and started to pace.

Wyatt had heard stories from his dad over the years of just how twisted and vile the human condition could get. Although his blood boiled that this had touched Hope, he wasn't surprised at anything Agent Burton and Jo were concluding.

"Right now it's all speculation. Once we find Mr. Lewis, we'll have our answers."

"I'm sure he's long gone."

Agent Burton offered a sly smile. "We'll find him. Every perp leaves a path. It's our job to find it."

"He left a witness," Wyatt muttered.

The small group went silent.

It felt as if everyone had ducked into their own heads after Hope had revealed the series of events leading up to her "fall" down the hill.

Jo had handed Melanie a notebook before returning to River Bend with Agent Burton, Miss Gina, and Luke. Any time Melanie remembered even the slightest detail of the bastard that hurt her daughter, she wrote it down.

Zoe had found a physician's shower that Melanie could use, and after three days in the same clothes, she finally had on something clean. Eventually, she knew she was going to drop. But as the afternoon started to slide into the evening, she had another shot of adrenaline forced on her.

An unavoidable shot of adrenaline.

Doctor Bellingham walked through on his evening rounds. The pediatric neurologist sat somewhere between fifty and sixty with a receding hairline and a thick waist.

"Good news," he said with a smile as he walked over to the light box and flipped on a switch.

Hope was awake but groggy after her full day of tests and visitors.

Zoe and Wyatt had sweet-talked their way into the room with a plate of cookies for the staff, so Melanie had the distraction of friends while she sat by her daughter's bedside.

"Looks like Hope's second CAT scan is showing improvement."

Melanie stood beside the doctor as he showed her a series of images side by side. "This is last night's, and this is today's." He ran a pen alongside the spot on the film the doctors had told her was the bleeding inside Hope's head. "It's tiny, but it's going in the right direction." He pointed to a few other things on the film they were watching, but he didn't anticipate any problems with a full recovery.

When he was done going over the images, he approached Hope with a smile. "It's good news, kiddo. Looks like you have a pretty hard head."

She lifted her purple cast. "My arm is soft."

He laughed.

Melanie watched as he checked Hope's eyes, her reflexes, and a few things that Melanie didn't understand the need for. He asked Hope a few random questions that she was enthusiastic to answer. Hope told him she still had a headache and her arm *pulsed*.

"I will see *you* in the morning, Hope."

"M'kay."

"Mom." He looked at Melanie. "Let's have a chat."

"Be right back, baby."

"Want us to go with you?" Zoe asked.

Melanie shook her head. "I'm good."

Doctor Bellingham walked her into a conference room, where she was met with two other people, one man, one woman . . . both in business attire and not hospital scrubs.

"What's going on?"

"This is Ms. Gomez, head of risk management here at the hospital, and Mr. Coban, one of our attorneys."

"Risk management and attorneys?"

"Miss Bartlett, Hope's father is creating quite a fuss about being denied access to his daughter," Ms. Gomez told her. "The scene he caused last night and the report from the nursing staff in the ER have given us what we needed to keep him away temporarily."

"Hope doesn't know her dad."

"We understand that." Mr. Coban leaned forward. "When your daughter was in less stable condition, the doctors had no problem suggesting his presence could hinder her recovery."

Melanie picked up on one key word. "Had . . ."

"Right." Doctor Bellingham sat in the chair beside hers and placed a hand on her forearm. "I can keep Hope in the ICU tonight, but tomorrow I'm going to downgrade her to the pediatric floor. Chances are she won't be there very long before I discharge her home. While I'm sure meeting her father will be a shock, my medical opinion about it harming her recovery at this point is that it won't."

Melanie squeezed her eyes shut.

"Without a restraining order, there isn't much we can do about keeping a father from seeing his child in the hospital," Ms. Gomez said.

"I've spoken with Mr. Stone's attorney and they've agreed to wait until Hope is out of the ICU before forcing the issue."

So Nathan had hired one of his own to push his way in.

"There's nothing I can do to stop him?"

"If he causes a scene, becomes a threat, we have full rights to make him leave."

She knew when Nathan had shown up in River Bend it wouldn't be the last she'd see of him.

"If it's any help, I'll request child services to be present when Hope's father arrives tomorrow."

"That's not a bad idea," she whispered.

Mr. Coban and Ms. Gomez stood to leave. "Thank you for your cooperation."

They didn't bother trying to shake her hand as they left the room.

Doctor Bellingham held back. "There's something I wanted to tell you about without Hope listening."

"Oh?"

"One of the things we see a lot in head injuries is a change in temper, personality. I've seen extreme cases where patients become violent for no apparent reason, bouts of anger, sometimes depression. Families report a shift in behavior that wasn't present before the head trauma."

Melanie stopped thinking about Nathan and once again focused on her daughter. "She seems fine. The same sweet girl I had yesterday. More tired than normal, but the same girl."

"And she may be. I just don't want you to be shocked if she does something, or says something out of character. Try and be patient and let me know what you see. There are some great websites that talk about post–head trauma issues. I'll have the nurses print you a list."

"Thank you, Doctor."

He patted her shoulder and left her in the room by herself.

When Wyatt walked in a few minutes later, she let him hold her while she told him about Nathan. In the end she said the part that scared her the most. "He's hired an attorney."

"To force access to the hospital?"

"What if it's more than that? What if he wants more? Custody? The things he said in the ER . . . I can't afford a lawyer, Wyatt. His family has connections."

"What kind of connections?"

"He is Nathan Stone the Third. Both his father and grandfather are lawyers. I remember early on him saying something about his father wanting to run for governor. Nathan would bitch about senator this and mayor that and how he had to attend all kinds of fancy parties when he was a kid."

"Those kind of connections." Understanding filled Wyatt's face.

"What am I going to do?"

Wyatt placed his palms on both sides of her head and kissed her briefly. "You're going to go back to Hope's room. You're going to eat whatever Zoe puts in front of you. And then you're going to read Hope a bedtime story before curling up on that god-awful recliner chair and try and get some sleep."

"But—"

He placed his thumb over her lips. "Melanie, you've been doing this by yourself for a really long time. You have a large network of friends here who aren't going to let some daddy-come-lately take your kid away. You concentrate on Hope, and let me see what we can do about Nathan Stone the Third." When he said Nathan's name, he added a little aristocratic lift to his voice.

Chapter Twenty

Once Hope was moved to a private room on a regular floor, her room exploded in color and scent. Balloons and flowers, stuffed animals and candy. Some of the treats were hand delivered by friends and visitors, while a local florist brought others in. Hope had never been a hand-held video game kind of kid, outside of the kind she found for free on Melanie's phone. But when Wyatt handed her one of those gaming devices Melanie could never afford, Hope's face lit up and out came her excitement in spades.

Wyatt had accepted the one-arm hug and told her the device was to replace her climbing trees for a while.

Nathan had agreed to postpone his visit until child services could be present. As that turned out, it was going to happen just after noon.

Melanie watched the time tick down slowly until she couldn't avoid the conversation any longer. Wyatt kept glancing at the time as if he, too, was worried about the outcome. It warmed her heart that he cared enough to be nervous.

Although she loved her friends, Melanie knew better than to have them in the room when Nathan showed up. Zoe wanted a piece of him in a big way, and Jo was armed. All things considered, she accepted Wyatt's support when everyone left for lunch.

"Hope, sweetie. I have some news for you." Melanie attempted a smile to put her daughter at ease.

"Yeah? What?" She reluctantly put the game down.

"You're going to have a special visitor today." Melanie had practiced the lines in her head the night before until after two in the morning.

"Another one?"

"Yes . . . you see . . ." Getting the words out was impossible. She took a deep breath and tried again. "Your father is coming to visit you."

Hope's jaw dropped.

"He heard you were hurt and was concerned."

"The daddy that left us?"

Melanie glanced at Wyatt . . .

"Right."

Hope moved her big blue eyes to Wyatt and blinked several times.

"Is he nice?" The question felt strange, the answer even stranger.

"If he isn't, we can have him leave."

"You and Uncle Wyatt are going to stay when he's here, right?"

Melanie patted her arm. "Of course, sweetie. I'm not going anywhere."

Hope bit her lip. "M'kay."

It wasn't long before Melanie heard Nathan's voice in the hall outside the room. She stiffened.

Wyatt glanced at the clock on the wall and tapped his fingers on his knee.

"Miss Bartlett?"

CATHERINE BYBEE

"Yes?" Melanie stood and acknowledged the young woman who entered the room.

"I'm Pamela, the social worker with child services."

"Oh, hi."

Pamela offered a genuine smile to Hope. "Did you tell Hope who is coming today?"

Melanie nodded.

"Good. Well, Hope . . . are you ready to meet your father?"

Hope just shrugged.

Pamela pushed back the curtain and waved Nathan inside.

He wore a suit, complete with a tie and polished shoes. Beside him was another man, slightly taller, just as smartly dressed.

Nathan acknowledged her with nothing more than a passing stare; his eyes found Wyatt and a tiny smirk lifted from his lips. Then he finally looked at his daughter. His face softened, and for one brief moment Melanie thought maybe, just maybe, Nathan truly gave a crap about his little girl. "Oh, darling . . . look what she let happen to you."

"Mr. Stone." Pamela's warning voice brought his attention to the social worker.

"It hurts me to see her like this." Knowing Nathan the way she did, she saw through his insincerity and hoped the social worker did too.

"You're my father?" Hope asked.

"Yes . . . I'm your daddy."

Hope shook her head. "Daddies don't leave. You left."

Nathan forced a smile. "I know that's what you've been told. I'm here now, and I'm not going to leave."

Hope peered closer and narrowed her eyes. "I've seen you before."

Melanie held her breath.

"When I was in the emergency place." Hope looked beyond Nathan and at her. "You were yelling at my mommy."

Nathan glanced at the man he'd arrived with. "I was upset, honey."

Hope started to frown. "I'm not your honey."

She shook her head. "And you were yelling at Auntie Jo."

The seconds ticked by as Nathan tried to back his way out of his actions, which clearly Hope remembered. "When parents hear their children are hurt, it makes them upset, Hope. I'm sorry I yelled."

Melanie was sure part of Nathan died with the strangled apology. He was sorry for nothing, never had been.

"Why do you care if I got hurt? You don't even know me." Hope's questions were incredibly thought out and well articulated. Both took Melanie by surprise.

Clearly she wasn't the only one.

"Of course I care, honey."

Hope narrowed her eyes.

"Hope," Nathan corrected. "Now that I've found you, I'm going to take care of you."

Hope pushed back into the bed and Melanie reached for her daughter's hand.

"Mommy takes care of me. Mommy and Uncle Wyatt and Miss Gina."

Nathan's voice turned cool. "Yeah, I see how well they're doing that."

"That's quite enough, Mr. Stone."

Nathan offered half a nod and stood. "I'll be back tomorrow, Hope."

Hope just stared and didn't bother saying good-bye when he started from the room.

"Melanie? Can I have a word outside?"

She considered telling him to screw off but decided it was best to keep Hope away from the hatred boiling in her veins.

"Wyatt and I will be right back, sweetie."

Pamela lingered behind. "I'll be here."

Melanie grasped Wyatt's hand, squeezed, and pulled him alongside her.

Once they moved away from Hope's door and hopefully her ears, Nathan turned. "You have her quite brainwashed, Mel."

The man at Nathan's side placed a warning hand on his shoulder. "Keep it cool, Nathan."

"You're not going to wiggle away from me again," Nathan kept talking. "I will be back tomorrow, and the next day, and as often as I can until we have this settled."

"Have what settled, Nathan?"

The elevator doors behind them dinged.

His anger snapped shut with her question and his hand fished into the inside pocket of his jacket. With a sleazy smile he took her free hand, which she nearly snatched away, and shoved the envelope between her fingers. "Divorce and child custody! Consider yourself served."

"What the—?" She glanced at the envelope and started to tremble. "You have to be married in order to file for a divorce." She wasn't a lawyer, but she understood that.

Nathan looked at the man to his side. "See what I mean? Complete denial."

Melanie clenched the papers in her fist and stepped closer with the full intent of shoving them down his throat.

Wyatt wrapped an arm around her waist, and a new voice to the mix interrupted the scene. "Hold up there, young lady."

Nathan twisted his attention behind him and paused.

"What do we have here?" The man had to be in his late fifties, with dirty blond hair that shone with a little silver-gray on the sides. Other than that, all Melanie caught at first glance was his height, his suit that looked like a million bucks, and his easy smile.

An easy smile she'd seen before.

Wyatt pried the papers from Melanie's fist and handed them to the stranger.

"Who the hell are you?" Nathan asked.

The man lifted a finger in the air as he ripped open the seal on the envelope and read the first few lines.

"Tsk, tsk, bad form, Counselor."

Nathan thumbed in the stranger's direction. "Who is this guy?"

"This is about as unethical as it gets, serving papers while one is in the hospital. Proves you're very wet behind the ears."

"Oh, crap." The man behind Nathan finally spoke.

"William Gibson," the stranger introduced himself to Nathan, took a card from his pocket, and handed it to the man at Nathan's side. "Miss Bartlett's counsel."

When Nathan went to grab the card, Mr. Gibson lifted it from his reach. "And if I see another stunt like this, I'll bring you both up with the review board."

Nathan snatched the card and glared.

"C'mon, Nathan."

Nathan's attorney pushed him into the open elevator and glared as the doors closed.

Pamela emerged from her daughter's room. "I was about to call security."

"We're okay," Wyatt told her.

Melanie was never so happy to see the man leave.

Once Nathan was gone, Wyatt let go of her waist and grasped Mr. Gibson's hand in a firm shake and then a double-armed hug. "Thanks for coming, Dad."

It took a full fifteen seconds for everything to click into place.

"Gibson . . . Gibson . . . this is your dad?"

Wyatt gave her his fullest smile, and when his dad did the same, the similarity was striking. Both handsome, both tall, both charming . . . wow.

"You must be Melanie."

She didn't know what to say. "I am."

"I've heard a lot about you."

"You have?"

He winked, just like his son often did, and then his gaze moved behind her.

"And you must be Hope."

Melanie turned to see Hope standing in the doorway of her room. The hospital gown she wore went past her knees, her slippered feet stood in place.

"Hope, sweetie, what are you doing out of bed?" Melanie took the few feet that separated them and knelt to her daughter's level.

"I had to pee."

Melanie took her hand. "You were told to ask for help."

Hope kept staring at Mr. Gibson. "Are you really Uncle Wyatt's daddy?"

Mr. Gibson laughed. "I am."

"Did you teach Uncle Wyatt how to climb trees and build things?"

"Climb trees, yes. Build things . . ." he cringed, a fully animated expression Melanie knew was for Hope's benefit. "Mrs. Gibson, Wyatt's mom, hides the hammer from me. It's embarrassing."

Hope gave a full-tooth smile. "It can't be that bad!"

"Yes, it can," Wyatt said behind his father.

Hope shook loose of Melanie's hand and grabbed Wyatt's father's. "I'll show you my room. I have lots of presents."

Melanie watched, slack-jawed, as her daughter took to a complete stranger and disappeared into her room.

"Your dad's an attorney."

"Yeah," Wyatt said as he draped his arm over her shoulders.

"And you called him to help."

"Yep."

Melanie took a step in front of him and reached both arms over his shoulders. "Thank you." She reached for his lips with hers and sighed.

From behind her, Hope's voice was full of sass. "Yeah, they do that a lot!"

William Gibson, otherwise known in the court and judges' world as Wild Bill, was a tornado. There was no other way to describe how he worked. He kept most of his primary questions about Hope and her safety and security. The barely controlled anger of Nathan and his unethical way of pushing his way into Hope's life threatened an already frightened child. At least that's how William worded the papers he filed in order to keep Nathan away until the custody battle could be decided.

Melanie didn't even want to acknowledge the ludicrous request for a divorce. She, Wyatt, and William were sitting in the corner of the hospital cafeteria close to the end of visiting hours. Hope was entertaining Aunt Zoe and Melanie's brother, Mark, who had shown up a few hours before.

"It clearly states he is filing for a divorce."

"How can he do that if we were never married?"

"No trips south of the border . . . too many drinks?" William was half joking.

"No."

"Trips to Vegas . . . fake chapel?"

"No Vegas, chapels, or anything."

William twisted the papers in front of her and pointed. "This date mean anything to you?"

According to the paperwork, Nathan claimed they were married a couple of weeks after Hope was born.

"Sure," she told him. "Diapers, breastfeeding, colicky baby, sleep deprivation. I measured that first year after Hope by the milestones she reached and the hours of sleep I managed every night."

"No wedding?"

"I'm telling you. It never happened. Nathan was pushing a lot those first few months. I didn't feel right about it and told him we needed to wait at least a year. If we could make it that first year, I'd give in."

William sighed. "Yet he told everyone you were married."

"He did. At first I'd correct him, tell people we were engaged at best. But after a while, especially once it was apparent I was having a baby, it was just easier to go along with him. I regret it now."

"Your friends thought you were married."

"I was young, William. I was embarrassed. The lie was easier than the truth. But I promise you . . . I never married Nathan. A girl doesn't forget that."

William patted her hand and winked. "I understand. We'll see what he has to say about the order to stay tomorrow. If he really wants custody, he won't wait to strike back."

"What I don't understand is why. Why now? What does he have to gain by taking Hope away from me? He doesn't want her."

"I have to agree with Mel on this, Dad. The man's about as sincere as a devil offering three wishes."

"He keeps saying things like *I finally found you*, and *now that I found you*. I was never hiding. He always knew where I was, or could have gotten ahold of my friends here if he didn't have my address."

William jotted down a few notes on his legal pad of paper. "He's going to try and say you hid Hope from him. That he couldn't pay you because he didn't know where you were. That's simple to see coming."

She thought as much.

"Why? I keep asking myself *why?*"

William put his pen down and started to tuck the notebook into his briefcase. "I don't know. I have enough to get started on. I'll have my people track down the alleged marriage certificate, if we can prove it fraudulent, or forged, we might be able to negate all of this. I've also got a team working on Nathan Stone the Third, the Second, and the

First. We might find something motivating this whole movement. You need to be patient."

They all stood, and Wyatt shook his father's hand. "Thanks again, Dad."

William sighed, "Yeah, yeah . . . so." He lifted his chin. "You gonna tell me how you managed that shiner?"

Melanie hardly noticed the healing bruise over Wyatt's eye.

Wyatt huffed a laugh. "A fist."

William closed his eyes. "Son!"

"Not Nathan's. It was in the bar."

"Oh, ho, ho . . . it just gets better."

"No one was arrested," Wyatt explained.

William snapped shut his briefcase and grasped the handle. "Well that's a good thing. I don't rescue sons from bar fights."

They were all laughing.

"Thanks again, William." Melanie gave him a brief hug.

He smiled. "Damsels in distress call, I'll come runnin'. We'll talk tomorrow."

"I like your dad," she said as they watched him walk out of the cafeteria.

"He's ruthless in the courtroom."

"Yet he raised such a kind and considerate son."

Wyatt nudged her with his arm. "You haven't met my sister or mother."

Chapter Twenty-One

The day they drove Hope home, Nathan struck back.

"You must be Hope."

Melanie was holding her daughter's hand as she walked up the steps to the inn. Behind her, Wyatt was removing an armful of get well gifts from his truck that Hope had accumulated over the past week.

Miss Gina stood behind the woman who greeted Hope before acknowledging Melanie. She had slicked back brown hair that was pulled into a tight bun and a pinched face that looked anything but inviting. The woman had to be in her sixties, with plenty of wrinkles that would do better with a little Botox.

Melanie hesitated on the top step and glanced at Miss Gina.

With hesitation, Miss Gina introduced the scowl-faced woman. "This is Ms. Pensky with Child Protective Services."

Damn you, Nathan!

"I'm here to assess the living arrangement for your daughter, Mrs. Stone."

Melanie cringed and offered a tight smile. "I go by Ms. Bartlett." Arguing the fact she wasn't a Mrs. and explaining she was still a Miss was useless when Nathan was spewing to the world that she was his wife.

Ms. Pensky attempted to win a staring contest before snapping her gaze to Hope. The forced smile had Hope stepping behind Melanie and gripping her hand tighter. Why CPS would hire a woman who looked like the witch from *The Wizard of Oz* before the green makeup was beyond her.

"I'd like to ask you a few questions, Hope."

Melanie was getting tired of playing nice. "Can we get into the house first?"

Ms. Pensky stepped aside and let them pass.

Wyatt jogged in behind them, eyeing the stranger. "Who is she?" he whispered in Melanie's ear as he walked past her.

"Child Protective Services. Damn Nathan," she gritted out in a voice only he could hear.

"Stall her. I'll call my dad."

Even through her building anger, Wyatt's instant support made her wonder how she'd lived without him.

Wyatt set a bouquet of flowers on the hall table and a bag on the floor before going back outside.

Melanie all but ignored the stranger in the room while she gently helped her daughter out of her sweater. "She looks mean," Hope whispered in her ear.

Amen to that, honey.

"I guess we'll find out, huh?"

"Do I have to talk to her?"

Good question . . . Melanie didn't really know her rights. Chances were, Wild Bill Gibson did and she'd find out soon enough.

"Should we get comfortable in the sitting room?" Ms. Pensky interrupted their private conversation.

Play nice, play nice, play nice.

Her internal chant wasn't working. "It's a long drive from Eugene, Ms. Pensky. Hope needs to use the bathroom."

The woman wasn't convinced.

"Mommy, I—"

"I know, sweetie, let me help you." Melanie didn't let Hope finish her sentence before taking her by the hand to the downstairs bathroom.

"But I don't have to go."

Melanie glanced behind her, saw Ms. Pensky watching them.

"Try, and take your time. So I can talk to the mean-looking lady."

Hope peeked around and then shrank into the small room and shut the door.

Melanie pulled in a deep breath and squared her shoulders. *Play nice, play nice . . .*

Ms. Pensky met her in the doorway to the sitting room; Miss Gina glaring at her side. "I really don't have that many questions, Ms. Bartlett."

"Yeah, well, it's been a very long week, and putting my daughter through anything more is asking too much."

"As a public servant, I'm obligated to investigate every report."

"And who requested you to question my daughter?"

Ms. Pensky did that staring thing again. "I can't reveal that information."

"Yeah, I'm sure you can't."

Ms. Pensky lifted her nose to the air and sniffed. "Who smokes?"

Miss Gina sat forward. "I do on occasion. Outside, away from Hope."

Oz Lady didn't change her stare.

The sound of the toilet flushing down the hall brought their attention to the door as Hope left the bathroom.

"Ladies?" Ms. Pensky spread an arm wide to encourage them to sit.

Hope was practically crawling into Melanie's lap when Wyatt hustled into the room.

He wore a wicked grin as he strode past Oz Lady and stood in front of her. "Hello, Miss . . .?"

Her thin smile stayed firmly in place.

"Pensky."

Wyatt held out his hand, palm up. "Can I see your paperwork?"

"Excuse me?"

"From the court?" Wyatt waited, did the staring thing with the woman, before she broke.

"I don't have a court order. This is a preliminary investigation."

Wyatt dropped his hand. "As you can see, Hope is in no grave danger at this moment, and without a court order, no one is obligated to answer any of your questions."

Ms. Pensky's jaw tightened. She obviously didn't appreciate being denied an audience.

"The child has a broken arm and bruises all over her face."

"From a highly publicized fall." Wyatt's smile slid. "Now, if you don't mind." It was his turn to spread his arm wide and indicate she should leave the room.

Miss Gina huffed as she walked in front of the woman and opened the front door.

Ms. Pensky glared over her shoulder. "I'll be back."

"You do that."

As she left, Melanie let her shoulders fall.

"So I don't have to talk to her?" Hope asked.

"Not today."

"Good." She popped off Melanie's lap and started to leave.

"Where are you going?"

Hope shrugged. "I have to pee now."

Wyatt and Miss Gina entered the room as Hope left.

"What kind of crap is he trying to pull?" Melanie asked the question running in her head.

Wyatt pulled her into his arms and held her. "Whatever he can."

"She's coming back, isn't she?"

"Yeah, probably."

Melanie rested her head against Wyatt's shoulder and closed her eyes.

Melanie was napping alongside Hope after a much-deserved shower and hot meal. Miss Gina was researching what CPS looked for in order to find a home unsafe for a child, and Wyatt was on the back porch, talking to Luke on the phone.

"Who is the pinched-faced woman going around town asking about you and Mel?"

Wyatt explained the situation. "Where did she go?"

"Sam's. Then I heard she was at R&B's asking a thousand questions."

"This ex of Melanie's is a real piece of work," Wyatt said.

"From all the stories we heard, none of us understood what she saw in him. You're sure he's the one who called Child Protective Services?"

"Is there any other suspect?"

"I guess you're right."

"Any more word from Jo about Mr. Lewis?"

"I haven't seen Jo in two days. Zoe told me she's done nothing but beat herself up for letting Mr. Lewis leave."

"She couldn't have known. None of us suspected a thing." It ate Wyatt up that he'd smiled at the man and shaken his hand when he expressed his concern for Hope's welfare.

"How is our little patient?"

Wyatt felt a smile on his face. "She's a trouper. Keeping her down might prove difficult."

"Hard to climb trees with a broken arm," Luke said with a laugh.

"Doesn't mean she won't try."

"Well, she's getting a hero's welcome tomorrow afternoon. Zoe is coordinating a huge barbeque. Her way of thanking all the volunteers who stepped up."

The effort had been huge. "You know, Luke . . . we live in a great town."

"Yeah . . . we do. Well, bud, if you need something, I'm a phone call away."

"Thanks."

He no sooner hung up the phone when it rang.

"Hey, Wyatt."

It was Josie.

"What's up?"

"Just wondering who this uptight bitch is asking questions about you and Mel."

River Bend needed a small newspaper, then he could just put out word on the front page and eliminate the calls.

Her head was splitting and her neck was so stiff that looking in the rearview mirror took effort. Sleep was something for the weak, and Jo wasn't giving in.

The FBI had taken over the investigation, but that didn't mean she couldn't dig into the criminal mind of a sleazebag who lured a child into the woods and pushed her off a cliff. Because the case was personal to her, Agent Burton did a fair job of keeping Jo informed of their progress.

Not that they'd gotten very far.

A sketch artist had drawn a picture based on the collective recall of everyone who'd seen Mr. Lewis. The image had been aired all over national television without any real hits. "It's easy to change your appearance," Agent Burton had told her. She'd gone on and shown Jo just how easy it would be to make their so-called Mr. Lewis into a balding thug with fake tattoos on his face and neck that would distract most people from really looking into his eyes to see the color. Mr. Lewis might have worn a wig once he left River Bend, donned a pair of shorts, and jumped on a party bus to Vegas. The possibilities were truly endless.

Between Jo and the FBI, they'd sat through countless hours of airport security cameras out of Eugene and come up empty-handed. The man either disguised himself as a woman, which wouldn't have been all that easy with the body scans and pat downs, or he didn't bother with the airport at all.

The rental car company had been given the same information that Miss Gina had received when booking Mr. Lewis's room. The car had been returned at the airport rental location, and by the time they'd tracked it down, it had already been released to another customer.

The room he'd used at the inn had a forensics team dissecting it for the better part of twelve hours. It was apparent that some surfaces had been wiped down before Mr. Lewis left the inn. Because he'd taken time to do that simple task, Agent Burton and Jo were convinced he'd had a prior that put him in the database. They both agreed that Mr. Lewis had used the back stairs from the kitchen up into his room unnoticed, and the front stairs when he faked concern for Hope's disappearance. An unusual amount of dirt was found on the back staircase, laying evidence to their claim, along with a couple of prints that partially matched those in his room. They just needed a break from the many prints they'd lifted to get the man's real name.

So far, the only print that lifted clean and had a match was Zane's. And it had come from the kitchen, where he'd been in and out the night of Zoe's going-away party.

Jo was clicking through mug shot after mug shot when she was told she had a visitor waiting to speak to her.

Instead of inviting them into her office, Jo left her desk and came to the front of the station.

Her clerk offered the briefest of introductions. "Sheriff, this is Ms. Pensky."

Jo's first thought was *Doesn't that hairstyle hurt?* From the pinched face, she imagined it did.

"How can I be of assistance, Ms. Pensky?"

The woman tapped a card she had been holding and handed it over. "I'm with Child Protective Services, investigating a case I believe you're familiar with."

Jo glanced at the card briefly and hid all the emotion from her face. Much as she'd love to tell the woman to leave, she didn't think that would bode well for Mel and Hope. "Perhaps we should talk in my office."

Ms. Pensky followed her inside and sat on the very edge of the seat.

"I don't think this will take long," Ms. Pensky told her.

The woman stared at her for a long minute before continuing. "I'm investigating the welfare and living conditions of Hope Bartlett."

One of the things Jo had learned in the academy, and from her father, was the art of silence when she truly wanted information. "Oh?"

"A complaint came through our office stating that she's in physical danger in her current living situation."

Oh, Nathan . . . when I get my hands on you.

"That's absurd."

Ms. Pensky had a flatline smile. "How can you say that? Aren't you searching for a recent guest of the inn in which Hope lives?"

"I am. So is the FBI."

"Didn't the man walk in, ask for a room, sleep under the same roof as Hope Bartlett, yet no one knows who he is?"

Jo felt herself being led down a rabbit hole. It was time to hide behind the law.

"The details of the investigation are not for public knowledge."

Ms. Pensky did that staring thing.

Jo matched her.

"Are you not personal friends with Melanie Bartlett?"

"I am."

"Has Hope ever slept in your home, Sheriff?"

"Why do you ask?"

Ms. Pensky let her eyes sweep up and down Jo's frame. "Do you leave your weapons at the station when you go home, Sheriff?"

Jo's back teeth started to hurt for all the grinding she was putting them through. "You're wasting your time, Ms. Pensky." She stood and indicated that Ms. Pensky do the same.

"One more thing, Sheriff. Did you recently respond to a disturbance call at R&B's?"

Jo pulled a slow breath, replied with a hiss she wished she could control. "Yes."

"And did you not bring into your station Wyatt Gibson, Ms. Bartlett's current lover? The man she was with the night before Hope's disappearance?"

"Mr. Gibson wasn't charged with anything."

"But he was involved in a bar fight, was he not? Indicating a propensity for violence. Something the office of Child Protective Services is very interested in since he is in close contact with that *poor* child."

"Wyatt Gibson is a well respected and law-abiding citizen of River Bend, Ms. Pensky. You won't find one person in this town who will disagree with me."

Ms. Pensky stood and cracked the line of her lips with a sneer. "I do believe you might be a little too close to the victim's mother to be objective, Sheriff."

"It's a small town, Ms. Pensky. I've known most of the residents all of my life. Safe to say I'm close to all of them. That doesn't stop me from doing my job."

"I'm sure you're right." She dripped with insincerity.

Jo followed her out.

Her clerk offered a smile and instantly dropped it when she noticed Jo's pained expression.

They'd just about made it out the door when Ms. Pensky fired her last shot. "Oh, Sheriff, one more thing."

"What might that be?"

"Isn't the suspect who put poor Hope Bartlett in the hospital still on the loose?"

"We haven't apprehended him yet."

"I was told that Hope was found on the side of a cliff, *left to die*, I believe those were the words from many of the volunteers that were present the day she was found."

Jo found herself rubbing her thumb and index finger on her right hand. "Do you have a point?"

"How safe is the only surviving witness to a crime?"

"Every precaution is being made to ensure Hope is safe. No one wants that more than the residents, family, and friends of this town."

"Good. Good. My only concern is Hope's welfare."

As much as Jo wanted to see the last of the woman, she went ahead and stopped her from leaving with a question of her own.

"Oh, Ms. Pensky?"

The woman showed surprise when Jo called her back.

"Yes?"

"How well do you know Nathan Stone?"

Ms. Pensky lifted her chin, didn't smile, and stared.

"Who?"

Gotcha! The woman could interrogate, but she was shit for lying.

"Have a nice day, Ms. Pensky."

"You do the same, Sheriff."

Chapter Twenty-Two

The street between Sam's diner and Miller's Auto was blocked off to traffic. Miss Gina's special lemonade bridge club started setting up tables by ten. Backyard barbeques were lined up on the street outside of the only market in town. A staple of any small town festivity was the American flag, several of which the volunteer fire department pulled out and flew on every streetlight in town.

River Bend was too small for a mayoral office, but there was a chamber of commerce . . . or a half a dozen busybodies who helped legislate some of the simple squabbles the town would come across.

"I didn't know you owned a pair of jeans, Dad." Wyatt gave his father crap as they lugged bags of ice from the market to fill the buckets lining the beverage station.

"Do you own a suit?"

Wyatt thought of the tie holding the PVC pipes together on his truck. "Define *suit.*"

His father laughed as he dropped the ice into one of the waiting buckets and went back for more.

"So, all this for one little girl."

"Yeah," Wyatt said with a sigh. "Great, isn't it?"

His father patted him on the back. "You really have something special here."

"I love it. I really do."

"I can see why."

Sam walked out of the market as Wyatt and his dad were going back in for more ice.

"Hi, Sam . . . have you met my father yet?"

Sam offered a handshake. "No, but I've heard plenty about you."

After his father exchanged pleasantries, Sam glanced back over to his diner with a scowl.

"What's up? You don't look too happy."

"Zoe's on a terror in there. She needs fresh basil and I don't have it."

"None here?"

Sam shook his head. "I bought them out last night, but she needs more."

Wyatt scratched his head. "Check with Mrs. Miller, she has an herb garden, and if that doesn't work, call Mrs. Kate."

Sam's eyes lit up. "Your son is brilliant," he told William before running across the street.

"All for a little girl," he heard his father utter again.

"She became everyone's little girl when she went missing. This day could have been very different." He shuddered to think about what could have happened had they not found Hope when they did. "This celebration is for the town. A pat on the back for watching out for each other. You don't get this in the big city."

"You don't get it in every small town either."

"Then you're living in the wrong town."

"Not a lot of need for a high-powered lawyer in a place like this."

Wyatt had to laugh. "There is this week."

His father conceded with a nod. When his smile grew bigger and his eyes traveled to a space behind him, Wyatt turned.

Melanie walked up the middle of the street with Hope's hand in hers. The two had the same smile, the same hair pulled back in a clip.

And Wyatt's heart warmed.

The woman had wiggled inside him and taken up space he didn't know he had available.

"If it isn't the special guest of this shindig," William said as they approached.

Hope lifted her arms to his dad, who hoisted her up as if she were four.

The movement had Melanie gaping and Wyatt doing a double take.

Hope kissed his father's cheek and giggled. "Did you see the balloons?"

"No, where are they?"

"Over by Uncle Luke's." Hope pointed with the arm she had slung over his father's shoulder.

"Wanna show me?"

"Okay." Hope jumped down from his dad's arms and pulled on his hand.

William winked at Melanie. "We'll be back."

Melanie stood with her mouth open as her daughter ran off with Wyatt's dad.

"What is that all about?"

She shook her head. "I don't know. She's infatuated. I've never seen her like this."

Wyatt took in Melanie's profile. There was still a measure of tired behind her eyes, but she looked as if she'd managed a few hours of sleep.

She must have felt his eyes on hers. When she twisted in his direction, she grinned and ran a hand down the back of her hair.

He smiled.

"Hey."

"Hey." He stepped into her personal space and pressed his body next to hers. "Getting some sleep?" he asked in a gentle voice.

"A little."

"Anything I can do?"

She glanced over her shoulder at her daughter. "Nothing you're not already doing."

When she twisted back his way, he closed the space between them and kissed her. Like every time, his body responded with a desire for more, not that this was the time, or the place.

She pressed a bit closer, and he suffered a groan.

Melanie broke their kiss and smiled. "Happy to see me?" she asked with a knowing smirk.

"Miss you," he told her.

She lowered her eyes. "Now's not the time."

He placed a finger under her chin and forced her eyes to his. "Just holding you is enough . . . right now," he added.

Wyatt wrapped an arm over her shoulders and walked her in the opposite direction from Hope and his father.

When Melanie looked behind them, he stopped. "She's safe with my dad."

"I know. It's just . . ."

"It's hard."

"It's impossible. I worry in my sleep."

Wyatt kept walking and let her talk.

"I wake up in the middle of the night dreaming that we didn't find her. I see her cold and broken on the side of the cliff."

He held her closer.

"I see Mr. Lewis coming back and checking in at the hotel and none of us being the wiser to what he is up to."

"I don't think he's coming back," he told her.

She snuggled closer. "I still worry. Then there is Nathan and that pinched-face Oz woman."

Wyatt stopped in the middle of the street and laughed. "Oz woman?"

"Yeah, didn't Pensky look like the witch from *The Wizard of Oz*?"

Now that she mentioned it . . .

"I see her taking Hope away and Nathan laughing."

"Oh, darlin'. Stop doing this to yourself."

She shook her head. "I'm not. It's my dreams. I feel so damn helpless. Like I'm not in control of anything right now. Like someone is going to reach in at any moment and take everything away."

"You know what you need?"

She laughed. "For Nathan to jump off a bridge, or relocate to Alaska where he can't get to Hope?"

"All good ideas. No, what you need is to remember the power you do have." They were already walking back around the block and on the opposite side of the street. "You need to take control and do something other than react."

Her laugh wasn't convinced. "Like what?"

"I don't know . . . sue Nathan for child support. Use the media that has been wanting to talk to you since all this happened to fight against Oz Lady and all those like her. Take control. It might not stop everything Nathan is doing, but it will make you feel better."

Her feet met the street and didn't move. "I can do that." It wasn't a question.

"You can."

"Stop being a victim," she said with a sigh.

The smile on her face said it all.

"You're brilliant."

He chuckled. "Second time today I've been told that."

"Humble, too."

He accepted her kiss, mourned it when she broke it off and disappeared inside Sam's diner.

In the middle of the main street in River Bend, Wyatt realized how hard he'd fallen.

And he smiled.

~

Melanie sat beside Wyatt's father, sinking her teeth into some of the best barbeque ribs she'd ever eaten and feeling as if the food was gas in a car that had been sitting in the front yard for twenty dry years.

She'd eaten enough to survive in the past week, but not enough to fuel her brain.

With Wyatt's infusion of confidence and watching the town come together to celebrate her child . . . she was ready to fight.

"I'm angry, William. The man refused to give me a dime, said he was barely living off the funds his parents gave him for college. When I suggested he get a job like me, he couldn't be bothered to tap into the hours set aside for his social life. We had a child. A social life takes a backseat to that."

William stopped chewing on his corn on the cob to respond. "That it does."

"Now he's back and for what reason? And even if we don't learn what's behind all this, what makes him think he's parent material? And you know . . ." she pointed the end of the rib bone at William, "that social worker has to be in his pocket. Hope was being cared for by a respected, sane, responsible adult when she . . ." The thought of Hope on the side of the cliff made her pause. "She wasn't neglected. *Isn't* neglected."

"Hope is a polite, well-adjusted young woman. It's clear you're doing a fine job raising her," William said.

"She is . . . isn't she?" They both looked into the middle of the street. Hope played alongside a handful of other kids her age. All kids she would have eventually met when she started school in the fall. She was smiling and laughing, despite the broken arm and the events of the week.

"I may not be able to provide her with all the toys and all the junk a lot of kids have. But she has what she needs. I've sacrificed my own crap so she could have enough." Melanie lifted a hand in the air. "I'm not trying to toot my own horn. I just do what every other parent out there does. Except Nathan. He never sacrificed squat. So yeah . . ." she paused, set the bone on the plate. "I'm pissed he even showed up. It isn't like he handed me a check, or God forbid, health insurance." The thought of the bills that were coming her way hadn't even hit her yet. The hospital social workers had set her up with a contact to help tap into some funding for the needy to help minimize the debt. Bottom line, she didn't have the money for gas for her car when she had one, and health insurance wasn't a priority when she could stand in line at a clinic. Yeah, it sucked, but she didn't have many options.

It was William's turn to point food at her. "You know the good thing about anger?"

"No, what?" She bit into another rib.

"It's the perfect motivator. Not happy with the current president? It motivates you to go out and vote for the next. Gas prices too high? Buy an electric car, hug a tree, put in solar. Tired of bullies? Learn to fight, take control, don't allow yourself to be a victim."

Melanie looked into the eyes of the man and saw his son. "Did Wyatt tell you to say that?"

William offered a look of shock. "Remember who raised whom, darlin'."

She giggled. "He calls me that."

"Calls you what?"

"Darlin'. Always makes me think he was raised in Texas and not California."

William glanced toward the cloudless sky. "Guilty. Born and raised outside of Houston. I'd like to think some of me chipped off the block."

She couldn't help but laugh and search the block chip out of the crowd. She caught him across the street, standing beside Luke and a man who looked familiar but she couldn't place.

Wyatt offered a wave and she smiled back, waving her rib.

Well, what was left of it.

She returned her gaze to William, then snapped back to Wyatt and narrowed her eyes. "Is that . . . Alan Crane?"

William glanced around, saw his son, and shrugged. "Looks like it."

Melanie tilted her head. "You knew he was coming?"

He finished off his corn and wiped his mouth with the red and white checkered napkin before placing it on the table. "I might have had my people contact his people."

"But my daughter's not missing." And Alan Crane was the face of missing children. After the murder of his young daughter many years ago, Alan's life revolved around finding missing children and the perpetrators who harmed them. He was the media face of the forgotten.

"Mr. Lewis is," William said.

She stared at Wyatt's father without humor. "But Wyatt asked you to help with Nathan."

He laid his hand over hers. "No. He asked that I help with you. And Melanie . . . my son has never asked a thing of me since before he was in college. Even then . . ."

Tears were close, but she pushed them back. "I'll pay you back someday."

Hope took that moment to climb up into the chair she had beside them. She shoved food in her face and smiled at them both before scrambling off.

"You already have."

Zoe snuck up behind her and slid into a chair. "Well, do I pass the test?" Zoe asked the question to William.

"Just like back home." He waved a rib before taking a bite.

Melanie questioned her friend with a lifted brow. "You knew he was from Texas?"

"Oh, please. The minute the man opened his mouth I knew where Wyatt got all that swagger and charm."

"I may not have the accent I once did, but I'd have to turn in my born and raised card if I'd lost my swagger."

They were both laughing at the twang William put behind his words.

"I guess the name 'Wild Bill' makes a little more sense," Melanie said.

"When do you fly out?" William asked.

Zoe sighed. "Tomorrow early."

Melanie leaned her head on her friend's shoulder. "It means so much that you came."

Zoe offered a one-arm hug. "Always, anytime."

And before Melanie let her friend go, she told her, "And tell Luke your plans. The guy goes a little nutty when you leave."

With a heavy sigh, she said, "He knew I was leaving the last time."

"Two words . . . Bar. Fight."

"Fine!" Zoe pushed herself off the seat and searched the crowd. Once she caught sight of Luke, she darted across the street.

"Your friend is a fine chef."

"Yeah . . . and you've only tasted her barbeque. She makes things I can't even pronounce."

"And lives in Dallas?"

"Yep. Left town shortly after we all graduated from high school." When she left again, Melanie would miss her all the more. Seeing Zoe's face around town made it feel more like home.

"I'll have to find out where she works when I go again. I wouldn't mind sampling her other menus."

Melanie stood and grabbed her plate. "You won't be disappointed. Can I grab you anything while I'm up?"

"No, no . . . I'm good. Why don't you go enjoy your town?"

Such a thoughtful man. "Wyatt's lucky to have a dad like you," she told him.

William smiled and cocked his head to the side. "Where are your parents, darlin'?"

The thought had crossed her mind a dozen times once she realized Hope was going to be okay. "My mom called, her boyfriend took her on a cruise . . ." Melanie was too embarrassed to tell him that her mom didn't offer to jump off at the nearest port to join her. When she'd called and heard Hope was going to be okay . . . she suggested Melanie call her if things changed. "My dad didn't get word from my brother, Mark, until night before last."

"And is he going to visit?"

She paused. "Not all family is helpful, William."

She heard Zoe laughing from across the street and turned to see her talking with Wyatt, Luke, and Alan Crane.

"It's a good thing you have such a tight circle of friends."

"Yeah . . . a very good thing."

Chapter Twenty-Three

They'd been filming all day.

Crane and the crew showed up at the inn before dawn with two huge trucks and a crew of no less than twenty-five people. There were shots taken as the morning fog lifted from the ground, and they filmed the sunrise from the vantage point of where Hope had been standing the last time Miss Gina saw her.

A small company of actors resembling Miss Gina, Melanie, and Hope were brought in, as well as a man who had the same body type and general look of Mr. Lewis.

The fake Mr. Lewis went through the motions of being checked into the inn by the fake Miss Gina for close to two hours before they got it right. Melanie stood to the side and watched as her double told the Hope's double to stop running through the inn. It took four takes before getting it right, and each one was a tiny knife in her side.

In the dining room, Mr. Crane had set up the interview room for the real players in the *American Fugitive* program.

Watching Miss Gina fidget under the hand of the makeup artist was almost comical. Eventually she settled down to recall, for the camera, as many details as she could about Mr. Lewis.

Mr. Crane was a gracious host who asked questions with real concern for the answers. He didn't ask her to repeat anything in any way other than how she felt. "What went through your mind when you realized a guest in your inn was the one responsible for Hope's disappearance?"

Her eyes glossed over and a blank stare went beyond Mr. Crane and to the wall behind him. "I'd rather not implicate myself on national television," she said, deadpan.

Mr. Crane laughed . . . a knowing sound you knew he'd felt to his bone. "It's time to get this scumbag off the street," he said as he covered Miss Gina's hand with his.

Someone yelled *cut* and everyone moved except Miss Gina and Mr. Crane.

Melanie didn't hear what they said after that since the noise in the room elevated by fifty percent. But whatever it was, it ended in a hug that lingered before Miss Gina turned and left the room.

Wyatt stepped in through the same door Miss Gina exited, found Melanie with his eyes, and walked her way. "How's Hope doing?"

"A little clingy, but liking the attention I think. Between the town picnic and this . . . she's been the center of attention for some time."

"It's going to get really boring when all this settles," Wyatt said.

"I could go for boring right about now." Sleep still wasn't happening without hours of tossing and turning. It only took a couple of days for Hope to kick her out of her room. And since Miss Gina all but refused anyone at the inn until they could figure out a way to stop what happened to Hope from ever happening again, with the exception of

Mr. Crane and his assistant, the place was empty. Even William stayed with Wyatt at his house.

"Are you ready, Miss Bartlett?"

It was her turn for the minute or two clip that would go on the actual footage of the show. She didn't think about the audience that would watch . . . she thought about the man needing to be caught.

"You look beautiful," Wyatt said, pulling her out of her thoughts.

She smiled and he brushed a strand of hair off her cheek.

The man had hardly left her side. Somehow she and Hope had become a priority for him, and they'd known each other for such a short time. She cautioned herself, worried that maybe he was acting out of obligation since they'd hooked up while all the crazy unfolded around them. Then a voice inside her head slapped her around. Nathan, even on his best day, never acted the way Wyatt did around her. He never put her above himself.

More, she'd never felt about Nathan the way she did about Wyatt.

She shook the comparison from her head and leaned into Wyatt's hand before he released her.

Wyatt winked and gave a gentle push toward the waiting chair and crew.

Sitting under the lights was a little intimidating at first.

A makeup woman stepped in and took ownership of Melanie's face. All the while she chatted about absolutely nothing. The weather, the state of Oregon. The color of the walls.

At one point Mr. Crane sat opposite Melanie while the crew scampered around them, adjusting the light and attaching a small microphone to her shirt. At some point one of the crew started lifting said shirt to tuck the wires out of the way. Melanie ignored the uncomfortable moment and tried to smile when he was finished.

Mr. Crane waved off the makeup lady after a few seconds and started to talk. "Like I told you earlier, Melanie, I just want you to answer everything as naturally as possible. Pretend the cameras aren't here."

There were three of them pointed at her, and one at him. "That's a little hard to do."

"I know . . . but try. Just look at me. Ignore the camera behind my head."

"I'll try."

Someone fiddled with his hair. "You grew up here."

It wasn't really a question. And she knew he already knew she had. But she started talking her nerves off anyway.

"I did. Just a few miles from here."

"Did you spend a lot of time with Miss Gina?"

Melanie smiled. "She was like the aunt none of us girls had. The cool aunt. The kind you could really talk to and not get into trouble with."

Someone pushed a glass of water in front of her and moved away as Mr. Crane made conversation.

"An adult you could turn to . . ." Again, it wasn't a question, and Melanie just kept going.

"She was. I didn't have any real issues growing up. But if we had a boyfriend problem, or a teenage 'everyone hates me' problem, this was where we could come to find some advice."

Mr. Crane accepted his glass of water and set it aside. "Safe to say you always felt safe here."

"Oh, God yes. It was the first place I thought of when I decided to return."

"Why did you leave in the first place?"

"Typical reason. College."

"Why did you come back to River Bend?"

The cameras started to fade as Mr. Crane asked his questions. "It started out as a promise. One I made to my best friends our senior year. We'd all return to our class reunion regardless of what was happening in our lives. I wasn't sure I wanted to at first. My life hadn't really turned out the way I thought it would."

"How so?"

The room had gone silent as people started listening to their conversation.

"College ended up being a bust. Funds dried up. I met a guy." The thought of Nathan put a frown on her face.

"And had your daughter."

She smiled. "Hope was my blessing. Things with the guy didn't work out, but Hope was there."

"It must have been hard. Single mom. No college degree."

"And a crappy car," she added. "We can't forget that."

Mr. Crane smiled.

"So you return to River Bend in a crappy car with your daughter."

"With Hope. The crappy car died en route."

His smile turned into a slight laugh. "So no car, your lovely child . . . and Miss Gina's beautiful inn."

"And my friends. Friends I knew were there, but I had forgotten meant so much. True friends, the kind that will drop everything to help when you need them. You know what I mean?"

Mr. Crane had a quick moment of sorrow . . . or maybe it was memory that flashed over his face. "You returned *home*."

Melanie glanced around the dining room. "Yeah."

"A better life for your daughter."

She nodded. "I couldn't let Hope walk to school where I was living before. The crime rate in River Bend is nothing compared to the big city. Every town has issues, but this small town's big news is when a house is littered with toilet paper."

That had Mr. Crane laughing.

"You think I'm kidding."

"No, I think you're telling the truth." He controlled his mirth and continued. "When did you first meet Patrick Lewis?"

Her laughter died instantly. "A couple of weeks ago. He was traveling through on business. At least, that's what he told us."

"By now you're working at the inn, is that right?"

"Yeah. Hope and I share a room when the inn is full, or I take one across the hall when we're slow."

"So Patrick Lewis was a guest. Did you ever feel anything was off about him?"

She bit her lip, tried to think of something . . . anything. "No. It kills me that I didn't catch something about him."

"Just a businessman traveling through town."

"Yeah. Left his room clean. Almost like he didn't use it. Drank his coffee black." A detail she was just now remembering. Another scratched at the surface of her memory that she attempted to remember. "Yolks. He didn't like egg yolks. Asked that we scramble whites for him. I'd forgotten that."

"So a tidy man who drank his coffee black and ate egg whites."

"Yeah, then he'd pack his stuff and say he'd probably stop back down when he was on his way through again."

"There aren't a lot of places to stay in River Bend."

Melanie shook her head. "A place north of town. But more of a motel kind of establishment."

"Let's talk about the visit preceding your daughter's incident."

"He was on his way through. His face felt familiar. He even reminded Hope not to run in the house. Not in a weird way, just an adult being an adult."

"Nothing abnormal?"

"Nope. Nothing."

"That all changed when you returned home one morning, after leaving your child in the trusted hands of Miss Gina, and found your daughter missing."

She paused. The room was silent.

"Everything died in the moment I realized Hope wasn't out playing."

"So when Patrick Lewis left the inn, you didn't think it was strange?"

Melanie shook her head. "I didn't think about it at all. He was just a guest at the inn. He ran outside when he heard me screaming Hope's name. At least that's what Jo told me."

"Jo would be Sheriff Ward?"

"Right."

"But Patrick Lewis wasn't simply a guest at the inn, was he?"

Melanie shook her head. "No. He lured my daughter out into the woods, telling her he was rescuing a puppy." She stopped and stared at Mr. Crane. "A puppy."

Mr. Crane leaned forward and placed a hand over hers. "Then what happened, Melanie?"

"We searched for hours. Jo . . . I mean Sheriff Ward called in K-9 units and they sniffed Hope out. We found her on the side of the cliff. Another foot and she could have . . ."

"Yet Patrick Lewis denied any involvement."

"He said he saw her that morning for breakfast, and that was it."

"He lied."

Melanie moved her stare into Mr. Crane's. "He left my daughter on the side of a cliff to die. Her body temperature was so low she wouldn't have made it the night."

"There wasn't a puppy, was there?"

"There isn't even a Patrick Lewis. The man lied about his name, gave us a fake ID, fake credit card. I don't know exactly what kind of sicko he is, but this didn't happen at random. He set us up for this."

"Why?"

"I don't know."

"One more thing, Melanie. What would you say to Patrick Lewis if you had a chance?"

Her nose flared and her temples beat with the pace of her rapid heart. The image of him calling Hope across the street as she recalled it surfaced in Melanie's head. "I used to think that only murderers were capable of murder. That only heroes were capable of walking through fire . . . then I became a mother. I would walk into a burning house to save my child. Walk over broken glass in bare feet to keep my child from one single cut." Melanie narrowed her gaze. "I don't think I would have much to *say* to Mr. Lewis."

Mr. Crane paused and someone yelled *cut*.

～

"My fee just tripled."

"Relax. I have everything under control."

The voice on the other end of the line attempted to respond with ease. But he'd been around much longer than the man paying the bills and saw through it.

He released a slow, mechanical laugh, one that would intimidate a saint. "Control? You don't know what control is."

"You weren't supposed to throw her down a cliff."

"You didn't tell me who she was."

"I paid you to check in, check out."

Liar! The man knew his priors, knew his propensity for the company of little girls. The part about being a smart criminal . . . is the intelligence part. The man paying the bills might have the money to pay him, but he had the intelligence of an ex-con on skid row. "Have you ever played chess?"

"What the hell are you asking?"

"Chess . . . you know, the king, the queen . . . all those pesky minions?"

"I know the fucking game, what's your point?"

He paused, thought of the moment his hand touched Hope's shoulder. Thought of the moment he didn't give in to his need. "Your minion put you in check. Her trip down the bloody hill put you in check. My fee triples daily until I see it."

"I need time to think."

"You might consider doing that promptly."

"Fuck you."

He wasn't fazed. "No, thank you . . . I prefer . . . well, you know what I prefer."

"You're sick."

"Recovering, actually. I'm starting to think picking on someone my size is a more respectable occupation. Triple, mate. You have my account information."

"You son of a bit—"

He didn't give the man time to finish before hanging up.

Jo called an emergency meeting the day after *American Fugitive* aired. They met at the inn, to avoid anyone strange being around Hope. Melanie had tucked Hope into her room with her TV and a DVD of a cartoon.

"The phone is ringing off the hook." Even though the number on the program suggested people call the Feds, many of them went straight for River Bend, and Jo had been inundated with tips and threats. "I was told to expect it, but this is out of control."

"Anything worth pursuing?" Melanie couldn't help but think they'd find out something within a few days of the airing of the television show.

"There isn't one lead we're not following up on." Jo had let the ass go one time too many. She wasn't about to let him slip through her fingers again.

"So why did you call us all together?" Luke asked.

Luke and his father, Wyatt, Melanie, and Miss Gina all sat around the sitting room in rapt attention. "I'm going to be busy with Agent Burton for however long it takes to exhaust this search. I have Emery running patrols."

"You're going to have to sleep sometime, Jo," Melanie told her.

"I can sleep when I'm dead." Jo leaned forward with her elbows on her knees. "I brought you together because I need your help."

"What kind of help?"

Jo stared at Melanie for a moment, then tilted her head. A pit formed in the bottom of Melanie's stomach. "I'm not going to like this, am I?"

Jo offered one curt shake of her head. "A handful of threats, Mel."

Wyatt tensed beside her.

"I think they're all a bunch of crap. I really do, but we have to take them seriously."

"What kind of threats?" Miss Gina asked.

Jo pinched her lips together, and when she opened them, Melanie knew she didn't tell the entire truth. "Someone called, said he was Mr. Lewis, and he was coming back to fix things."

"Fix things?" Mr. Miller asked.

"Finish things . . ." Jo corrected herself.

"A woman called, said her son was Mr. Lewis, and none of us know what really happened. That she wouldn't see her son in jail again."

"Sounds like a statement, not a threat." Wyatt reached over and held Melanie's hand as he spoke.

"What she said next was definitely a threat."

Melanie released a long breath. "And what was that, Jo?"

She shook her head, nudged closer to the edge of her seat. "Doesn't matter. You just need to know there have been a few of these types of calls and I want to take some precautions."

"And that's where we come in?" Luke asked.

"Yeah. I need an extra set of hands here at the inn. Not that I think Melanie and Miss Gina can't handle themselves, but more help if something does go down is better."

Melanie wasn't so far up her ass, thinking *I'm a woman, I can do fine without a man,* that she didn't see the wisdom in what Jo suggested. "A deterrent, if nothing else," she said under her breath.

"Exactly. I was hoping between the three of you, you can work out a schedule."

"I can put my side jobs on hold," Wyatt said.

Melanie squeezed his hand. "You'll have to work eventually."

"She's right, bud. I can bring some of my work here, so long as Miss Gina doesn't mind a little oil in the gravel."

Miss Gina pointed a finger at Luke. "Long as you clean it up."

"Might not be a bad idea to park the tow truck in the drive. Make people believe you have a full house," Mr. Miller added.

"Perfect. Another thing, Mel . . . I need you and Hope to have company when you're driving into town."

"You're really worried," Mel said.

"No, I'm being safe."

"So Wyatt and I will tag team it during the day, Dad, you can keep the shop going, and if I need you to bring me parts . . ."

"I'll bring you parts." Mr. Miller winked.

"And I'll set up in one of your rooms," Wyatt rounded out the plan.

Melanie offered a sly smile and Jo chuckled.

"However you guys make it work," Jo said.

"Works for me," Miss Gina said. "When will those cameras come in, Wyatt?"

"Any day."

"What cameras?" Jo asked.

"Security cameras and a security system." The idea had been Miss Gina's, and no one argued the need. The entire place needed to be wired, but Wyatt said he could do it.

"Perfect." Jo then turned her questions to Wyatt. "How are things going with the custody case?"

"The social worker wasn't willing to file for an immediate removal of Hope, knew the grounds wouldn't hold up . . . but she didn't close the case either. My dad has met with Nathan's lawyers and he is coming back this weekend to go over what's next."

Melanie couldn't believe there was any *what's next*.

"Do we have any idea of what we might expect?" Jo asked.

"I might have to show up in court in LA sooner than later. With Nathan's connections and all the press, he's pushing for Hope to return to California. Even claiming I left the state without his knowledge. Like he somehow cared where we were." When William had called to tell her that Nathan was pulling every conceivable ploy to force a preliminary hearing in front of a judge, and refused to meet and settle anything in a boardroom, Melanie knew he was doing something underhanded. One of the things William had said was that she was not going to bring Hope back into the state of California without a court order. Right now Wyatt's father was in Southern California playing endless rounds of golf with friends and colleagues of Nathan's father. When he broke for the afternoon, he spent his time doing some "good old-fashioned elbow rubbing" with some of the Stone clients.

Melanie wasn't sure how any of that was going to assist her in keeping a hundred percent custody of her daughter, but Wild Bill Gibson had the reputation of winning his cases, so she didn't question him directly.

The radio on Jo's shoulder squawked and captured everyone's attention.

"Sheriff?"

Jo lifted the mic and squeezed. "I'm here."

"Josie just called, requested you stop on by."

Melanie did a quick head count. Nope, no one she was close to was in a bar fight tonight.

"Is there a disturbance?"

"No. She just asked if you could come by real quick like, maybe help keep one from starting."

Jo lifted herself off the couch, her heavy belt following her up like a chain. "I'm on my way."

Luke stood with her. "Need some backup?"

She patted his shoulder. "Your bruises just went away. I think I have it."

"You know where we are," Wyatt offered.

She pointed two fingers in Melanie's direction. "Just keep an eye on Mel so I can find Mr. Lewis."

"Got it."

Chapter Twenty-Four

Jo didn't bother trying to find a space to park at R&B's, and pulled up behind several motorcycles that took up a handful of spaces. High-end Harleys mixed with a couple of BMWs, and at least one Ducati rounded out the average bike. She was fairly certain this was the doctor and lawyer crowd Josie normally had pass through toward the end of summer. They didn't often cause any concern, but it wasn't unheard of for those who used bikes as their daily vehicle to cause a little trouble for those who only did on the weekends.

With her hat on her head, her arms loose at her sides, she stepped into the busy bar and swept the room with her eyes. Sure enough, a big crowd of fortysomethings surrounded one of the pool tables, swigging back beer. All of them men, short hair on top, a few rebels with a couple days' growth on their chins. Most couldn't stand the itch and didn't bother with the act. They wore black leather, but it wasn't well-worn with cracked elbows and dirt around the collar. Doctors and lawyers. No doubt about it.

A couple of locals sat at the bar, several groups of the early twenty-plus crowd did the jukebox thing. She'd make a point to swing by that group before leaving to make sure one of them was sober and driving.

The place was loud, but it didn't feel edgy, which made Jo ask why Josie called.

"Hey, Sheriff?"

She turned to find Zane. His eyes were a tad glossy, but he had a soft smile on his face. The fact he called her Sheriff actually warmed her heart. His respect for her badge was nil ever since she put it on.

"Hi, Zane."

"It's been a little crazy around here lately, wouldn't you say?"

"Understatement of the year. How is Zanya doing?"

He actually shuffled his feet. "Gonna be an uncle any day now. And don't worry, I walked here."

"Good to hear, Zane. Let me know how your sister is coming along."

"I will." He offered a timid smile and turned back to his group of friends.

Jo wasn't sure when his switch happened, but she liked it. She reached the bar, caught the bartender's eyes. "Josie?" Jo asked.

She waved her thumb toward the other end of the bar before noticing Josie's frown.

When she stood in front of her, she asked, "What's going on, hon?"

Josie nodded her chin to one of the tables in the corner of the room.

It took a second for Jo to realize who she was looking at. "What the hell is he doing back here?"

"Keeps looking out the window like he expects company."

"What's he drinking?"

"Jack."

"How many?"

"One. Wouldn't have allowed that but my waitress didn't know who he was."

Jo patted Josie's shoulder before weaving through the crowd to the lone man sitting by the window. Last time she saw him he was cooperating enough to keep Luke and Wyatt from being booked. She pulled the chair opposite him across the wooden floor with a scrape loud enough to catch the attention of several tables around them.

His eyes shot to her from where he had them pinned against the window.

"Jesus. Little warning there, Officer."

"It's Sheriff."

He didn't bother correcting himself.

"I thought I told you to avoid River Bend and especially this establishment if you drove through again."

He picked up his whiskey, which looked more like melted ice at this point, and looked beyond her for a second.

"She's not serving you again," Jo told him.

He went ahead and finished his melted ice and slapped the glass on the table. He paused for a second. "Saw that news program."

Jo went still.

"Which one? The news vans have been all over town."

He glanced back out the window. "Couple of them. Glad you found that little girl."

Jo did a little mental Rolodex search. The man's name was Buddy . . . strange last name she didn't remember. Friends called him Big. For obvious reasons. Unlike the lawyers and the doctors in the bar, this man owned a beard he'd been growing most of his life. Kept it fairly trimmed, but you could see the yellow cigarette stains that took plenty of packs to create. On the top, complete chrome dome. Priors were assault, armed robbery, a few catch and release on drugs. He was either working his way up the chain gang or deciding it might be better to live on the outside of barbed wire fencing.

"We all are."

He twirled the rest of the ice in his glass. "People shouldn't fuck with kids, man. That shit's off-limits."

Honor among thieves. "Too bad not everyone gets that memo, Buddy."

He seemed surprised she'd called him by his first name.

She did what she always did, and waited for him to talk. It was obvious from the fact he hadn't left that he had something to say.

And Jo wanted to hear it.

"I have a kid."

"Oh?"

"Twelve. Her ol' lady won't let me see her. Can't say as I blame her."

Jo felt some of the tension in her body relax. "Hard to explain jail time to a child."

Buddy nodded, looked into the melting ice.

"Saw the news . . . heard the name of this town. Crazy . . . I've never been through here before . . . what's the chances of hearing it twice in a week?"

A little too coincidental for Jo's world.

He glanced out the window of the bar. "I—I ah, saw that guy."

The hair on Jo's arms stood on end. "Which guy?"

"The brown-haired surfer-looking guy . . . the one we roughed up."

Jo felt the air go out of her lungs. She wanted to hear Mr. Lewis's name so desperately she could scream. "You mean Wyatt?"

Buddy shrugged. "Is he the little girl's dad?"

"No. Why do you ask?"

"Saw the mom on the news. She was clinging to him." He sucked down the rest of the melted ice, crunched on what was left.

It wasn't like her to share with someone she didn't know, but there was something driving this conversation that had yet to appear, so Jo went ahead and told the man what everyone in River Bend already knew. "Wyatt's dating the mom."

Buddy started to tap the edge of his glass. His somewhat easy expression hardened on the edges.

"I don't like it when people fuck with kids," he said again.

"No one does."

"I mean . . . a grown man, he can have enemies. Done wrong by someone else. But a kid . . . shit's just not right."

Patience was such a hard line to stand on.

"Couple more hours and she would have been dead . . . that's what that *American Fugitive* guy said. Is that true?"

Jo offered a slow nod.

"Still looking for the guy who pushed her?"

"We'll find him."

"Good. Bastard should fry."

On that, they both agreed.

"Do you think he was working alone?"

Again, gooseflesh pimpled on her skin in the warm bar. "What makes you ask?"

He shrugged, looked out the window again.

"Buddy?"

"Yeah?"

"Who you expecting?"

"No one." Which was a lie and they both knew it.

They sat for another solid minute in silence before Jo moved to stand. "Well, Buddy. I need to get back to that little girl." Since children were his hot button, she pressed it hard. "Someone out there wants her dead, and until we find him, she needs all the protection she can get."

She actually turned around and took a step before he spoke. "I was paid."

"Paid?" she asked over her shoulder.

"The boyfriend. We were paid to rough him up."

What the—? She kept her expression stoic as she turned. "Paid to fight Wyatt . . . by who?"

"Don't know. Ty set it up, saw D-Man and knew he'd help. It was an easy grand."

Ty was one of the other guys with him the night of the bar fight.

"Someone paid you and Ty to fight Wyatt Gibson here . . . and you don't know who, or why?"

He shook his head. "Didn't really care. Couple punches, make sure the cops were called. Don't press charges. Just like Ty said, we all left."

Her head scrambled. Who the hell would pay this thug to fight Wyatt?

"Then I saw him on the news . . . saw the kid. Thought . . . wait, is someone setting this guy up and using the kid? What kind of sick fuck does that?"

Yeah, her thoughts exactly.

"Feds are really good at tracing shit. Only a matter of time before they realize I was here fighting this dude on purpose."

"So you came back to make sure you're not accused of more than a bar fight."

Buddy ran his hand over his beard. "Yeah. Probably kick myself when the Molly wears off . . . but yeah."

Good to know what kind of drug he was on.

"Do you know who paid you?"

"No. Ty might, but I haven't seen him since that night." He glanced out the window again.

"Is that who you're looking for?"

He shrugged.

She wasn't sure how the dots connected, but she'd find the link. "You know I need you to come in and give a statement."

He didn't seem like that was on his list of things to do.

"I'm working with the Feds to find Hope's assailant. I need him off the street before he comes back to finish the job or hurts another innocent little girl."

He stood at that point and slowly followed her out. A small path cut through the crowd as they passed. Jo caught the whites of Zane's eyes, which narrowed at the man following her.

Outside, she suggested, in the firm way cops do, that he take the ride with her . . . in the back.

Buddy had been around long enough to understand what that meant.

Thankfully he didn't argue and suggested she remove the pocket-knife he had tucked into his boot.

The pat down was quick, and she went ahead and opened the back door without placing him in cuffs. The cage separating them was enough for her.

Three hours later, after Agent Burton drove in from Eugene, they'd learned that Buddy and Ty had cased Josie's for three nights waiting for Wyatt to walk in. They were instructed to involve Wyatt in a bar fight and each of them would walk away with a thousand dollars. According to Buddy, Ty wasn't concerned about a little jail time with a thousand dollar return. Buddy had been a little more anxious with his record. In the end, the money weighed out. A moment, he said, he wasn't proud of.

The question Buddy kept asking throughout his interview was the same one that Jo kept asking herself. Did Mr. Lewis hire Ty to fight with Wyatt? Or did someone hire Mr. Lewis to hurt that little girl and Ty and Buddy to fight Wyatt? Either way, a child was involved and that was the line Buddy didn't cross. Buddy must have said the words *don't fuck with kids* a dozen times.

The guy had been hard and edgy the last time she'd seen him. Probably the combination of drugs he'd taken, but something in the air was changing the criminal element in River Bend. Between Zane's unusual acceptance and Buddy's appearance and statements, Jo felt like she was Mayor Giuliani turning around the crime element in New York. More importantly, she felt as if they were at the breaking point of the case.

"You can taste it, can't you?" Agent Burton asked.

Jo closed her eyes and lifted a hand in the air. "It's right there." She made a little invisible dot in the air with her index finger. "Right fucking there!"

"We need to find Ty."

Jo couldn't agree more. They'd put out an all points on the man for questioning. Buddy seemed convinced that Ty wouldn't have a lot more information. He didn't have the criminal connections Buddy had . . . but he'd recently been stung, though it hadn't stuck, according to the drunken stories they'd shared.

It was easy to conclude that had Ty seen the stories of attempted murder, seen Wyatt on the news like Buddy had, he might be running scared at this point. "Or," Agent Burton pointed out, "our Mr. Lewis, or the one who hired him, wants to clean up loose ends."

That was *not* what Jo wanted to hear.

Jo pulled out her personal cell phone and sent a text to Melanie.

Is Luke or Wyatt there?

It took a moment before the dot dot dot of a pending message appeared.

Luke just left, Wyatt is here with a suitcase.

Jo sighed. She knew Miss Gina had a shotgun. There weren't too many people in town who didn't. But the chances of Mel using it were slim to none. *Okay.*

Thanks for all you're doing, Jo. Love you.

Love you back.

Jo tucked her phone in her pocket.

"Where is Mr. Buddy staying?" Agent Burton asked after Deputy Emery drove Buddy back to R&B's to retrieve his bike.

"The hotel outside town. I checked in with the owner. He's been there for a couple of days now."

They'd asked him to stay close for more questioning. Hopefully once the drugs wore off, he wouldn't take another that would cause him to freak out on a massive level and flee. Only time would tell.

Agent Burton rubbed the space between her eyes. "Well, it's a long drive back to Eugene. I should be going."

"You know, I have two extra rooms in my house, Burton. You can crash there."

The other woman hesitated, then said, "Sure. I'll take it. Save time."

Jo grabbed her keys. "Follow me."

Melanie and Miss Gina were washing dishes and cleaning the kitchen when Melanie received Jo's text.

Wyatt was upstairs unpacking a small bag to hold him over. He took the room at the very top of the stairs so he could hear any comings and goings inside the inn.

Melanie thought about how much of her life had been turned upside down, and how just by knowing her, her friends were in a constant state of chaos as well.

She handed Miss Gina a wet pie pan and shoved her hands back into the water for another. "I'm sorry," she said without preamble.

Miss Gina kept drying dishes as she spoke. "What the hell are you talking about?"

"Everything. You hire me and look what happened. I've closed the doors of the inn, interrupted your income—"

"Stop. Just shut the hell up right now. You didn't bring any of this on yourself."

"Doesn't stop me from feeling guilty about how this has affected everyone around me."

Miss Gina slammed the cupboard after placing the dish inside. "And what is that guilt doing for you? Is it solving anything? Making you sleep better at night?"

"No."

"Then let it go. I want you and Hope here. I wouldn't have it any other way." Miss Gina shook off her anger and placed a hand on Melanie's shoulder. "I never wanted kids because I've always felt I had several. You're like a daughter to me. Don't ever forget it."

Her heart leapt in her throat, and she hugged Miss Gina, soapy wet hands and all. "Does this mean Hope can call you Grandma?"

"Hell no! I'm much too young to be a grandmother."

Chapter Twenty-Five

Melanie turned off lights and double-checked the doors to make sure they were locked as she passed through the downstairs of the inn. She reached the top of the stairs to find Wyatt's door open and voices coming from inside.

When Hope started to giggle, Melanie paused.

"You can't be Snow White," Wyatt was telling her daughter.

"Why not?" she asked.

"First, you have the wrong hair color."

Hope giggled.

"Second, your mom would never let you live with seven tiny men."

"You don't have a very good imagination," Hope told him. "The seven dwarfs are all my mom's friends. Like Auntie Jo is Doc . . . in charge and a little bossy. Luke is Happy. Actually, Mr. Miller is Happy, too. Auntie Zoe is . . ." Hope lowered her voice. "Grumpy. She yells when she's cooking."

Wyatt laughed. "Who is the queen?"

When the conversation paused, Melanie snuck a peek behind the door to find Hope snuggled up to Wyatt on his bed, their heads buried in a book. "That guy who says he's my dad."

Wyatt stared at Hope. He opened his mouth as if he were going to say something a couple of times before anything came out. "What makes you say that?"

Hope shrugged and turned the page. "I'm a kid, but I have ears. I know he wants to take me away from here." The sadness in her voice sliced through Melanie as she listened to their conversation.

"He might just want to get to know you."

"Then he should come for dinner or something . . . like normal people."

Her daughter was so smart.

Wyatt messed up Hope's hair and pointed to the book. "Who is the huntsman?"

Hope tried to hide a yawn. "That's your dad."

Melanie closed her eyes and thought about her daughter's cast of characters.

"What about the prince? The one who saves Snow White?"

"There is no prince." Hope was adamant.

"No prince?"

"Nope . . . that's where all these stories are messed up. Princes don't save anyone. It's the knight that comes to the rescue. And he doesn't do it by kissing." Hope made an animated face as if kissing was like eating mud. "The knight sweeps in and keeps Snow White from eating the apple and pushes the queen off the cliff before she can push Snow White."

Melanie found herself holding her breath. That went very dark, very quickly.

"If my knight was here, he would have kept Mr. Lewis from pushing me."

Melanie must have moved. Wyatt's eyes snapped to her once Hope's words sank in. She'd never once said aloud that Mr. Lewis had pushed her.

"How did Mr. Lewis push you, sweetie?"

She turned the page, unfazed by the question. "He pushed my butt with his hands." She sighed. "Maybe Mr. Lewis is the queen, too."

Hope snapped the book shut, gathered it with her unbroken arm, and kissed Wyatt's cheek. "Thanks for reading me a story."

"You did most of the reading."

Hope smiled as she slid from the bed. "Good night."

"Night, sweetheart."

Melanie took a step back before Hope made it to the door. "Going to bed?" she asked Hope.

"I'm tired. Uncle Wyatt already read me a story."

Melanie smiled at Wyatt through the door before walking her daughter to her room.

"Did you brush your teeth?" Melanie asked while she turned down the bed.

"I forgot."

She waved her daughter toward her bathroom and went about tiding up the room. She placed the book on the shelf beside the others while the sound of water running kept her company. She knew Patrick Lewis, or whatever the hell his name was, pushed her daughter. The doctors had said she might remember . . . or she might not. Somehow, Melanie had wished Hope wouldn't recall that moment when her trust had been broken.

As much as she wanted to shelter her daughter from all the evil in the world, it was obvious she couldn't.

The water turned off, and Hope walked past her and jumped into bed.

Melanie painted on a smile, one she didn't really feel, and tucked her daughter in.

"I'm glad Uncle Wyatt is here."

"I am, too."

Hope placed her arm on a pillow. "Mommy?"

"Yeah, honey?"

"If the queen comes again . . . I'm going to push her down the hill first."

What was she supposed to say to that? "I think you'll have to get in line. You have a lot of dwarfs who want to push her for you."

Melanie kissed her daughter and left the room, leaving the door open.

Wyatt waited outside in the hall. "You heard all that, right?"

She nodded toward the stairs to lead the conversation away from Hope's room.

As soon as they rounded the stairs and Wyatt turned on the lights in the sitting room, Melanie let him gather her into his arms.

"She's going to be okay," he whispered into her hair.

"Her fairy tales are littered with black clouds. I hate that he did that to her."

"None of this is right."

The weight of Wyatt's arms around her grounded the world. "We should call Jo, let her know what Hope said."

"We all knew the man pushed her."

She moaned and Wyatt leaned back to look down.

"We'll call Jo in the morning. I'd hate to wake the woman if she found time to sleep."

Melanie agreed with a nod.

Wyatt ran his fingertips down the side of her face. "Hope isn't the only one with dark clouds in her fairy tales."

"I don't believe in fairy tales."

"Oh, really?"

She shook her head. "Magical kisses and princes who save the day? Doesn't happen."

There was a twinkle in Wyatt's eyes. "What about the knight?"

She paused.

"You mean the man who offers to put his responsibilities aside to protect the princess?"

"Yeah, him . . . do you believe in him?"

He was fishing.

And Melanie needed to laugh.

"No, he doesn't exist either."

Wyatt pretended shock by placing a hand over his heart.

"Oh, you mean you?" She grinned.

Wyatt reached around and pinched her ass.

She squealed and hopped away from his hand.

"I'll get you for that."

She scrambled around the couch and put several feet between them. "Have to catch me first."

He bent his knees and acted as if he could hurdle over the couch, then darted right and chased her around the sofa. She caught herself squealing and muffled the sound.

"Are you ticklish, Mel?"

She did a little hop, step, jog over a cord to avoid toppling a lamp.

"I'll never tell." She placed a high-back chair between them and used it as a shield to keep him from grabbing her. Problem was, she was literally cornered. Distraction would be the key to getting away.

"Now where you gonna go?"

"I have superpowers," she told him.

"Oh?"

She stopped pretending like she was going to run and brought both hands to the top button on her shirt.

Wyatt's eyes were drawn to her chest, and he paused.

After releasing one button, she teased the top of her breast with the back of her index finger.

Then she ran from behind the chair to the right. She made it three feet before Wyatt's arms wrapped around her waist, his fingers dancing over her, making her giggle.

"You are ticklish!"

"No I'm n—" He found a spot under her arm and had her doubling over.

She tried to twist away, but his grip wouldn't let her go. Wyatt relented the tickle attack and lifted her off her feet. When he set her down, her back met the sofa and he was on top of her, pinning both her arms with one of his hands.

And the tickling continued.

"Oh, my . . . Wyatt, I'm warning you . . ."

He didn't stop. "What are you going to do?"

She attempted to buck him off. He didn't budge.

"I don't know, but I'll figure it out."

Wyatt sighed and eased up his efforts.

And Melanie was smiling. It felt so good to laugh and forget, even for a few minutes.

"You have a beautiful smile," he whispered.

"Says the man with dimples."

He flashed them and Melanie felt her entire body relax. When Wyatt released her hands, she lifted one to his face and brought it closer to hers.

The taste of him was becoming familiar, the feel of him missed when he wasn't beside her. The need for him, in these quiet moments that didn't happen often enough, was something Melanie was finding hard to live without.

Wyatt kept his full weight off of her as he sank deeper into the kiss. His tongue darted around hers until he found the spot he wanted to explore longer. There was no hurry in his pursuit as he heated her body from the inside out.

Melanie wiggled one of her legs out from under his and wrapped him close.

The fully clothed, full-on make out session on the couch hadn't been something Melanie had experienced in over a decade. Although the weight of Wyatt's erection teased her, he made no move to remove her clothes. He kissed her breathless, then moved to tease her ear and neck with his tongue.

She, however, didn't have the same restraint. The space between his shirt and his jeans became her playground. The edges of her fingernails ran up and down his back, the motion of her hips providing some contact.

Melanie forced her lips away from a never-ending kiss. "I need you inside me."

Instead of saying anything, he pushed into her, captured her lips, and didn't let her breathe.

The constant pressure on her core, the movement of his hips, was doing the job. The beat of her heart sped with his against her chest, the angle of his hips shifted and pressed closer. It wasn't perfect, but it was close enough to taste the edges of an orgasm.

"What are you—"

"Shh," he hushed her, rode her fully clothed, and she came.

Her frame trembled and her mind went blank.

Wyatt released her then, pulling her to her feet. "C'mon," he said against her hair. "I'm not done yet."

"That was crazy," she managed once they were in his room, the door closed.

"And fun," he said as he pulled his shirt from his shoulders.

She leaned against the door and watched him undress. His confidence in his nudity was absolute.

Once he kicked the last of his clothing free, he stood tall, a cocky smile on his face. "What are you waiting for, woman?"

Good question.

~

Wyatt used his time staying at the inn to map out the project Miss Gina planned. What started out as a space for her was starting to look more and more like a guest house to accommodate Melanie and Hope.

When he questioned the woman, she just shrugged and told him something else she wanted the place to have. Two bathrooms, maybe a kitchen after all.

"You're suggesting I build a second house."

"You can do it, can't ya?"

He lifted his hands to the large home behind them. "You already have a big house."

She waved him off and walked inside.

Wyatt moved on with the project, happy with the distraction.

Melanie was in the kitchen, determined to master a few meals with the aid of a microwave, she told him. The fact that she was on the phone with Zoe while doing so made him laugh.

Hope had moped around the backyard for a good hour, complaining about being bored and the itch inside her cast. It didn't help that it was in the high eighties with a fair amount of humidity usually reserved for the South.

He thought he heard the sound of a car on the gravel, and was confirmed when Melanie poked her head out the back door. "I think it's your dad," she told him.

"I'll be right there."

He left his notepad on an outside table, wiped his feet, and walked through the main hall of the house right as Hope was running down the stairs.

"Careful. You don't want to break your other arm."

She laughed as she fled through the front door.

Melanie's gaze was fixed and a little troubled.

Hope screamed, laughed, and screamed again.

When Wyatt looked to see what the fuss was about, he stared.

"For me?" Hope yelled as she ran down the steps of the inn.

"Well he isn't for me." William opened the back door of his rental car and out ran a four-legged, panting bundle of energy that pounced on Hope with oversize paws and a pink tongue.

Hope attempted to avoid some of the puppy saliva by turning her head. It didn't work.

"He didn't," Melanie muttered under her breath.

"Looks like he did."

"Can I keep him, Mommy? Can I?"

The screen door opened and Miss Gina's voice followed. "Well look at that."

Hope giggled and fell on her butt, which gave the yellow Labrador puppy the platform he needed to lick every inch of Hope's body.

"William!" Melanie said his name with a warning.

William flashed the same dimples Wyatt saw every day in the mirror and Melanie sighed.

"He's cute, isn't he?"

"I might have to kill you." Because watching the shadows lift from Hope's eyes when the puppy barked, licked, and came back for more wasn't something Mel would make go away, and Wyatt knew it.

Miss Gina sat on the edge of the top step. "What are you gonna name him, Hope?"

The puppy took notice of Miss Gina sitting at his level and bounded up the steps and into her space.

The woman allowed the assault of tongue and wagging tail before the puppy decided Hope was a better playmate.

Wyatt placed an arm over Melanie's shoulders.

"I'm going to kill your dad."

"No you're not."

"Okay, I'm going to *think* about killing your dad."

He laughed.

"I know the perfect name for him," Hope announced.

"What is it, darlin'?" William asked with his elbows resting on the top of his rental car as he watched her play.

"Sir Knight." She looked into the puppy's eyes. "Do you like that name?"

The puppy barked his approval.

Chapter Twenty-Six

"The troublesome thing about court battles is the long waits of nothing happening. As lawyers, we try and hammer out as many of the details in private before bringing anything before a judge."

"And did you get anything hammered out?" Melanie asked over her coffee.

"Hammered? No . . . figured, yes. I think I might have determined what is motivating Nathan to seek custody."

"Don't keep us waiting." Wyatt sat across the table in rapt attention.

"As you know, Nathan is the third attorney in his family. In line with his father and grandfather. But unlike his predecessors, there isn't a lot of respect for the youngest Stone. It took him three times before he passed the bar exam. When he did, he thought he'd immediately begin working with his father and those in his firm. Not so." William sipped his coffee and continued. "Not in the complete sense in any event."

"What does a lawyer do if not practice law?" Melanie asked. She couldn't imagine the blow to Nathan's ego after finally passing the test and not being able to do the job. Then again, he hadn't really shown a lot of joy in pursuing law in the first place.

"He's been shadowing a newer associate for the better part of a year. Word is, his temper is starting to flare at not being able to do more."

"Sounds like Nathan."

"How does all this turn back to Melanie and Hope?" Wyatt asked.

"A couple of ways. There's a woman. Miss Gregory . . . who happens to be the daughter of one of Stone's partners. I think he's trying to ensure his place in the firm from a couple of different angles."

Melanie lifted her hands in the air. "Okay, how does that fit?"

"Nathan needs a divorce."

Melanie placed her palm on her own forehead. "We are *not* married!"

William reached under the table where he'd placed his briefcase and removed a folder. "Actually . . ."

"Oh, God, what did he do?"

William removed a paper with the words *Certificate of Marriage* on the top and twisted it toward her to see.

Her name was there, as was Nathan's.

"I never signed this."

"I studied the signature, it looks like yours."

She peered close. It would have passed, no doubt. "I'm telling you . . . I never agreed to marry Nathan. I never said *I do*. There was no judge, no minister, priest, or rabbi."

William tapped the paper. "This is a contract. Two people sign it, a court approves, and the paper is filed. The pomp and circumstance is nothing more than a party, I'm sorry to say. This is the part that Nathan needs to go away."

"That's karma slapping him in the ass then. He knows damn well we never got married. If he forged this, or somehow managed to get me to sign it when I wasn't paying attention, then the joke's on him."

"Joke or not, he needs a divorce to marry Miss Gregory."

She sat forward. "All right. Say we were married. Fine, file for a divorce. But leave Hope out of it."

"He can't."

She narrowed her eyes. "Why?"

"Miss Gregory is from a big Catholic family, and when word got out that Nathan was a father . . . and quite possibly a deadbeat one at that, their future engagement was put on hold until he made a few things right."

Wyatt turned to his father. "Why would Nathan forge this?" He tapped the marriage certificate with an index finger.

Unfortunately, Melanie had an answer for him. "I met Nathan's parents once. I think they considered me a threat to him finishing law school. What they didn't know was the only threat to that was Nathan himself. He told me his parents didn't think he could commit to anything. When we found out I was pregnant he started telling everyone we were married. That he was settling down. A lot of that was all show for his parents."

"Didn't you say you only lived with him for a year?"

"Barely a year. After Hope was born he was gone more than he was home. Eventually he moved out altogether and I had to move to a smaller place I could afford alone."

"Did you ever speak with Nathan's parents after that?" William asked.

"No. I didn't see the need to reach out. They weren't my in-laws. They were about as interested in Hope as . . ." she was about to say her own parents, but didn't. "They didn't seem to care."

"It certainly appears as if Nathan has wrapped himself in lies and is trying to dig his way out and earn some respect along the way. If he can prove you took Hope away from him, that he attempted to help you and you refused—"

"None of that happened."

"He said, she said. Courts have to look at everything presented in front of them. The divorce is the easy part. It's Hope Nathan needs for leverage. Proving you're unfit gives him that leverage."

"I'm not!"

"Of course you're not, darlin'. We all know that. Let me tell you what a court is going to hear when it's all in front of them."

She waited, knew he wasn't going to be kind.

"He will start with the marriage that you say never happened. The court will show you this," he tapped the paper and continued, "and ask you to prove it's a lie."

"He said, she said," Melanie muttered.

"Exactly."

"Then he'll say you left him . . . or moved when he was away . . . or whatever he needs to do to look good in court."

"All a lie."

"Did you move away?" William asked.

"Well, yeah, like I said. I couldn't afford where we were without his help."

"Nothing he can't twist. Nothing I couldn't twist if I were on his side," he explained. "So you moved away, he continued with school, maybe he shows a little remorse about not trying harder to find you and his daughter. Or maybe he has something up his sleeve to make him look good at this point. Then you leave the state with his daughter without his knowledge."

She was afraid of what he was going to say next. "I didn't kidnap my own kid."

"I doubt he'd use that. But it has happened. Nathan finds you here, decides you're not doing right by his child. You have a home for Hope, but that has proven unsafe in the current situation. Your boyfriend." William nudged Wyatt's arm with a frown. "Your boyfriend here enjoys bar fights."

"No charges, Dad."

"Right . . . because the town sheriff is an old friend of Melanie's. And small towns take care of their own. Lots of witnesses saw that the fight happened. And how safe is Hope in a house with a man who drinks in a bar and gets into fights."

"Dad . . . it didn't happen like that."

"I know that. But the court will hear every detail of that fight from several people. The job of Nathan's lawyer is to paint Melanie as a bad and unfit mom. Cases have been won on less."

Melanie ran a hand through her hair. "How do I fight it?"

William tapped the marriage certificate. "We stop it here. If we can prove this is fraud, that Nathan is lying from this point forward, the rest will be easy."

"How do we do that?"

William's smile flattened to a straight line and a shiver went up her spine.

"You want me to talk to him."

"Confessions are best obtained by those who know the truth."

"Recordings without the other person's approval aren't admissible in court," Wyatt said.

"Glad you've been paying attention. You're right. But once the jury hears of a confession and are told to 'forget' about it . . . do they? No. That's why lawyers let things *slip* from time to time."

The last person she wanted to talk to was Nathan. "So when do we schedule this little meeting?"

"The sooner the better."

That's what she was afraid he was going to say.

Clouds were starting to roll in, and according to the forecast the rain would come and go for the better part of the week. The weather fit Wyatt's mood.

Hope, Miss Gina, and Melanie were playing with Sir Knight in the thick of the lawn, while he and his father continued to chat.

"Has Jo had any luck with the investigation?"

"She's been quiet lately. The Feds have a couple of things they're following up on."

"Anything you can share?" his father asked.

"The ink on Lewis's arm came back. An Englishman . . . aristocrat kind of guy who served some time when he was younger but has evaded prison ever since." Wyatt wasn't convinced he was the same man they were searching for.

"Did Lewis have an accent?"

"No. Not that I heard. But he did seem to have a superiority about him. And according to Melanie his table manners stuck out as strangely elite."

"You mean he had them?" his father asked with a half grin.

"Yeah."

"So what was the man's crime of choice?"

Funny how his father had a way of making a criminal sound like he was picking candy from a counter.

Wyatt closed his eyes briefly. "An early accusation of messing with his young niece had his hand slapped. Another incident had him booked but the charges were dropped."

"Damn, son." William glanced again at Hope. "You don't think . . ."

"No. Hope remembers him pushing her down the hill in great detail but has said nothing about anything more." As if trying to kill her wasn't enough.

His father stared at her for a few minutes before asking, "Why are you staying here?"

"Threats against both Melanie and Hope," Wyatt said. "Luke is here when I need to leave. The girls are going a little stir-crazy. I wish they'd just find this guy already."

His father didn't look too excited. "Problem with that is what follows. Charges, court . . . it won't be over for a while. And with everything else on her plate . . ."

"Much as she's gonna hate cleaning up after that thing, the dog was a really good idea."

"I didn't do it alone."

"Oh?"

William nodded across the lawn. "Miss Gina suggested a four-legged playmate for a sad little girl."

About then, Hope let out a contagious giggle.

"I'd say Sir Knight was a good call."

"Labs are known to find one favorite owner and stick by them. The more time Hope spends with him, the higher the chances are he'll stick by her. Not sure how much of a guard dog he'll be, but you'll always know where she is."

Wyatt smiled. "I like how you think, Dad."

"She's brave, you know."

"Hope is a smart girl."

"I didn't mean Hope," his father said.

Wyatt watched his girls run around the yard, playing tag with a puppy that was sure to grow into those big paws. *His girls* . . . since when did he look at them and think that?

"You're going to win this case, right?"

"Don't I always?"

Wyatt glanced at him, then moved his gaze back. "I don't know, do you?"

"I'm going to win. And even if she has to go through a divorce, this should all be tied up by the holidays."

"Tell me you're joking."

"I'm pushing for action now. No guarantees. Chances are Nathan wants to move fast, too. My guess is he'll only push for custody for so long. It's the divorce he wants and the illusion that he isn't a shit."

"He is a shit."

"Yeah, I got that the first time we met."

The phone rang from inside the house and Melanie ran toward the back door. "I'll get you for that dog later," she warned, smiling as she passed to get the phone.

Wyatt heard her answer the inn's phone with a pleasant voice, then she went silent. "Yes, I did."

His radar went on and he turned to watch her from the back door. "I'd like to talk, Nathan."

She'd left a message at his office shortly after Wyatt's father had arrived, and apparently the call went through even on the weekend.

"You know I can't do that right now. Hope needs me here."

Wyatt saw her clenching the phone as she paced. "I don't want to fight. We need to talk. This doesn't have to get ugly."

"No lawyers. No police . . . no, he won't."

Wyatt tried to figure out what the ass was saying on the other side of the line and only caught half.

"Fine."

When she hung up the phone, she leaned against the counter and sucked in a deep breath.

Wyatt walked through the back door and stood opposite her. "You okay?"

"That was Nathan."

"So I guessed."

"He agreed to meet me."

"That's good."

"Not in town, he doesn't feel comfortable."

Wyatt didn't like that.

"No lawyers, no Jo."

He narrowed his eyes.

"I need you to stay here with Hope," Melanie told him.

"Yeah, that isn't going to happen."

Her eyes met his. "You have to. He won't meet with me if you're there."

"I'll stay in the car."

"I need you here. Luke can take me, or Mr. Miller."

Wyatt shook his head. "I'm not letting you go without me, darlin'."

"Excuse me? You're not *letting* me?"

Maybe that wasn't the best way to put it . . . but damn right, he wasn't letting her.

"Be reasonable. This guy is a threat."

"Mr. Lewis is a threat. Nathan is just a prick. I'm going without you and that's it. If you won't stay with Hope, I'll find someone else to do it."

He ran both hands through his hair and felt his pulse race. "When is he coming?"

Melanie placed both hands on her hips. "I'm not telling you."

"Oh, for God's sake."

"You have to promise you'll stay away. If he sees you, he'll think I lied and question why I even want to talk to him."

"Sure, fine . . . when is he coming?"

"I can handle Nathan."

He didn't believe that either.

"What? You don't think I can, do you?"

"I didn't say a thing."

She turned away and started toward the back stairs to the rooms.

"We're not done, Melanie."

"Yes we are."

She stormed up the stairs as Wyatt's father said, "Well that went well."

~

"I don't like it," Jo mimicked Wyatt's concerns.

"See?" Wyatt waved in Jo's direction as he tried triple hard to get everyone in the room to suggest he accompany Melanie to the meeting with Nathan.

"We need him to talk," William told them. "Now, I know you want to be by her side, son, but if the guy clams up, it's all for nothing."

"I'll be there, bud. Nothing will happen," Luke said.

"Why you and not me?" Wyatt felt like he was whining. "Jo, tell them."

Jo passed a few glances around the room. "You misunderstood, Wyatt. I don't like the fact that he asked that I not be there."

"You're a cop. That makes sense," he said.

"You're sleeping with her, that makes sense," Luke stated the obvious.

"Please, guys, I'm right here. This is all ridiculous. I will meet with Nathan; Luke will drive me and wait in the car. I'll wear that wire thing Jo has. The most that will happen is he won't say anything about the marriage certificate that implicates him. He might catch on without everyone being there. He will know something is up if the place is littered with familiar faces."

It didn't feel right, and Wyatt didn't like it.

"I'm going to be okay, Wyatt. I know how to yell *fire* and call attention to myself if I feel threatened. We will be in a public place."

"Agent Burton is due back in Eugene on Monday, maybe I can get her to blend in close by."

"She's still here?" Melanie asked.

"Yeah, there's a lead on Ty she's going to check out."

"Who is Ty?" William asked.

"Remember the two guys you got into it with at R&B's?"

Luke and Wyatt exchanged glances. "Kinda hard to forget. Weren't there more than two?"

"Yeah, but one of them came back when he heard about what happened to Hope. Seems that little bar fight wasn't random."

"What?" Luke asked.

"Buddy, the one who came back, thought it was a little too coincidental that he and his friend Ty were paid to pull you into a bar fight. Then he sees what happened with Hope on the news, saw you in the feed. He has an issue with people hurting kids."

"Why would someone pay to force me into a fight?" Wyatt had a hard time wrapping his head around that.

"That's what we're working on. The running theory is Mr. Lewis was casing the place, wanted to see that you weren't around. Finding the second guy is key since Buddy didn't deal with the person who paid them."

Melanie stood. "See why I need you here?" she asked. "I need to know Hope is safe, Wyatt. She trusts you above everyone."

"You think you can get your FBI friend to follow Mel?" Wyatt asked.

"I don't see why not. She's been at my house for the better part of the week."

"Great." Melanie pushed off the couch. "Show me how that wire thing works, Jo, and let's go. I want to get this over with."

"Let me call Burton, have her drive ahead of us so she's in place before Nathan even shows up." Jo left the room.

"Keep her safe, Luke."

"She's like a sister, dude. I won't let anything happen to her."

"Better not." He hated being benched.

"Jeez, he has it bad!" Luke said to William.

"Sure does."

"Screw you both," Wyatt said as he left to follow Melanie.

He met her in her bedroom while she was changing her shirt. He didn't bother knocking and didn't offer any privacy when he saw her undressing. "I'm going to be okay," she said over her shoulder.

"You haven't been out of my sight for more than a few hours since all this happened."

She tossed her shirt on the bed, grabbed another. "How do you think I feel? I haven't left Hope at all. I couldn't do it if I thought she wasn't protected."

"Jo can stay."

"Yeah, but you know what?" She stopped messing with her shirt and placed both arms on his shoulders. "It's you Hope asks about. It's you she feels safe with."

He leaned his forehead against hers. "I hate this."

"If I can get Nathan to say something . . . anything that proves I didn't sign that damn paper, think of how much less time either of us has to deal with this. I'd love to focus on one thing . . . finding Lewis and putting him in jail for a long, long time."

"Fine. But if you're not back—"

"Ready, Mel-Bel?" Jo walked into the room. "Oops, sorry."

"Stop, we were just saying what needed to be said." Melanie placed a quick kiss against his lips and pushed him away.

Jo moved into the room and started taping the wire on Melanie's delicate skin. Once it was secure, the bulk of the device tucked into her bra, she put her shirt on and buttoned it up. "The receiver will be in the car, with Luke recording the conversation."

"He can hear the whole thing?"

"Yeah. Remember, if you start to feel uncomfortable, tell Nathan you have a headache and leave. If at that point you don't walk out, Luke will come in and get you."

"Sounds simple."

"It is. Agent Burton will be close by, but you probably won't see her. Don't stress that."

"Okay. Now, everyone needs to act normal or Hope is going to catch on," Melanie told them both.

"I'll see you outside then, and make sure Luke knows what's going on."

Jo left, leaving Wyatt and Melanie alone.

His palms itched, his head screamed with worry.

"Kiss me," she told him.

He didn't have to be told twice. His kiss didn't linger, it just said he cared. "Be safe. Don't take any chances."

"Wyatt. I'm not wired to speak with a drug lord. It's Nathan . . . a putz, but hardly a criminal."

He didn't feel any better.

He kissed her again. "Be safe."

"I will."

She was actually nervous. They were driving north of River Bend to Waterville. The only real meeting place was a burger joint that doubled as a pizza parlor. It was public, and often loud, but it wasn't in River Bend and it wasn't all the way in Eugene, which Melanie refused since it was too far from Hope.

Luke drove around the restaurant before finding a space close enough to pick up a signal from the wire.

"He's going to see me out here," Luke said.

"I told him you were with me and that you'd stay in the car. He seemed to understand the threats and didn't argue."

"Good."

She saw him step out of a rental car a few slots away and head inside. "Here goes nothing."

"I'm right here."

She winked and stepped out of the truck.

A pair of dress slacks and a pullover shirt replaced Nathan's normal suit. He saw her approach and looked around. "No posse this time?"

She pointed toward the truck Luke was driving. "Just Luke."

Luke shot his hand in the air with a little wave and a smile.

Nathan shuffled his feet before stepping inside the burger joint. It was after two, and the place wasn't filled to the brim, but it was noisy.

They found a small table by the window and sat.

"Thank you for meeting with me."

"My attorney suggested I not," he said.

"Mine, too," she lied.

"Why am I here, Melanie?"

"I need to know why. Why are you doing this?"

He looked around the restaurant. The place was filled with teenagers and young twentysomethings. No police or lawyers to be found.

"I want to know my daughter."

If that was so, then why wasn't he asking about her?

"Why now?"

"I'm in a better place now."

Words he said the first time he walked into town.

"Okay."

His eyes swung to hers. "Okay, what?"

"I think you should get to know Hope, too. Maybe you should come over for dinner."

He seemed shocked.

"You're serious?"

"Right now she's scared to death you're going to take her away. I can't have her afraid of her own father, can I?"

"I don't think my attorney will think that's all right."

Scurrying away already. What a shock.

"It doesn't have to be tonight."

His head nodded like one of those bobblehead dolls. "Probably something we should plan."

"Right, for Hope's sake."

His untrusting eyes narrowed. "Why the change of heart?"

Melanie attempted to act unaffected. "I know I'm not going to win."

"Why?"

"You're smarter than me." He always told her how his intelligence outweighed hers when they were together. A part of his ego she didn't feed then.

"You didn't used to think so."

"Yeah, well . . . I do now. You managed to come up with a marriage certificate, and we both know that didn't happen."

He left a smile on his face but didn't say a thing.

A smile wasn't being recorded.

"What I don't really understand is why. Why fake that kind of thing?"

He leaned forward, lowered his voice. "I told you I wanted to get married."

"I suggested we wait."

"Well, I'm a man of action, not words."

"But I didn't sign that paper."

He huffed a small breath. "Yes, you did."

"When?" *C'mon Nathan . . . be cocky you son of a bitch.*

"Right about the time you were signing all the papers for Hope's legal name after she was born."

Melanie had one of those moments when the light bulb goes on and everything makes sense. The delivery had been hard, and the doctors had given her medications for pain. She remembered signing stuff, like every new parent. They argued about Hope's last name, but Nathan had relented after she signed . . . like it didn't really matter.

"You slipped the papers in the mix. It makes sense now."

"So let's talk about making this divorce happen as quickly as possible," Nathan said.

"Considering I didn't know I was married, I think that's a brilliant idea."

"You'll cooperate?"

No, but he didn't need to hear that. "Sure. I never thought I'd keep Hope to myself forever. Are you really ready to be a dad?"

He hesitated. The man couldn't even say the words. "O-of course. Hope needs a dad."

It was time to wrap this up . . . she had what she wanted. "Do you think we might give her some time? After all, there's been a lot of drama in her life."

"I think that's reasonable. No one could argue she's been through a lot." And he would look like a caring father if he didn't push at this point. All he really wanted was the divorce and good standing with his family. After the *American Fugitive* program, he probably realized that sympathy would lie in her court. He really wasn't stupid.

An asshole, but not stupid.

"They have a lead, by the way."

"A what?"

She placed the strap of her purse over her shoulder, knowing he cared about the case of finding their daughter's attacker about as much as he cared to buy pizza from a burger joint.

"Yeah . . . apparently the fight Wyatt and Luke got into at the bar wasn't an accident."

Nathan sat silent.

"You know about the fight. That social worker you sicced on me told you, I'm sure."

"I heard about the fight. What do you mean it wasn't an accident?"

Good, he wasn't playing stupid. She hated when he did that.

"One of the guys involved came into the station after he saw the footage on TV."

Nathan's face turned white.

"Which one?"

"Which who?"

She saw his white face start to turn red. Something he never did control when he got mad. She used to tease him that he'd make a terrible attorney if his parents ever convinced him to finish law school because he had a horrible poker face. "Which guy came in?"

"Buddy. Jo said it was Buddy."

Nathan's shoulders slumped, the smile reappeared. "So they are still looking for Ty." It wasn't a question.

"Yeah, they think they have a lead . . ." Her palms started to itch. "How did you know his name?"

Nathan removed his phone from his pocket and appeared to check the time. "Whose name?"

"Ty."

He hesitated, looked down. "You told me."

"No. No, I didn't."

"Just now. You told me Buddy and Ty watched the footage . . ."

"No, Nathan, I didn't say their names."

And suddenly his body language made sense. Shock, surprise, unease . . . poker face fully disengaged.

"Why would you do that?"

"I didn't send anyone into that bar to fight your boyfriend."

It was time to call in a little help. "Jeez, you give me a headache. Was it just to make Wyatt look bad? To make me look like a bad mom?"

He reached across the table and grabbed her arm. "I didn't do anything."

She yanked free. "Is that what Ty is going to say when they pick him up?"

Again, his face lost color.

"It's kinda hard to practice law when you're behind bars."

He reached for her again, and a hand came down on his. "No touching." Luke offered a deadly stare.

Nathan scrambled out of Luke's grip and glared. "You're both crazy." He pointed at Melanie. "I'll see you in court."

"Look forward to it."

They both watched as he walked out and stormed to his car.

"Did we get all that?"

Luke smiled. "Every word."

Chapter Twenty-Seven

They'd been gone for over an hour and the rain was pelting the side of the inn like an unrelenting hammering from a bad neighbor on a Sunday morning.

Wyatt jumped for the phone when it rang. "Yeah?"

"It's me." Hearing Melanie's voice sounded so sweet.

"Hey, darlin'. How did it go?"

"I definitely got what I came for."

"He told you about the marriage certificate?"

"Yeah, but I don't think we'll need it."

"Really, why?"

"Put your dad on the other line."

Wyatt walked to the foyer phone and handed the receiver to his father.

"What did you find out?" William asked once they were both listening.

"I think Nathan hired the guys to pull Wyatt into the bar fight."

"Are you sure?" Wyatt asked.

"Luke came to the same conclusion and he didn't even see the reaction on Nathan's face when he was trying hard to hold back his thoughts. Bottom line, he knew the names of the guys who fought you both. Luke didn't even know and he was there. When I told Nathan that Ty was getting picked up for questioning, he—"

"Started to get rough!" Wyatt heard Luke yell from what sounded like the inside of the truck.

"He did what?"

"He grabbed my arm. I'm fine. But yeah, he was pissed. Then Luke came in and Nathan stormed off."

"And you have that all on tape?" William asked.

"Every word."

"We need to call Jo."

"Already done," Melanie informed him.

"Are you on your way home?"

"Yeah, pulling onto the main road now. Raining like crazy. I didn't want you to worry."

Wyatt placed a hand over his chest. "I'll worry until you're back. But take your time, I don't want a delay due to an accident."

It was hard to hang up, but he did anyway.

It took a few minutes for the gravity of Melanie's words to sink in.

"Talk about setting your ex up for a fall." For a moment, Wyatt thought his father was giving Nathan kudos. "Makes me wonder just how far the guy would go."

"Hiring a couple of guys to beat me up is really out there, don't you think?"

Wyatt watched his father pace. "Yeah, but it isn't like you and Melanie are living together. One piece of the puzzle helps the overall case . . . but you alone, bar fighting wildcard and all, wouldn't give a judge what he needs to take Hope away from her mom."

"He needed to stack the deck," Wyatt assumed. "After all, at the end of the day, he's just a deadbeat dad who skipped out on his girlfriend and their child. He wants to come out looking like the better of the two parents, and what better way than to suggest the ex is hanging around with criminals?"

Wyatt's father paused, looked around the room. "But how far would he go? Hire one thug, two . . . what about three?"

"Are you suggesting Nathan hired Mr. Lewis?"

"I'm suggesting anything is possible. You were here when Lewis showed up the first time. Was that before or after Nathan came around?"

"After."

"Well, I'd be interested in hearing what Nathan Stone has to say to the FBI when they pull him in for questioning."

"You and me both."

"You need to disappear," Nathan yelled into his cell phone as he took the corner a little wide.

"What makes you think I haven't?"

Why couldn't the man just do what he'd been paid to do? Why did he have to improvise along the way? "You're still answering your phone."

"That's because every time I see your call I picture another payday. You paid so well the first two times, why say no to a third?"

"I don't have any more money to shell out. Take what I gave you and get out of the country. If they can't find you, they'll have nothing on me."

The windshield wipers were going at Mach speed, the road winding as he made his way back to Eugene.

"I wouldn't be too sure. That pretty little ex of yours was wearing a wire, you know."

Nathan slammed on his brakes. "What?"

"Whoa, careful, mate, you wouldn't want a car accident on this road."

Oh, fuck, oh, fuck... Nathan twisted in his seat, looked around the car, and spotted the shadow of one following from behind. The fog and rain brought down his visibility to almost nothing.

"What the hell?" he said into the phone. "Why are you even in the state? Everyone is looking for you."

"No, mate . . . everyone is looking for Mr. Lewis."

And Ruther, aka Patrick Lewis, was a man of many disguises, which was why Nathan had hired him in the first place. His family had money but had cut him off years ago, and Ruther had a little problem. A problem that Nathan could use to gain respect from his family. He'd sent Ruther into Miss Gina's inn as a spy . . . find the dirt on Melanie and report back. Yeah, he knew about his unusual taste in little girls, which he had every intention of using in court to make the judge see Nathan's need to remove Hope from Mel's care. But then the pervert decided to murder his kid. A part of him hurt with that, but a bigger part of him worried that everything would come back on him. That Ruther would say he was hired to remove Hope from the equation, or something equally disturbing.

"Why are you following me?"

"Making sure you get back safely. Keeping that FBI agent from following you."

The car sat idling, the smoke from the exhaust the only visible sign that there was someone in the thing. "What agent?"

"You really have no idea how deep you're in, do you?"

Nathan was shaking, couldn't control it. "Stop following me."

He hung up and put his foot on the gas.

Ruther followed. The road continued on a steady incline and narrowed. At the top, he knew it leveled out, which would give him the space he needed to pick up his speed.

Ruther pulled close behind, making Nathan's blood pressure shoot high.

When his phone rang, he jumped.

He answered without looking at the number. "Yeah?"

"Nathan?" The voice was that of a woman.

"Yeah?"

Ruther flashed his lights and Nathan picked up speed.

"It's Sheriff Ward. We'd like to ask you to come into the station and answer a few questions."

"Screw you, bitch."

"We can do this the hard way, Nathan."

He took his eyes off the road as he ended the call and tossed the phone aside.

When he looked up, he felt the back end of his car lurch and the wheel jerk to the left.

And then, as they often say in basketball . . . it was nothing but air, but there was no net to catch him as his car tumbled off the cliff.

"He hung up." Jo pressed End and smiled at Agent Burton.

"Not surprising."

"I'll have a warrant and court orders by tomorrow afternoon."

Burton had driven back through town after watching the interaction between Melanie and Nathan from across the street. When she saw Nathan speed out of the parking lot, she ran to the back of the restaurant to retrieve her car, only to find one of her tires flat. By the time she had it changed, Nathan was long gone and Jo had already called her.

"I'm going to go ahead and drive to Eugene tonight and get this going. We don't want any delays."

"I don't want Nathan getting away. He's bound to find a flight to Mexico tonight if in fact he hired Mr. Lewis to kill his own daughter." The thought made her sick to her stomach.

Burton left the station with the promise of calling the next day.

An hour later a call came in to the station about a car off the side of the road. It took thirty more minutes for her to reach the scene. When she did, Jo realized she was the last one to talk to Nathan before he died.

Poor Agent Burton didn't even have a chance to check into the standard hotel room before Jo was calling the woman back. The point on the road where Nathan's car had gone off was on a curve, making it more dangerous to get a team down to retrieve his body.

"You think he drove off on purpose?" Burton stood on the muddy road looking down at the wreckage.

Jo looked down. "I think he was too much of a pansy to end his own life. This guy hired people to do his dirty work."

Burton walked over the road, an umbrella covering her head. "No skid marks."

"He could have hydroplaned."

"The gravel on the side of the road is barely kicked up. If he was on his brakes, we would see it there," Burton said.

"No obvious evidence he was trying to stop."

"Kinda suggests suicide."

"If the man knew the area, I'd agree. But unless he knew this road clipped off like this . . . there aren't any other places the road narrows this much all the way to the main highway."

"If he didn't do it on purpose, and there are no marks on the road to suggest he was swerving to avoid hitting something . . . then what, brake failure?"

Jo turned to look at the landscape. "If your brakes failed, wouldn't you aim for the other side?" There was a good five yards of a sloping face of the hill off to the right. "I'd take my chances with a wall. Air bags being what they are."

"What does that leave . . . homicide?" Burton asked. "Sadly, the main suspects I see all live in River Bend."

Jo nodded. "And all were present and accounted for at Miss Gina's. Which leaves . . ."

"An accomplice?"

"Someone cleaning up loose ends."

"Yeah, someone worth dying for."

Jo did not like where her thoughts led. Could their tattooed Mr. Lewis have returned? "How often do assailants return to the scene of the crime?"

"C'mon, Jo . . . you're a smart cop. You're jumpy because you know the victims in all this."

The rain was dripping off the slicker Jo had over her uniform—without a gutter on her hat—it dripped over all sides.

"I'm saying . . . Nathan didn't commit suicide. He is a wimp . . . *was* a wimp. He didn't have the stomach to start his own bar fight, so he hires a couple guys. Then he hires someone else to drive up and down this very road." Jo pointed to the pavement. "You only have to drive it a few times before you know this curve and cliff are here. This guy acts as some kind of salesman, and stays at the inn. We know all that was a lie. We know Mr. Lewis rented a car using the same ID he had at the inn and then disappeared from there. The man didn't even have a destination on the other side. He simply drove through for the purpose of what? I don't think for a minute he stumbled upon Miss Gina's inn, do you?"

Agent Burton shook her head.

"And who is Mr. Lewis? We have one match on the tattoo. That match has some connections that could link him to Nathan. I think you were the one who suggested that our guy could be a child molester who is trying to avoid his crime of choice. Didn't the profile of our only possible suspect have an affluent, aristocratic family?"

Agent Burton nodded. "Yeah. Big money."

Jo wiped rain from her face. "If our dead dirtbag here did hire Mr. Lewis and knew he had priors . . . then he could claim his daughter was in danger of all sorts of ugly people who walked into the inn and booked a room."

It was Burton who spoke next. "So Nathan hires Ty and Buddy, my guess is we'd find one or both of them on a list of clients Nathan represented at one point or another. Has Mr. Lewis showing up randomly. Mr. Lewis might have only been hired to be inside eyes at the inn . . . someone trying to find dirt. Only Mr. Lewis is a hired con man. He wipes down the inside of the room." Burton was pacing, her sensible blue heels splashing in the puddles. "He sees an opportunity. Maybe he means to hurt Hope, or maybe he just wants to blackmail this one for more."

They both turned to look at the tarp where underneath, Nathan lay.

"And when there is no more to take, and Nathan starts running scared . . . who will be the person ratted out?"

"Lewis."

Jo pointed two fingers in Burton's direction. "With Nathan dead, that leaves only one person who can positively identify the man and his actions."

"Hope."

Jo twisted around in the middle of the street before sprinting toward her car.

Burton jumped into the passenger seat and tossed the umbrella on the side of the road.

"This is a patient man, chances of him doing anything tonight are slim."

Jo turned on her lights, filled the night air with sirens. "I'm not taking any chances."

Melanie shot out of bed with the first pounding on the door.

She slammed her hand against the side of the bed to find the light switch, and clicked it several times before remembering that the power had gone out hours before. From the sound of the rain outside, it wasn't back on.

Footsteps in the hall accompanied Wyatt's voice. "I think it's Jo. Her squad car is in the drive with the lights on." He kept his voice low to avoid waking Hope. Or more importantly, the tiny, four-legged barking machine that had finally stopped yipping a couple of hours before. Between the events of the day, the rain, the power outage, and the new addition to the family, Melanie wasn't going far from Hope's room.

Sure enough, Jo pounded on the front door one too many times and Sir Knight started to bark from inside Hope's closed door.

Melanie tossed on a bathrobe and checked Hope's room.

On the bed, Sir Knight took up residence. Already the room started to smell like wet puppy.

"What is it, Mommy?"

"I don't know, honey. Auntie Jo is here. Just go back to sleep."

Sir Knight barked.

"You, too."

Hope placed her unbroken arm on the dog and quieted him down. Miss Gina met Melanie in the hall with a flashlight. "What's all the fuss?"

They both walked down the front stairway to find Jo and Agent Burton saturated and talking with Wyatt.

When Melanie and Miss Gina joined them, they went silent. "What is it?"

Jo glanced up the stairs. "Is Hope okay?"

"Attempting to sleep with a puppy pouncing on her."

There was relief in Jo's stance.

"Let's go sit down."

That was never good. "Jo? Cut the crap, what's going on?"

"It's Nathan, Mel . . . we, ah, we found his car off the side of the road."

Melanie knew she was half-asleep, but it was the next words from Jo's mouth that woke Mel up.

"He's dead, Mel."

She placed a hand over her mouth. "Oh, God." Her stomach lurched and her head started to spin. "I need to sit down."

Wyatt was there, his arm around her waist as they all moved into the sitting room.

Miss Gina moved around and twisted on a couple of vintage oil lights.

Dead? She felt herself start to rock. Guilt for wishing he'd just jump off a cliff started to wiggle inside with the thought of him gone. Her eyes started to swell with emotion. Much as she disliked the man, hated him even, death wasn't really an option. "You're sure it was him?"

Jo cringed. "I saw him."

A numbness rolled over her, the reality that her daughter would now grow up without her father sank in.

"There will be a lengthy investigation," Agent Burton told her. "We need to rule out suicide."

Melanie shook her pounding head. "He wouldn't have had the stomach for that."

"Told you," Jo said to the agent.

"So it was an accident?" Miss Gina asked.

When Jo and Agent Burton didn't respond quickly, the three of them stared.

"If not an accident, then . . ."

Rain started to pour outside, giving the silent room a level of background noise that hummed.

"We need to rule out homicide, too."

It took a few minutes for Jo and Agent Burton to explain their theory, and their haste to return to the inn that night to make sure everything was all right.

"If what you say is true, you think Lewis is still close by."

"We have to assume he is."

The room lit with a splash of light, and a few seconds later shook with the sound of thunder.

Sir Knight protested from Hope's room upstairs.

Ruther watched as the sheriff and the Fed walked into the house.

Picking the lock on the back door was elementary level breaking and entering. Old houses like this littered the countryside where he grew up, making his ease of entry absolute. It helped that as a guest at the inn, posing as Patrick Lewis, he'd practiced picking the lock to ensure his entry at a later time.

The back route to the upper floors invited him. Voices from the parlor indicated the players he expected. When he heard his alias, he stopped and listened. He heard Lewis, and homicide. His palms itched. Getting rid of Stone had the blood in his veins pounding. The image of a tiny blonde with perfect skin and innocent eyes blurred his vision and had him standing on the back stairs of the inn.

He took the stairs slowly, even though the rain drowned out the squeaky steps.

The closer he moved toward the room, the more he felt alive.

Outside her bedroom door, Ruther took a deep breath.

When lightning hit, he opened it quickly as thunder shook the house.

The sight and sound of a dog stripped the smile from his face.

When the barking didn't stop, Wyatt stood to check on the puppy. "I'll be right back."

Melanie offered a tiny smile she didn't feel as he walked from the room. "I can't believe he's dead. I'm . . . jeez, I don't know what I am."

Miss Gina patted her knee. "You cared for him once. It's okay to feel sad."

Melanie glanced at the candlelit face of her friend. "Hope. What am I going to tell her?"

"Damn it!" Wyatt's voice from upstairs had everyone on their feet. "Jo!"

Sir Knight was barking above his voice.

"Hope isn't in here."

Melanie hardly registered Agent Burton removing a gun from behind her back before Mel jumped to her feet and ran toward the stairs.

Melanie climbed over Jo to look inside Hope's room.

The window was closed; the dog ran in circles before darting out from under their legs toward the door.

Don't panic . . . don't panic. "Hope?"

"She was just here."

Sir Knight barked obsessively toward the back stairway that led to the kitchen and back door. They heard a loud thud and rushed to the noise. There they shone a flashlight toward the narrow space and paused.

The sight of Hope, standing at the top of the stairs, her little dog running up and down the back steps, nipping at the edges of her daughter's nightgown, would sit with Melanie for years to come.

"Mommy?" Hope's tiny voice called to her.

"Sheriff?" Agent Burton called from the bottom of the stairs.

"What are you doing out here, sweetie?" Melanie reached her daughter and knelt.

Hope all but jumped into Melanie's arms, and that's when she noticed the moaning from a man at the bottom of the steps.

Jo pushed past them and none too gently helped Agent Burton cuff the man.

"Bloody dog," she heard him saying over and over again.

Melanie picked Hope up and took her away from the scene going on below. Melanie placed her in the center of her bed and let the dog jump up onto her lap. After lighting every candle in the room, she took stock of her daughter.

She was shaking like a leaf in the wind and hugging the puppy within an inch of its life. "Sir Knight saved me, Mommy. He bit the queen and I pushed her really hard."

Melanie placed her daughter in her lap and rocked her until all the shaking went away.

Epilogue

It took Wyatt a week before he moved his stuff back to his house. Even then, he didn't leave the Bartlett girls' sight for very long. It helped that he was laying the foundation to the new guest house and needed to be on the property during most of the daylight hours.

Lewis was in custody, wearing orange and doing his best to avoid extradition. His crimes in the UK superseded those in the past few months in Oregon. As the ends of the case tied up, they did find a money trail from Nathan to Lewis. And Ty had no problem calling Nathan out even before he found out the man was dead.

Melanie didn't attend Nathan's funeral. Wyatt could see the doubt in her decision until after it was over. Then she seemed to come to terms with the man and their combined past.

It was Hope that shocked everyone. Two days after Lewis had attempted to take her from her room, she tossed all her fairy tale books in the trash. More surprising, not one of them asked her why she did it.

They all understood perfectly.

Summer was fading into fall when Wyatt finally asked Miss Gina the question everyone wanted to know. "So when are you going to open for business again?"

She pointed across the lawn. "When are you going to get that house built?"

"There's a correlation?"

Miss Gina shrugged her shoulders and went back into the house.

One particularly breezy afternoon, Wyatt sent the small crew he brought in for the framing home early for the weekend.

Sir Knight barked from inside the rough framing of the house, which told Wyatt that Hope was close by. Sure enough, he found her climbing between the studs, her dog barking at her feet.

"What are you doing, young lady?"

"Climbing."

"I can see that." He swiped her off the wall and placed her on her feet. "Your arm just got out of the cast, remember the doctor told you no climbing trees until Halloween?"

"Well the doctor isn't here, and I feel fine."

She started to climb again, and he took her by the waist and set her back down. "Enough."

Her chin came out in defiance. "You can't tell me what to do. You're just my mom's boyfriend. You're not my dad."

Her words stung, but he used them anyway. "One day I'm going to be your dad, and you'll eat those words, princess."

Hope lowered her defiant little chin and narrowed her eyes. "Really?"

Considering he couldn't leave Melanie and Hope's side for a night without texting Mel until midnight and finding an excuse to come over daily . . . yeah, it was safe to say he was in for the long haul.

"Yeah, so don't make me spank you."

Hope made a perfect little O with her lips. "You won't do that."

"You're right." He snatched her around the waist and started to tickle her. "I have much better ways to punish disrespectful little girls."

Sir Knight barked and ran in circles around them for the few minutes Hope giggled in her attempts to get away. She cried "uncle" before the two of them ran off.

When Wyatt turned back to his work, he saw Melanie standing in the soon to be doorway, her arm leaning against the frame. How long had she been standing there?

"Hey, darlin'." He moved in for a kiss, didn't linger long. The fact she never unfolded her arms told him she had something on her mind.

"Hey."

"What brings you out here?"

"Do I need an excuse to see my *boyfriend*?"

He chuckled and turned away. Oh, she'd definitely heard his conversation with Hope. How to play this?

"Is there something you need to say to me?" she asked, not moving.

"Nope, not really. Did you have something on your mind?"

She pushed off the two-by-four. "Anything you wanna ask me?"

"Yeah." He pointed to the drill behind her. "Can you hand me that?"

She lowered her hands from her hips, grabbed the drill, and thrust it into his hands.

Pretending disbelief, he looked at the drill, then her. "Did I miss something? Why are you mad?"

When she let go of the drill, he nearly dropped it. "You're infuriating sometimes. You know that?"

She twisted to leave and he caught her hand. "You're adorable when you're angry."

Melanie actually growled at him.

Any minute she would stomp her foot the way her daughter did. Instead of waiting for it, he leaned in and kissed her. "I love you when you're angry."

"Whoa . . . what?"

He'd never said the words aloud and knew they sank in slowly. "Yeah, the way your eyes crinkle right here." He tapped the space between her eyes. "The way you glare with that attempt at a stink eye." He squinted his left eye and not the right. "I love you when you're angry."

"When I'm angry?" She did the stink eye thing, and he was hard-pressed not to laugh at her.

"And when you're laughing. Like when I'm tickling you or when you're watching TV and talking to it. I love you then, too."

She was starting to catch on and folded her arms across her chest. "So you love me when I'm angry, and when I'm laughing?"

"And when you're doing that thing you're doing with your arms right now. That's pretty adorable, you have to admit."

She looked down at herself.

"And when I'm making love to you. That noise you make when I'm making you—"

He didn't finish before she grabbed him by his shirt and kissed him hard.

Wyatt bent his knees and lifted her off her feet. She took his lead and wrapped her legs around his waist, laughing into their kiss. "I love you, Melanie."

"You picked a funny time to tell me."

She kissed him again. This time when she pulled away, an expectant look crossed over her face.

"What?"

There was that stink eye was again.

He laughed.

"One day," he started to say . . . "One day, that isn't today, I'm going to ask you to marry me."

Her stink eye faded.

"And on that day, you're going to say yes."

She bit her bottom lip. "Am I?"

"Yes, you are."

"How can you be so sure?"

"Because you love me."

She made herself comfortable in his arms as he placed her back up against the partial wall. "How do you know I love you?"

"You talk in your sleep."

The stink eye made another appearance.

"Well, I could say no."

He kissed her briefly. "You won't."

"You're so sure of yourself."

"Yeah. A little cocky. But I happen to know you came back to River Bend for a do-over. And that do-over is with me."

She smiled, tilted her head to the side, and kissed him again.

When he finally let her back on her feet, her cheeks were flushed and he told her he loved that part, too.

He swatted her butt as she turned to leave. "Now get out of here so I can get this done."

Melanie swatted him back and kissed him briefly. Then against his lips she told him what he already knew. "I love you back."

Acknowledgments

A huge shout-out to Grants Pass . . . if not for the lovely experience of breaking down on the road, at the ripe young age of eighteen, at two o'clock in the morning, before cell phones had been invented . . . I may not have become a writer.

Note to self: Never ignore lights on the dashboard. They're not lit up for Christmas.

To my agent, Jane Dystel, for your constant support and understanding during this crazy year.

For Kelli Martin, and all those at Montlake, for understanding my delay as I begin my own personal "do-over."

Back to Kari:

Friends were often the only family I had growing up. And you were at the top of that list. I considered waiting until Jo's book to dedicate one of these to you . . . since you do pack a weapon in your profession . . . but I felt the title of this one screamed your name. When I developed this series in my head, I thought of the three good girls of S.I.R.: Kari, Brandy, and Cathy . . . and knew I had to write a story of true friendship. No matter where we land, or what challenges our lives face, we're always there for each other. And that is the definition of family.

I love and admire you more than you can ever know.

I offer my unwavering support as you move forward in your "do-over."

Catherine

About the Author

Photo © 2015 Julianne Gentry

New York Times, Wall Street Journal, and *USA Today* bestselling author Catherine Bybee has written twenty-four books that have collectively sold more than two million copies and have been translated into twelve languages. Raised in Washington State, Bybee moved to Southern California in hopes of becoming a movie star. After growing bored with waiting tables, she returned to school and became a registered nurse, spending most of her career in urban emergency rooms. She now writes full-time and has penned the Not Quite series, the Weekday Brides series, and, most recently, the Most Likely To series.